P9-DNQ-143

"What if we announce our engagement?"

It took Clara a moment to digest his words. "What are you talking about?"

John grinned excitedly. "It would be a fake engagement, of course. Just to get the wagging tongues to settle down."

Clara's mind raced at the suggestion. "What? Why would we do something like that?"

John sat down next to her on the settee. "It would explain why I've been at the shop so much in the past few weeks. Learning the business to take over from my future father-in-law."

This was all too much for Clara. This morning she was preparing to open the doors to the store for another successful day of sales, and now she was contemplating a fake fiancé.

"This plan seems like quite the burden on your part," Clara said.

John reached over and grabbed her hand. "For once someone should be doing something nice for you. You are usually the one who helps people."

Clara fought back tears: It had been so long since someone considered her needs that she didn't know how to react.

Julie Brookman is a former preacher's kid who started her career after college as the manager of a bookstore, before later becoming a journalist and public relations specialist. Besides writing romance novels, she enjoys hiking, reading and belting out showtunes at the top of her lungs. Julie lives in Arizona with her husband, her three awesome kids and her kitty, Pepper Potts. Visit her website at www.authorjuliebrookman.com.

Books by Julie Brookman

Love Inspired Historical

Their Business Betrothal

Visit the Author Profile page at LoveInspired.com.

Their Business Betrothal

JULIE BROOKMAN

LOVE INSPIRED
INSPIRATIONAL ROMANCE

If you purchased this book without a cover you should be aware that this book is stolen property. It was reported as "unsold and destroyed" to the publisher, and neither the author nor the publisher has received any payment for this "stripped book."

LOVE INSPIRED®
INSPIRATIONAL ROMANCE

PLEASE RECYCLE
THIS PRODUCT IS RECYCLABLE

Recycling programs for this product may not exist in your area.

ISBN-13: 978-1-335-41892-0

Their Business Betrothal

Copyright © 2022 by Julie Maurer

All rights reserved. No part of this book may be used or reproduced in any manner whatsoever without written permission except in the case of brief quotations embodied in critical articles and reviews.

This is a work of fiction. Names, characters, places and incidents are either the product of the author's imagination or are used fictitiously. Any resemblance to actual persons, living or dead, businesses, companies, events or locales is entirely coincidental.

For questions and comments about the quality of this book, please contact us at CustomerService@Harlequin.com.

Love Inspired
22 Adelaide St. West, 41st Floor
Toronto, Ontario M5H 4E3, Canada
www.LoveInspired.com

Printed in U.S.A.

For my thoughts are not your thoughts,
neither are your ways my ways, saith the Lord.
—*Isaiah* 55:8

For my Christopher.

If they gave an award to the most supportive husbands, you would definitely win. Without your children wrangling, pizza ordering and caffeine delivery services, this book would not have happened. Thank you for believing in me. I love you.

Chapter One

Independence, Missouri
January, 1846

Clara Morehouse looked up as the bell above the door jingled to signal someone was entering the store and sighed at the intrusion. She and her sisters had just reached a merciful lull in business and she had been looking forward to getting off her feet for a few minutes. But now there was a customer who would need their attention.

Her sigh turned into a scowl when she saw who it was. It was *him*. The man who had been in here all week and not spent a single cent. Clara had no patience for loiterers, even handsome ones.

At least he was well-groomed today, a stark contrast to when he first came in last week. Clara had guessed that he was one of the men who worked the wagon train, because he'd been covered in dust, with a wild beard and messy hair that hung in his eyes.

That initial time, he'd entered the store as if looking for something, or someone, and then turned and left.

Within a day he'd reappeared—though this time,

he was well-groomed, with freshly cut brown hair that fell neatly on his forehead. He cleaned up nicely. His beard had remained, but it was trimmed all the way to his very defined jawline. His flannel shirt had been replaced by a suit, and Clara couldn't help but blush at the time, when she'd noticed that his arms filled out both outfits quite well.

The first and second versions were so different she almost didn't recognize him, except for his brown eyes. *The color of chestnuts*, she'd thought.

Her sisters had not really paid much attention to the man who came in almost every day and didn't buy anything, other than giving him a curious look from time to time. They teased Clara mercilessly when she brought him up.

"Oh, so you are noticing handsome customers now. That is so unlike you," Eliza joshed.

And then, of course, the youngest Morehouse sibling, Hannah, had to add her dramatic flair. "Wouldn't it be so romantic if you fell in love with someone who visited frequently just to admire you?"

Clara waved her sisters away. "Oh hush, he's not coming in here because of me." Clara didn't want him admiring her. Even though she was twenty-one years old and everyone in town seemed to think it was well past the time she should find a husband, she didn't have the opportunity or the inclination to go on a hunt for suitors. And surely men didn't go to the local store to find their future spouse. So she wasn't looking for a husband, and this stranger wasn't looking for a wife. And whatever he *was* looking for didn't seem to have made an appearance in the past week, which meant the man's presence without a purchase was…irksome.

Today, he was perusing the grocery aisle and taking notes about the special crates they had organized for wagon-trail pioneers. As the launching point for the Oregon Trail, Independence's businesses had thrived with all the travelers that came through here, needing to stock up before departing for their new lives in the West. And the Morehouse General Store had made a reputation as the best outfitter for families journeying by wagon train. In a few short months, the next set of wagons would be packed to head out. Most of the passengers had not arrived yet, but the outfits who organized the expeditions had already started doing some of the preparation for the trips.

Maybe this man was researching prices for his employer. Still, in a fancy suit, he looked like he *was* the employer, not the employee. Also, he seemed very familiar for some reason—and not just because he'd been loitering this week.

Clara could take the mystery no longer. She flipped up the counter door, stormed out from her post and approached the man.

"Can I help you with something, sir?"

The man looked up at her in surprise and then maybe…alarm? Was he a thief? Had she caught him in the act?

"I'm sorry, ma'am. I'm just looking," he said politely. His voice was genteel and smooth, like he frequently used it to get his way.

"You've looked enough to have the entire store memorized," she muttered under her breath.

He smiled at her. Oh dear, he must have heard her. "Not quite, but I'm getting close to having the whole layout firmly planted up here." He tapped on his temple with one of his long fingers.

Clara ground her teeth. He was blatantly admitting

to loitering! And what need did he have to memorize their floorplan? Was he planning to break in during the night to rob them? "It is frowned upon to frequent an establishment without ever making a purchase. We are running a business here."

The man nodded. "And it's a fine business," he said. Clara forced herself not to blush at the compliment. She was doing her best to keep the store running effectively without her father, so the praise was a sweet balm to her heart.

Clara tightened her shoulders and raised her chin. "And were you planning on contributing to the bottom line of this business, or shall I contact the sheriff and have you taken away on suspicion of theft?"

She could be mistaken, but Clara thought she saw admiration flash through the man's eyes before his smile widened "I will make a purchase, ma'am. I apologize for loitering."

He grabbed a satchel off one of the shelves. "I know of a young man who is about to make a journey in a few months, so I think he would appreciate one of these."

Clara just nodded and carried it to the counter. She didn't say anything as she wrapped the item.

"You're still suspicious of me," the man teased.

"Well, yes—you've behaved questionably. You've been in here every day."

His fingers brushed hers when he laid a bill on the counter to pay, and Clara's breath quickened as she looked up to meet his eyes.

"Oh, so you've noticed me?" His lips quirked when he said the words. Arrogant man. She steeled herself against his smile and sparkling eyes.

"I make note of all potential thieves."

He just chuckled. "You're right. My behavior was

somewhat suspicious. I was actually in here looking for someone. I believe he is your father—Mr. Morehouse?"

Clara nodded. "Yes, that's my father and this is his store. But he's not in today. Is there something I can help you with?"

The man shook his head. "I really need to speak to him. Is he ill? He seems to be out every time I stop in."

Clara did her best to keep a calm demeanor. "He has a lot of errands."

He again quirked his eyebrow. "Every day?"

Clara scowled. "Running a successful business isn't just about sitting behind the counter. There are visits to the banks, messages to deliver to suppliers, private meetings with potential buyers of large stock."

The man raised his hand in surrender. "I'm sorry. You are right. I run many businesses myself, so I understand."

Clara just nodded. "As you should, Mr....?"

He looked embarrassed for a moment. "Oh, I'm sorry for all my lapses in manners today. Butler, John Butler. I've been a friend of your father's for a very long time."

John Butler, one half of the famous town-building Butler Brothers, and the man who had written the letter to their father encouraging him to sell his building and travel west to start a general store in their new town. The proposal she had rejected without even consulting Papa. She could tell from the letter the two men were on friendly terms—but she'd never expected him to show up to respond to her rejection in person.

Oh, this is not going to go well for keeping up the ruse behind father's absence, Clara thought.

"It's funny. He never mentioned you," she said with an air of snobbery, in an attempt to show no fear.

He just smiled. "That's interesting, because he *has*

mentioned you. In fact, I think I saw you as a girl when I first started coming in here, about six or seven years ago."

She gasped. "You must have been very young yourself at the time."

Mr. Butler nodded. "Some of us don't have the luxury of living with our parents into adulthood. I left home at sixteen."

Clara felt a pang of sorrow for him. She couldn't imagine having to leave Mama and Papa behind at that age. Still, she didn't like his tone.

"I'm not spoiled."

"I never said you were. In fact, I think it's very dutiful of you to put in so many hours of work in your parents' store. You've been here all week," Mr. Butler said kindly. "You all have." He gestured toward her sisters, who had stopped pretending to be busy with work and were paying their full attention to the conversation.

Clara just nodded. "It's the least we could do, given the circumstances."

As soon as she said the words, she wished she could take them back. Of course he would inquire, given that he claimed to be a friend of father's.

"Circumstances?"

Nearly two weeks after their store reopened following a death in the family, Clara was finally past the point where she had to talk about it every day. For a moment, the words stuck in her throat. But there was no delaying the inevitable.

"Our mother passed. About a month ago," she said in a soft voice, ignoring the sympathetic expression that immediately settled in Mr. Butler's eyes.

"Oh, I'm so sorry, Miss Morehouse. Your mother was… She was a very kind lady."

His words almost broke the hard shell that Clara had erected around herself. In all the weeks since the funeral, people had said so many things about her mother. That she was beautiful, that she was a fine woman and excellent homemaker.

But Mr. Butler was the first to note how kind she was. It brought to Clara's mind how she had always been there if anyone needed help. She'd handed out candy to all the neighborhood children. She'd brought in a woman she found on the street who was starving with a baby and helped her find a job and a home.

"She was. Thank you," her sister Eliza said from the other side of the store. Clara had almost forgotten her two sisters were even there. Embarrassed that she had let this man distract her, she felt her cheeks redden.

"You look like her," Mr. Butler said, never taking his eyes off Clara. She just nodded and tucked a fallen strand of black hair behind her ear.

"Was there something you wanted to tell my father? I can pass it along to him. Maybe have him send you a note at your hotel?"

The man studied her for a moment, and she forced herself not to fidget under his scrutiny.

"I'll wait."

Clara gasped. "Pardon me?"

"You said he was out running an errand. I really need to talk to him in person, so I will wait to see if he returns."

Clara gripped the counter. "It could be hours."

He leaned on the counter and grinned at her.

"I've got nothing else to do, ma'am."

She exchanged a look with her sisters, who both shifted nervously. They needed a plan, and fast.

* * *

John felt a momentary pang of guilt for the obvious stress he was causing the Morehouse sisters. But something was going on here, and he needed to get to the bottom of it. If the family was in trouble, he wanted to help them.

Arthur Morehouse was not running an errand, of that he was certain. John wasn't the mathematician his brother was, but even he could figure out that the odds of the man being coincidentally out on errands at all the random times he'd stopped by were very low.

John shifted his feet and leaned against the counter. The ladies had not offered him a chair to sit on, probably hoping he would become uncomfortable and leave. At first, they had been friendly and tried to reassure him that their father would contact him, so waiting wasn't necessary. When it became clear that he wasn't going everywhere, they started ignoring him.

It was very amusing, the way they had loud conversations around him as if he weren't there. A rush of customers came in, each looking at John with curiosity, but they took the lead from the Morehouse sisters and did not say anything to him.

He took the opportunity to study the eldest sister, Clara Morehouse, while she was occupied. She stationed herself behind the main cash register, making sure everything ran smoothly while her father was out. John noted that she did the work quite capably—and that she was striking.

She had her mother's coloring—raven hair and creamy white skin. But it was her vivid green eyes that drew him in. They met his gaze a few times when he entered the store, but she always had to turn away to help a customer.

When business slowed again, he set about restarting a conversation with the sisters. Ideally, he'd like to get more information out of them, but even if that wasn't possible, a restoration of dialogue would be nice. He wasn't very keen on spending the rest of the day being ignored.

"You know, you should put these new items more toward the front, maybe in the window," he said, hoping to draw the eldest sister into conversation.

She ignored him still, but he wasn't one to give up so easily.

"I recall your father telling me your names. Since I have nothing but time, I'm going to guess which one is which."

He noticed the two younger sisters hiding their smiles while the oldest pulled out a ledger and started updating the records. Interesting. So she was doing the bookkeeping as well as managing the store.

John knew that others would turn up their noses at the sight of a woman doing such things, but he found it admirable. He certainly had no patience for that sort of administrative task. That was what his brother Adam was for—doing the paperwork. Of the famous Butler brothers, who were known for earning their wealth by starting brand-new towns along the route of the wagon trains heading west, Adam generally handled the logistics. John was the one who worked with people the best. He used those skills now to evaluate the Morehouse sisters before turning to one of them.

"I know you are Eliza. The middle daughter. Your father always said you were his spirited child and I can see that you have flowers in your hair. Did you pick them from the field outside of town before coming in today?"

Eliza reached up and fingered a flower, giving him

a big smile. The eldest daughter just narrowed her eyes at him.

John turned to the youngest. "And you must be Hannah. Your mother used to brag about you, how well you read, and that you might make a wonderful teacher someday. You're about sixteen years old, right? You must be done with regular school by now. Are you going to pursue a teaching certificate?"

Hannah opened her mouth to speak, but the woman behind the counter whispered, "Don't answer him."

John turned toward her with a grin. He'd managed to get her to speak, even though the words weren't directed at him.

"And you must be Clara. Your father always praised the wise head on your shoulders and your beauty," John said. "Can't say he was wrong about either."

While most women would blush and be pleased with such compliments, Clara Morehouse seemed the opposite. She narrowed her eyes at him. He wondered why she was so annoyed with someone calling her wise and beautiful.

He liked her anger, though; the fire in her eyes made his heart beat faster. Liked the way she couldn't manage to ignore him when he irked her. John decided to goad her some more.

"Although I'm not sure you are so wise about everything when it comes to business. There are a few things I would change about this store."

Victory washed over him when she crossed her arms defensively and spoke to him at last. "And what is wrong with my store?"

He noticed she used the possessive term for it, even though the shop was technically her father's. Yes, Clara

Morehouse was definitely running this business. Only he didn't know why.

"Oh. Well, there was what I already mentioned about putting the new items out front."

She scoffed. "We put a mixture of new and old items out there to catch different kinds of customers. These items you noted came in last week, but we find they sell well by the cash register as an impulse purchase."

John couldn't help but be impressed, although he was quick to bring up another suggestion. Anything to keep her talking to him.

"Then, there are the supply crates for the wagon train travelers. You can barely see inside of them. How do people know what they are buying?"

Clara stormed from behind the counter and marched over to one of the crates. "There is a list of items included right here! And they can custom order a crate with specific supplies that they need."

John nodded. "That's good for business."

But Clara just continued on her rant. "Besides, we have been in business for so long that our customers trust that we know what will be needed on the trail. Morehouse General Store has been here longer than the wagons have been departing from Independence."

She clearly knew every aspect of the business. She was passionate about it. John was intrigued by her. But needling her didn't give him any more insight into why Arthur Morehouse had rejected his offer to join his new town in the West—and why he wasn't currently operating his own store.

"Your father is indeed a good businessman. And so is his daughter," John said.

This compliment made her blush. Ah, so giving her

praise on her entrepreneurial skills was the way to get in her good graces.

"Your father isn't out running an errand, is he?" He said it as softly and kindly as possible, hoping she would realize that he was on their side.

She opened her mouth to object, but he placed his hand over hers. It was a bit forward, but he could not resist.

"Miss Morehouse, please. I consider myself a friend of his. I've been coming into this store since I was very young, and I need to know that nothing is amiss with him. With any of you. I can help if you need it."

The last bit had been the wrong thing to say, though, because just as Clara looked like she was softening toward him, she pulled her hand away. "We don't need your help. We don't need anyone's help."

John looked around the store and nodded. "Yes, I can see you have indeed done a fine job here without him. But, please, miss, can you assure me that my friend is all right?"

Clara sighed, and gave in. "He's…sad."

"Sad?"

Eliza, eager to talk now that the barrier had been broken, stepped forward. "He hasn't been the same since Mama died. We can't get him out of bed."

John gave her a look of sympathy before turning to meet Clara's eyes. A hint of embarrassment flashed in them before the steel was back. She was such a strong woman.

"And your mother has been gone a month?"

Hannah spoke up next. "Yes, and ever since she passed, he barely eats and will only sleep."

Sorrow weighed on him as he remembered a time when his own father had been in such a condition.

"Can I see him?"

The eldest Morehouse shook her head. "No, I don't think he would like it if we brought anyone to visit him in this state."

"Please, he has always been so kind to me. And perhaps I could help," he said.

Clara scoffed. "You think that none of us have tried to help him? Haven't begged him every day to get out of that bed and embrace life again?"

He placed his hand on hers again. "Of course you have. I just thought maybe I could bring a new perspective."

She studied him for a moment before finally nodding. "You can come over for supper tonight, if you'd like. We close the shop at seven, so we eat at eight o'clock."

John's shoulders slumped in relief. "Thank you, ladies. I will see you then."

He gave them a nod and left the store, pleased with the progress he had made. Finally, he had figured out where the Morehouse patriarch was. And tonight, John would have a chance to discuss the proposal with him. A general store started by anyone else might still suffice for their new town, but he wanted one run by the Morehouse family because they were the best at what they did. He had learned from the past that having a good general store went a long way toward building a successful settlement.

With this town being farther west than he and his brother had settled, it would be more important than ever to keep those building new lives supplied by someone who knew what they were doing. And now that he knew about his old friend's condition, he had the hope that hearing about the territory and their plans might rouse Arthur's spirits. This could be good for all of them.

Suddenly, John's stride broke as a new realization struck. He had received a written reply from Arthur Morehouse about his proposal at his hotel just last week. From what the ladies had told him, the man was in no condition to be writing letters.

Which meant one of them had penned the rejection to his proposal.

Clara Morehouse. It had to be. The youngest sister was too timid to forge a letter in her father's hand. The middle Morehouse child was too adventurous to turn down such an endeavor, which left the eldest as his sole suspect.

Why had Clara Morehouse turned him down? Did she feel the time was wrong for her family to make a change? Was she too settled in the city to consider a life out in the frontier?

Hope sprang in John's chest at the idea that he still might have a chance to convince Arthur Morehouse to come with them.

But he had a feeling he would have to get past Clara first. Tonight's supper was turning out to be very important indeed.

Chapter Two

Immediately after Mr. Butler left the store, another unwelcome visitor arrived—though this customer, at least, was not one who came in every day. Sophia Emmers was one of the wealthier women in town and was rarely seen out shopping herself. She usually sent her cook or maid to gather her groceries for the week. "Clara! I'm so delighted to see you here. You are looking so lovely."

"Thank you, Mrs. Emmers. I'm surprised to see you here yourself today," Clara said politely.

The woman chuckled. "I know, but everyone in town was talking about stopping into the store over the past few weeks to support your family after such a tragic loss, and I didn't want to be excluded, of course." She walked over to a display. "What lovely new fabrics you have in stock. Did your mother pick them before...?"

Clara sighed and shook her head. "No, Hannah picked those. She has an eye for it, as well."

Mrs. Emmers smiled. "Well, that is very helpful. I would hate to take my purchases elsewhere."

The woman was ghastly, talking about not patronizing a business because of a family death, Clara thought.

"We're glad we can accommodate you," Clara said in her best customer service voice.

The society matron just nodded. "I'm sure Michael will be here to visit you later today. He has talked about you so much in the past few weeks."

It took everything in Clara not to let out a groan. Mrs. Emmers's son, Michael, visited the store often—and it wasn't to purchase groceries. He had started coming in about a year ago and made it clear that getting to know her better was his intention. Even the company of the annoying John Butler was preferable to that of Mr. Emmers's.

Her parents had been thrilled that the son of a prominent family, even better off than the Morehouses, wanted to court their daughter, but they had left the decision up to Clara—and she was careful to never give him any indication that she was interested.

Sure, he was handsome, rich and proffered all the expected compliments to Clara, but there was something about him that unsettled her. She could not figure out what it was, but her mother had told her to always trust her instincts. She was not interested in a match and had done her best to make that clear without offending the influential family. Michael had not gotten any of the hints, however, and still pursued her relentlessly. He even made overtures during her mother's funeral!

Clara had been so upset that she told him to leave and not come to their home again. She should have known that being at the business more than ever before meant providing another way for Michael to see her.

Even if he didn't make her uncomfortable, Clara had no time for romance. She had a business to run. She had sisters to care for. Her mother was in heaven, and her father was unable to care for anything at the moment.

Which meant it all fell to Clara. And she would not fail them, no matter what sacrifices she had to make.

"Well, we are very busy, so I probably won't have much time to talk to him," Clara hinted at Mrs. Emmers, hoping that would be enough to move the woman on her way.

"Perhaps in another day or so, then," she said with a predatory smile. Clara shuddered. The mother unnerved her almost as much as the son.

But she didn't have long to dwell on her thoughts. The store was indeed busy until the very end of the day, with them ringing up customers until soon after closing time, when they finally managed to close and lock the door at a quarter past seven.

"We did it. We survived another long day," Hannah said as the three collapsed onto chairs.

"We've worked at the store for full days before," Eliza said with a roll of her eyes.

Hannah grinned. "But not very often, and definitely not while running it by ourselves."

Though the store had reopened two weeks earlier, the town had been cautious about overburdening them at first. Many customers had come in, but their orders had been generally smaller than usual—as if the townspeople didn't want to trouble the sisters by making them work too hard. That initial hesitance seemed to have worn off, though, and the day they'd just concluded had been as busy as any Clara could recall.

"If the community knew that three women were running the business, and not father, they would be beside themselves," Hannah added.

Clara couldn't help but agree. Independence was where pioneers gathered to head to the new frontier, which made the community sound as if it was dominated by a bold and unconventional spirit—but the truth was that the town was as traditional as they came. Men ran the businesses and the women ran the homes. Sure, there were widows and some women who partnered with their husbands to become entrepreneurs, but it was unheard of for single young women of marriageable age and good social standing to be working independently, without their father's supervision.

But not anymore in the Morehouse family. Someone had to keep the store afloat—and it was going to be Clara with the help of her sisters.

The girls hurried home to prepare for supper with Mr. Butler. When they arrived, Clara peeked in on her father, thankful that half the food on the lunch tray by his bedside had been eaten. He must have felt a little better today.

Clara kissed him on the forehead. "We did well today, Papa. You don't need to worry."

He opened his eyes slightly and patted her hand. "I never worry about you, Clarabelle." And then he was out again before she could even warn him about their guest. She considered trying to rouse him but decided against it. If her father didn't wake up in time for supper, maybe Mr. Butler would just leave. Surely that would be best. Clara tiptoed out and headed to her room. Her feet ached as she took off her boots.

As she collapsed on the bed, grateful to finally rest her aching body, she thought about her father's words. He was right; he never had to worry about her. Or anything.

Clara would handle all the worrying for him.

She let herself relax for a little while before getting up to dress. She had just finished reordering her hair when their housekeeper, Betty, called up to tell her it was almost time for supper. Clara scolded herself for the number of frocks she had tried on to prepare for this family meal with John Butler. She didn't know what she was more nervous about, the conversation the man would have with her father or seeing him again. Something about John Butler made her feel different. Softer.

She wasn't sure she liked it. She could not afford to be soft. She had to take care of her family.

A husband could help you with that. He could take care of them with you—while caring for you, as well, she told herself.

But the thought rankled her. She was capable of tending to her sisters and father on her own. She didn't need a husband to come in and boss them all around. She had seen her friends from school marry off one by one, and had watched in dismay as each lovely, clever, independent woman slowly became just a dutiful wife. Her friend Mary had been so proud when she finally got her certificate and became a teacher, only to quit after a single year because her new husband didn't want her working.

It wouldn't have to be like that. A good husband would help share your load. Ease your burden. He wouldn't need to overpower you.

Clara shook her head at the thought. Such a man was rare, and it definitely wasn't John Butler. What kind of future could she have with a man who was such a rolling stone? She liked structure, dependability. Mr. Butler's life could offer neither of those things. Anyway, the man would be leaving to go back out to his new town in the West soon and none of this would matter.

They just needed to get through the night.

She heard the chime at the front door and hurried

from her room just in time to see the housekeeper come up the steps to tell her she had a guest.

Assuming it was Mr. Butler, she steeled herself and walked slowly into the parlor. Clara was surprised to see Michael Emmers there instead. He had never been forward enough to call on them unexpectedly at home.

"Mr. Emmers! What are you doing here?" Her unease around the gentleman pushed a polite greeting out of her mind.

"Clara, I have asked you to call me Michael," the man said. "You look lovelier than ever."

She seethed at his informality. While she didn't want to offend him, there were some lines she would not allow him to cross. "And I don't recall giving you permission to use my first name, Mr. Emmers."

A hardness entered the man's eyes, but it was quickly replaced by false charm. Clara was not fooled by it.

"My apologies, Miss Morehouse. We have been friends for so long that I had forgotten." His voice seeped with politeness.

The room, usually the warm center of their home, suddenly felt a lot colder. Mr. Emmers made it uncomfortable to be in the very place that was usually filled with love and laughter. She needed to get him out of here as soon as possible.

"I'm sorry to be impolite, but we are about to enjoy supper. Why are you here?"

He smiled. "I came to call on you, of course."

She steeled herself, knowing that she needed to be firm with him since he seemed to refuse to believe she wasn't interested in him.

"I did not give you permission."

Michael stepped forward and grabbed her hand. Clara's other one formed into a fist. How would it appear if she punched the son of the town's wealthiest family? Would they lose business?

"Miss Morehouse, please give me permission to court you. We could be wed within the next few months, and I could take on the burden of caring for your sisters."

Clara pulled her hand from his.

"My father cares for all of us. And I already told you no, Mr. Emmers, many times."

Michael's jaw clenched at that. He was angry. *Good. Maybe he will finally get the message*, Clara thought.

"Does he, though? Take care of you and your sisters? No one has seen your father in quite a while. People are starting to talk."

Clara's heartbeat began to race. Was it true? Was their ruse close to being discovered? If Michael was suspicious, then was the rest of the community too?

She schooled her emotions, giving Michael her coolest glare.

"As I said, my father cares for us, Mr. Emmers. I do not wish for you to court me."

Michael sighed. "I will keep trying. You will change your mind one of these days."

Clara wanted to suggest that there were plenty of other women in Independence to pursue, but she knew the words would fall on deaf ears. For his whole life, Michael Emmers had been the kind of person who rarely had been told no for anything. Once he fixated on something, he was hard to shake.

Clara sighed. "You're welcome to try, but really, I'm not interested."

"Can I at least stay for supper?" The man honestly would not give up.

"The lady said she wasn't interested, sir. Perhaps you did not hear her properly?" The two of them turned toward the parlor door, where the housekeeper had just shown in John Butler.

Michael stiffened at the sight of Mr. Butler, and the new arrival did the same in response. They reminded Clara of two dogs staring each other down over a bone in the street.

She was nobody's bone—but maybe she could use Mr. Butler's visit for her benefit.

"Mr. Butler, welcome. Mr. Emmers was just leaving. Did you want to speak to father before or after our meal?"

Her plan worked, evident because Michael narrowed his eyes at Mr. Butler. "He's staying for supper?"

She nodded. "He asked this afternoon if he could call on us." Mr. Butler's eyebrows rose when she used the phrase *call on us*, which implied that the visit was more than just a business meeting with her father, but he said nothing.

"And he's talking to your father?"

Clara gave him a sweet smile. "Oh yes, they are very old and close friends."

Michael walked over to John and held out his hand. "I don't think we've been introduced. Michael Emmers."

"John Butler." The men shook.

"It's funny how I've also been a friend of the Morehouse family for years, and I don't remember seeing you around here."

Mr. Butler smiled. "I travel a lot."

Clara hoped that she would be forgiven for the white lie she was about to tell. "Mr. Butler is here for a very special conversation, isn't that right?"

To her relief, Mr. Butler didn't contradict her or show any confusion. He merely nodded and Michael turned pale. "A very special conversation?"

For the father of three unmarried ladies, a gentleman coming calling could have only one reason for a special conversation supper—a marriage talk. She hated implying that it was happening, but she needed Michael to finally see reason and end his pursuit.

"Yes, and we should probably serve supper promptly. Will we be seeing you soon in the store, Mr. Emmers?"

With those words, Clara hoped he would finally get the idea that he was not invited to their home as a suitor. Boundaries were set.

Michael tightened his jaw and nodded. "Yes, I will stop by tomorrow."

He leaned forward and said in a low voice. "An engagement is not permanent. Remember that, Clara."

"*Miss Morehouse*," Mr. Butler said loudly, reminding Michael to address her properly. "I would love to have a word with you in private before we speak to your father."

Clara hid a smile at the scowl that appeared on Michael's face. He stormed out of the room, barely giving the housekeeper the time to open the door.

"I leave you alone for a few hours, and here I find you in another lie, Miss Morehouse. And you roped me into it too," Mr. Butler said. The words were reproachful, but his tone was teasing.

"I'm so sorry. He just would not leave and I panicked. You don't have to tell any more lies. I can tell him that I turned you down."

Mr. Butler's eyebrow quirked at that. "*You* turned *me* down? Why am I the one on the embarrassing end of this situation? More likely I changed my mind and never proposed."

Clara laughed. "Well, I guess we could try that, but I don't think the person who has pursued me relentlessly for the past year would believe that I had been rejected."

He smiled. "Arrogant and smart. I like it. He's pursued you for a year? Have you given his proposal consideration at all?"

Clara sighed. "Of course I have. You know about our situation now. An influential, rich man wants to marry me. My sisters would be taken care of. I wouldn't have to worry. And my parents encouraged me to allow his suit when he first started courting."

Mr. Butler regarded her with those warm brown eyes that made her want to confess all of her troubles. Clara was famous in her family for being the one who kept her emotions in check, so this was a new feeling for her.

"But you would still worry about your family, even if you were married and rich. It's part of who you are," Mr. Butler said, his voice soft.

Clara blinked at him. "And how would you know this?"

He chuckled. "Because you are the eldest. My brother worries about me like I'm still five, even though I've been a grown man for years."

"I suppose it comes with the job," Clara said with a laugh. She invited Mr. Butler to sit.

"Why did you turn Mr. Emmers down on his proposal, then?"

She leveled a stare at him. "Do you really need to ask? You met the man."

He grinned at her. "I was trying to be polite. What I really wanted to do was grab him by the ear and toss him out of the house."

Clara laughed. "Part of me would have cheered you on, but I don't need anyone fighting my battles."

The wink and smile he gave her made Clara's insides flutter. "No, I don't suppose you do."

She played with a bit of lace on her skirt, as a distraction. "Besides, even if his proposal was more palatable, I don't need any man to step in and take over my life. We have things well in hand."

He nodded. "So I saw at the store today. And I know your secret."

Clara looked up to meet his eyes in panic. Was he referring to the secret about them running the business without their father's oversight? Or the other one, that she had sent the letter rejecting his proposal? So many deceits, it was hard to keep them all straight.

"Oh?" She tried to keep her voice strong and steady.

Mr. Butler leaned forward and spoke in a conspiratorial whisper. "You *like* running that business. And you don't want to give that up."

She wanted to object but found that she could not. "And what if I do?"

He just shrugged. "Nothing wrong with that in my book."

Mr. Butler must have spent too much time in the wilds of the West. Things were different out there for sure, but not so much that he would have completely forgotten how society thought women should act. He could get himself in trouble if he said things like that in town.

"Most people would not feel that way. This is why I have no interest in getting married. A man would object to the idea of his wife running a business. He would either take it over or make her close it."

Mr. Butler was silent, contemplating her words. She heard the tick of the grandfather clock in the hallway, marking each second until his reply. There was no way he could deny that her words were true.

"Then I believe, Miss Morehouse, that you are not acquainted with the right sort of men."

John didn't know why he was sitting here flirting with Miss Morehouse. He had come to have a conversation with her father about his business proposal but had been pulled into her relationship drama. However, her declaration that she would never marry because no man would accept a working wife irked him.

"I'm not out looking for any sort of man," she replied to him. "I am perfectly fine without one."

He shook his head. "I wouldn't discount the idea completely, Miss Morehouse. Maybe say that you are not interested now because of your circumstances. A few years down the road, you could change your mind."

She regarded him coolly. "And why aren't you married then, Mr. Butler, if you are so in favor of the institution?"

He chuckled. "Oh, I will have a wife someday. I'm just not ready yet."

She raised her eyebrows. "And what would it take to become ready, in your opinion?"

This conversation had gone far off from where he'd intended it to go.

"I believe it is different for everyone. I live a life of travel right now, and have never had a home. Once I'm settled somewhere for at least five years, then I will find a wife."

She laughed at him and he bristled a bit. John didn't think the notion was that funny. "Why is that so amusing?"

She finally stopped laughing enough to answer.

"First of all, what if you never settle down? What if it's when you are an old man? Five years is such an arbitrary number, and you may not be able to wait that long because you would be too close to death."

He gritted his teeth. Who was she to question his carefully thought-out plan?

"My brother and I have moved many times throughout our lives. We find a place along the wagon trail, start a town and make sure it's established before we head to someplace new. This town we're working on now will be our last. My brother and I plan to make it our home."

She gave him a skeptical look. "How do you know for sure? What if another exciting new opportunity comes along?"

"That's why I have the five-year plan in place. So I know that I'm truly settled before I take a wife."

She chuckled. "What if you fall in love before then?"

He steeled himself. He wouldn't let himself fall in love before then. John had to ensure that he had not inherited wanderlust from his father. He wouldn't let his desire to move from place to place run his wife off like his father had done to his mother... "I won't."

"How do you know for sure?"

John tightened his jaw. "I won't let myself."

She sighed. "From what my parents have told me, sometimes you don't have a choice in the matter. Love just happens."

He shook his head. "It won't to me. I'm not going to subject someone to an unsettled life."

Miss Morehouse gave him a confused look. "Why not?"

"I have my reasons. Can we move on to the real reason I wanted to speak to you, instead of my love prospects?"

Miss Morehouse scoffed, "I see, you are all soft and caring when it comes to me talking about my ideas about marriage but an absolute bear when talking about yours."

John shifted uncomfortably. He needed to change the subject, now. "I know another of your secrets, Miss Morehouse."

She eyed him nervously. "I'm not sure I want to know what it is."

He pulled from his coat pocket the letter that had been allegedly written to him by Arthur Morehouse.

"This letter from your father, rejecting my plan to go out West. Did he really write it?"

She dodged the question. "Why does it matter anyway?"

John sighed. "You and I both know that the man has not signed anything in weeks."

Miss Morehouse cringed and leaned back in her seat. "Fine, I wrote the letter."

He blinked, having not expected her to admit to the truth so easily.

"I can't seem to evade the truth with you very well. Everyone else, yes. But you? Strangely difficult. I don't know why," she said in dismay.

He laughed. "Maybe I just pay attention better than others. Or maybe I'm just more clever than you."

She scoffed at that. "Now who's being arrogant?"

John folded the letter back up and handed it to her. "Can you tell me why you rejected my proposal?"

Clara arched an eyebrow. "Why on earth would I accept it? Selling a successful business and starting over in a brand-new town? It is too big of a risk, especially now."

He had to give her credit, she was thinking with her head and not with her heart.

"This is why I wanted to broach this topic with your father and not you." While in years past, Arthur Morehouse had shrugged off his suggestions to head to the West, John was convinced that he could change his friend's mind this time. Especially since this was the last town he and his brother were planning to start. He wanted to make sure his new community had the best. Arthur had always been interested in his adventures, and this would be his last opportunity to join John.

She glared at him. "Because you think he is more likely to make a bad business decision? I don't know whether to be insulted or complimented."

John sighed. "No insult implied to either you or your father, I promise. Mr. Morehouse has always been fond of my stories of the frontier, and I thought he might be interested in the adventure of it all."

Clara gave him a sad look. "He's not really interested in much of anything these days."

He stood up, and she followed suit. "Well, maybe this is something that will help rouse him. Miss Morehouse, I think it's time that I finally speak to your father."

She nodded. "He's not really dressed or prepared for company. He fell asleep earlier before I could even let him know you were coming."

John didn't care; he just wanted to see the older man, his friend, again. "I won't mind, I promise. Visiting with him will set my mind at ease. And while he may be avoiding the world right now, maybe it will do him some good to have the world brought to him."

"Very well, I will take you to him," she said, though her tone indicated she would rather take him out the front door instead.

As he walked up the stairs, John prepared himself for whatever he would see behind the bedroom door. Just what had become of the kindhearted man he had known?

Chapter Three

Clara knocked softly on her father's bedroom door, not surprised that she didn't receive a response. She turned to Mr. Butler, who was looking at her with concern.

"If you could give me a moment, I will light the lamp, and make sure he's at least awake."

He placed his hand on her shoulder as she turned. "No, it's all right, I will help you."

She wished he would let her at least clean up the room for a moment, without his scrutiny, but Clara had learned this afternoon that once Mr. Butler got a plan of action in his mind, he was hard to dissuade.

Their housekeeper had thankfully cleaned the room this morning, so it smelled like lemons when they entered, but there was a darkness to it. Her father was in the bed, not snoring. Maybe he was awake after all.

"Father? It's Clara, we have a guest."

He did not respond with anything other than a few mutters under his breath. Mr. Butler looked at her and nodded to the lamp on the bedside table. She walked over to it and lit it.

Her father groaned in response. "Too bright," he complained, but still made no effort to sit up.

"Father, we have company," Clara told him again, giving Mr. Butler an apologetic look. She had warned him about her father's condition, but sometimes seeing was worse than hearing about it.

"I don't want to see anyone, I'm not coming down" came a stubborn voice from the bed. They still could not see him among all the pillows he had surrounded himself with.

"You don't have to come down. He's already here, in this room," Clara said as kindly as she could manage. She didn't think this was going to go over very well with him.

Before her father could protest, Mr. Butler stepped forward. "Arthur, it's me, John Butler."

Father sat up in his bed and studied the man. "John?"

Clara knew that the men were acquaintances but hadn't realized that they were close enough to be on a first-name basis. Why had her father not mentioned knowing the famous town founder before?

Her father surprised Clara by reaching out to shake Mr. Butler's hand. "Oh, it's good to see you, boy. Clara, pull up a chair for our guest."

Mr. Butler gave her a knowing look, and she was too shocked to be properly irritated by it. These were more words than her father had spoken at one time in weeks. While she wanted to wipe that smirk off Mr. Butler's face, she couldn't help but be grateful to him for this moment.

She hurried to bring a chair closer to her father's bedside. She looked up in surprise to see that Mr. Butler had grabbed another one for her, as well.

"Oh, thank you."

"Stop flirting with my daughter and sit down and talk to me, boy," Father said, interrupting them.

"Arthur, I wasn't…"

Her father just chuckled. It was the first time Clara had heard that sound in a long while.

"I'm just teasing you. Now, come. Tell me about your latest adventure."

John went into a long story about his last wagon train journey out west. Clara found herself lost in the details he shared. Betty had called for supper several minutes before, but she couldn't tear herself away from this conversation. His descriptions of each person made her feel like she knew them.

"Wait, you're telling me that if their wagon is too heavy or full, they just throw things off the side and keep going?" The imagery was so humorous, she couldn't help but laugh. Still, she wondered about how cluttered the trail would be if it was littered with cast-offs along the way.

Although there were some funny things about life on the trail, much of it seemed quite difficult. Early to rise, late to bed. Being stuck for days on end in rainstorms, dealing with the same people day in and out. The same bland food over and over when fresh supplies ran out.

The saddest part was when the train ended and everyone went off in different directions toward their new settlements.

"People are going out farther and farther, and it's getting to be several weeks' journey to the nearest town for some of them," Mr. Butler explained. "So, Adam and I decided it was time to build a new community."

He explained that they had found the perfect piece of land and staked their claim. John had traveled back East in the fall to begin recruiting people in various essential professions to come live in the town. Independence was his last stop, and he would stay here making final preparations until the wagon train moved out in late April.

Her father sat up in bed with rapt attention. "How exciting, another town from the ground up."

Mr. Butler just nodded. "We've done this five times before, so I have a pretty good idea of what we will need. I'm recruiting my blacksmith tomorrow morning. Hopefully I can convince the young lad who is apprenticing for Mr. Johnson to finally start a business of his own and join us."

"Benjamin? He will be an excellent addition," Mr. Morehouse said. Clara couldn't believe what was happening. His eyes now gleamed with a passion that had been missed.

"Do you have a barber?"

Mr. Butler shook his head. "Not yet, but I have some leads. I did find a brave young preacher who wants to start a church."

Father gave the young man a look of approval. "And what about your general store? You have to keep those settlers supplied. It will provide their sustenance."

Mr. Butler didn't answer and Clara shifted uncomfortably in her seat. Father looked curiously between the two of them.

"What is going on?"

Mr. Butler cleared his throat, but Clara spoke first. "The Butler Brothers wanted you to run their store, Papa. But I responded to their letter and turned them down."

Father stared at her for a moment. "You didn't even bring it to me to read?"

Clara stared at her fingers twisted together in her lap. "You said you didn't want any letters, after..."

Father reached out and took her hand. "So I did, my

girl. But I'm also surprised you replied on my behalf. You and your sisters have taken on so much for me these last few weeks. I'm a terrible father to burden you."

Clara squeezed his hand back. "Oh hush, Papa. We're fine. But I didn't think Mr. Butler's proposal was a good business idea so I turned it down."

The family patriarch arched an eyebrow at that. "You rejected it because of business reasons and not because of my...condition?"

Clara nodded. "Your condition was a contributing factor, but it also doesn't make financial sense to sell a thriving enterprise to open an uncertain one."

Her father thought about her words before answering. "My dear, how do you think my 'thriving enterprise' started in the first place? I had to take a risk."

Clara gave him a confused look. "But now that we are successful, why would we give it up for something so unsure?"

"Oh, I know it would be a sure thing," her father explained. "Yes, there would be dangers on the way there, and it would be tough to start over from the ground up. But imagine being the only store for miles and miles. That is guaranteed success, at least until the competition rolls in. And if the location is as remote as all that, the competition may take quite some time to arrive."

Mr. Butler, who had been silent during the exchange, chimed in, "And by then, you will have established the loyalty of the community and a reputation for being the best. Just like you have here."

Clara looked between Mr. Butler and her father, the excitement reflecting in both their eyes. "Unfortunately, I am in charge of the store now and I say no."

Both men gave her a sad look. *Honestly, they are like children*, she thought.

"Now, Clara…"

"Papa, you agreed that I was in charge and could make all the business decisions until you were back on your feet. You said that you trusted me. Do you?"

He nodded. "Well, yes, I do. But this…"

She arched an eyebrow at him. "Do you think you'll be out of this room anytime soon?"

Her father deflated at that. "No, I'm not ready."

"Well, then, the answer is no. I'm sorry, Mr. Butler." The man's eyes reflected admiration and…stubbornness. Clara almost groaned. She should have known John Butler wasn't going to give up that easily.

The housekeeper called up again to let them know that it was suppertime. Of course Father asked for his to be served in his room.

She turned to their guest. "Will you be joining us at the dining table, Mr. Butler?"

The man looked torn, but her father made the decision for him.

"Stay with me, John. We have a lot of catching up to do."

Clara just nodded and said she would have a tray brought up to them. She worried a bit that Mr. Butler would put more foolish notions into her father's head, but she hoped that it had been made clear that she was the decision-maker for the family now. Part of her wondered what she would do when her father finally did feel better. She wanted more than anything for him to be back to his old self, but she also loved running the business.

I will just face that when it comes to it.

"If it's all right with you, Miss Morehouse, I would love to join you for dessert," Mr. Butler requested in a smooth voice as she was leaving the room. Clara just nodded and left. She took a moment to collect her thoughts before going to join her sisters for supper. Papa was awake and talking. They would be so excited to hear that news.

John exchanged pleasantries and small talk with Arthur Morehouse while they waited for their supper trays. He had yet to offer condolences on the family's loss, but he did not want to put a damper on the pleasant mood the man was in.

Judging from the surprised look on Clara's face during most of their earlier exchange, this level of engagement from her father had not happened in a while. Once their trays were set in front of them, Arthur quickly turned the conversation to business.

"I'm honored that you considered us to open the store in your town, John. You know I would love to go, if only…"

John nodded. "I could hold a spot for you, if you thought you might be well enough within a few months. We don't leave until the end of April."

Arthur gave him a sad smile. "I have no way of knowing. Losing my Violet was… Well, it was too much for me to bear."

John put his hand on the older man's shoulder. "I know, and I'm very sorry for it, my friend. But maybe a change of scenery would do you good?"

"You know, there may be some truth to that. I stopped leaving my room because everywhere I go in this house reminds me of her. Even here, but I'm slowly getting used to at least this area," Arthur said, apparently giving the idea some thought.

John was more convinced than ever that the Morehouse family should start anew in the West. "Then you should consider my proposal. I can help with getting the store ready for sale, and I'm sure Clara and I can come up with a list of all the inventory you will need to go—"

Arthur raised his hand to interrupt. "Clara already said no, and I have to respect her business decisions."

John's eyes widened in surprise. It was a rare thing for a man to give over control of his livelihood to his daughter, clever and capable though she may be.

"You really do trust her, don't you?"

Arthur nodded. "She's young and has a lot to learn, but she has a good head on her shoulders. And an excellent eye for business. I'm not going to be around forever, and I would rather have someone I know will succeed take over."

John regarded his friend. "You know some people aren't going to like that."

Arthur chuckled and sat up a little bit more in his bed. "Well, some people can mind their own business. I know you aren't like that…being an adventurous kind and all."

John gave his friend a grin. "The women out West do all sorts of things that would make polite society back here cringe. They are just as capable as their husbands, if they have them. Some of them even more capable."

A businesswoman like Clara would thrive in that setting, John thought.

Arthur smiled sadly. "I sure wish I could see it."

"Is there no way that we can change her mind?" John sat back in his chair, dejected. He would have to recruit another family to start a store, but his heart was still set on this one.

Arthur sat up straighter.

"Yes, that's it. You just have to change her mind. You

got me to fall in love with the West, and you are going to have to do the same with her."

John thought of the business-minded Clara. She would be a hard person to sway with stories of adventure.

"I don't know, Arthur, she seems like a tough sell. And besides, how would I be able to justify spending more time with her?"

Arthur gave the matter some thought. "I have a plan. Can you tell Clara that we need to speak with her?"

John got up to gather their supper trays so at least he would have an excuse to go downstairs. "Don't you think you should let me in on this plan first?"

Arthur just chuckled and told him to hurry. Clara looked up at him curiously when the housekeeper led him into the dining room.

"Your father wants to see you. And me. Both of us," John stammered. Why was he so nervous?

"What did you say to him? Did you try to convince him to do something that he's not ready for?" Clara hissed at him as they walked back up the stairs.

"Not at all, ma'am. All I did was regale him with tales of the West."

Clara sighed but put on a happy face when she opened the door to her father's room. John wondered how many times a day she had to put on a false front—cheerful for her father, pleasant for customers, calm and in control for her sisters—when she was secretly hurting inside.

John wished he could do something to ease the weight on her narrow shoulders, but he doubted she would let him.

"You wished to see me, Papa?" Clara's voice reverted from the annoyed woman he had encountered in the hallway to the sweet, almost childlike tone she used to speak to her father. It was funny because she had taken on an authoritative tone with the elder Morehouse when she had rejected their plans to move.

"Yes, since we will not be taking the business west for Mr. Butler's new town, we need to assist him."

Clara gave them both a confused look. "I don't understand. How can we help?"

John had no idea where Arthur was going with this, but if it meant he still had a chance to take them with him, he was not opposed to it. And, though he was hesitant to admit it to himself, the idea of spending more time with Clara was appealing.

"John will be working in the store with you for the next few weeks. You can show him how we do the books, order supplies, pack our crates for the wagon train, everything."

Clara gave him an annoyed look. "Won't any other businessman he recruits already know all of this?"

Arthur just shook his head. "Not necessarily. We are the best, as you know, and he wants the new store to run as the best. Besides, he may end up with someone inexperienced if others agree with what you said about it being too big of a risk to sell their current stores."

Clara considered his words, and John waited, holding his breath. It was a solid plan. While working together in the store for the next few weeks, he could convince Clara to see the beauty of a life in the West.

"All right, I will do it—but only if it's the last talk we hear about moving our business."

John grinned at her. "No promises, Miss Morehouse."

She gave him a stern look. "Are you coming down for dessert, Mr. Butler?"

He nodded but hesitated to follow. "I will be down in just a moment. I need to have one more word with your father."

Clara narrowed her eyes but didn't say anything. She left quietly.

"I told you that I had a plan. See? It worked," Arthur said after his daughter left.

John chuckled. "She seems pretty adamant that she's still opposed to the idea of even talking about going west."

"You can convince her. You are one of the best salesmen I've ever met." Arthur shuffled in bed so that he could lie down. John could tell he was getting tired.

"All right, I will give it a try, but if I'm going to do my part in this plan, you're going to have to do something for me too."

Arthur sighed. "I'm not really in the position to do anything right now."

"That's just it," John said, choosing his words carefully. "If I'm going to convince your daughter that you all need to move to the new town, you have to prove to her that you can be ready to go in April. You're going to have to make more of an effort to improve and get out of this room."

Arthur gave him a sad look. "I'm not sure I know how."

John told him to start with sitting up for a little while every day. "And I will come back in a few days to visit again. Maybe you can make it to the parlor. Just for a few minutes."

Arthur closed his eyes and lay back. "I'll try."

When John opened the door, he saw a rush of blue skirts and raven hair run by. Clara had been listening from the hallway. If his job to convince her before was difficult, it would be nearly impossible if she had over-heard their plans.

Either way, he suspected she would be making his life challenging in the upcoming weeks.

Chapter Four

Clara prepared the store for the day's opening, watching her sisters chatter happily about their father's progress as they worked. To say that she was conflicted about the entire thing was an understatement.

She was pleased that her father was finally excited about something but did not like that he and Mr. Butler were scheming behind her back to try to convince her to go west. She had overheard them last night, and it took all that was in her to not stomp in there and give the men a piece of her mind.

Clara had been fully prepared to refuse to allow Mr. Butler to spend time in the store after that, but their father had sat up this morning and asked for his breakfast. And he'd eaten it all! He was still in his bed, but this was more progress than they had seen in a long time.

So, she would allow him some hope and let Mr. Butler come into the store every day. But that didn't mean she was going to make things easy on him.

"Write down all the chores that you don't want to do here today. We will give them to Mr. Butler," she told her sisters.

Eliza laughed and happily took a few things off her work list. Hannah, however, was not as cooperative.

"I don't know if we should. Mr. Butler is very kind. And he's already helped Papa."

Clara scowled. She loved Hannah; she really did. But there were times when her sister's soft heart vexed her.

"Fine, Eliza and I will take care of it. You just do all the busy work."

Hannah bit her lip, considering, and nodded.

When Mr. Butler arrived, the two eldest Morehouse sisters had composed a work list that would make anyone want to turn in the other direction. Split among the three of them over time, the chores weren't normally that bad, but piled onto one person in one day—it would be grueling. To her surprise, Mr. Butler just looked at it and proceeded to take off his suit jacket, roll up his sleeves and get to work.

Clara didn't want to admit it, but it was nice to have someone stronger around the store to lift heavy bags of flour and restock the higher shelves. Less nice was how comfortable he was doing the work—so comfortable that he had plenty of time to make conversation with her sisters.

Eliza may have wanted to get out of the more unpleasant parts of her labor, but the adventurous woman also wanted to know everything about life on the wagon train and beyond.

"I wish I could go on a wagon. And see the West! It sounds so beautiful," Eliza said wistfully.

"Maybe you will someday," Mr. Butler said, giving Clara a mischievous look.

It was all Clara could do not to roll her eyes at the man, but she was an adult and didn't need to resort to childish behavior. "All these stories are lovely, but Mr.

Butler isn't telling you the bad parts. The disease, danger and death on the journeys. The uncertainty of life in the new frontier."

Eliza laughed. "Of course he isn't. Those stories aren't as fun. But I think we've all heard some of them. Have you had a lot of deaths on your wagon trains, Mr. Butler?"

For a moment, Clara regretted that she'd brought it up. Mr. Butler looked so sorrowful that it pulled on her heart. From his stories the previous night, she knew how close he got to everyone on each trip. He must take every loss hard.

"A few. I've traveled on the wagon train probably five or six times now, every time I come back to recruit people for a new town. The losses are sometimes staggering. Occasionally people get injured and sick and there is no access to a doctor if I haven't recruited one. Even if professional care is available, a prairie schooner is not an ideal place to do any real medicine. And, you have to worry about weather, animal attacks and other dangers. It's not an easy journey," he said.

Clara reached out and put her hand on his shoulder. "It's not your fault, you know. The deaths. Those people chose to go, knowing the peril."

He nodded and gave her a sad look. "Yes, I know. But it still hurts. When you are with people on the trail for so long, they start to become like family. It's painful when something happens to them."

Eliza's interest still wasn't dampened, however. "Do you warn people of the dangers ahead of time? What else do you do to prepare?"

John Butler dropped a heavy bag of flour into place and then sat down on a stool for a break. "Well, we do have a big talk with everyone that signs on about what we'll face. And I hire the wagon train masters with the best experience. They've already been through most of the bad things that can happen, so they know what precautions to take to minimize the risks. I also ask all the people going if anyone has any medical experience, so if needed, we know who we can ask for help."

Eliza looked intrigued. "And how many normal travelers have medical experience?"

Mr. Butler chuckled. "You'd be surprised. Sometimes we have someone who used to be the town's barber who can handle a few things. We always have several midwives. One time, we even had a man who was a doctor's son, who had decided he would rather become a rancher than follow in his father's footsteps. He knew more than enough to handle some of the minor injuries on the trail."

Clara scoffed, "What about the major injuries?"

"Those didn't always get fixed," Mr. Butler said in a quiet voice.

The girls sat in silence for a moment, no one knowing what to say. Finally, it was gentle Hannah who spoke up. "It's good of you, though, to take so many precautions. I've heard that there are some wagon trail outfits that are just in it for the money."

Mr. Butler nodded. "My brother and I are in it for the people. We want the towns we build to grow and prosper, and we need settlers in the area to arrive safely if we are going to do that."

After that, the conversation turned to what life was like for new arrivals out West, and how the Butler Brothers built their towns. Clara made every effort to focus all her attention on her customers and then her bookkeeping, but she couldn't help but listen with fascination to his stories.

She looked up at Mr. Butler and saw the passion in his eyes when he talked about his projects. It was the same excitement she had felt when her father told her she could run the business.

No, she refused to think she had anything in common with the man who lived his life taking risk after risk.

Customers who came in the store throughout the day gave Mr. Butler curious looks. No one asked after him, but Clara knew people were talking about the young man who was spending a lot of time with the Morehouse sisters, because they had more busybodies than usual stopping in to purchase small items just so they could get a good look at him.

Someone must have told Mrs. Emmers, as well, because she was the one who finally stepped forward to get answers to the mystery.

"I wasn't aware you had family in town, Miss Morehouse. Is this young man helping out while your family recovers after your mother's passing?"

Clara just shook her head. "No, Mr. Butler is just a friend of the family who is interested in learning more about operating a store."

Mrs. Emmers studied John, who was at that moment hauling supply crates out from the back room.

"Oh, how nice of your father to show him the ropes. Opening a store yourself, Mr. Butler?"

John looked up at the woman in surprise, almost as if he hadn't noticed her before. Clara hid her smile behind her hand, because with her high status in town, Mrs. Emmers was used to everyone paying her immediate attention.

"No ma'am, but I may need to help someone else open one someday."

Clara made introductions between the two, and she

could see when it finally dawned on the older woman who she was talking to. "You're not John Butler, of the famous Butler Brothers, are you?"

John nodded. "I sure am. And I'm a good friend of the Morehouse family. You wouldn't be related to Michael Emmers would you?"

Clara groaned inwardly, remembering the encounter Mr. Butler had had with Michael the night before. Mrs. Emmers narrowed her eyes.

"He's my son. Do you know him?"

"I made his acquaintance last night," John said, his smile oozing charm. Clara could now see that there were two versions of Mr. Butler's smile. One that he reserved for when he was trying to make an impression on people, and his genuine one. She found that she preferred the latter.

"Oh, you're the gentleman he told me about who interrupted his call on Miss Morehouse. How good of a family friend would you say you are?"

John leaned forward, smiling. "Very good. Almost like family. Wouldn't you say so, Clara?"

For once she didn't mind someone using her given name without permission. She stayed quiet, but Eliza stepped forward, grinning. "Yes, almost like a brother."

Mrs. Emmers huffed at this, but did not say anything else while she paid for her purchase.

"That family is something else," John said after she left.

Clara just nodded. "I imagine we will be getting a visit from Michael this afternoon too. Now that he knows you are here, he's going to want to come in and spend time with me, as well."

John regarded her. "You know, you can just tell him to leave you alone."

Eliza laughed. "She's tried. Believe me. That man just can't seem to get the idea into his head that anyone might not want to marry him."

Clara really wished they could change the subject, but that seemed impossible. Mr. Butler stiffened. "Do you think he could be dangerous?"

Clara chuckled and waved him off. "No, he's just a bored gentleman who has a fascination. I keep hoping he will find someone else to obsess over and move on. For now, however, I'm the one he's fixated on."

The others looked doubtful, but she shrugged them off. "You can pretend that we are engaged, like we said yesterday, if you want," Mr. Butler said. Her sisters exchanged a look, and Clara had a feeling they would be attacking her for information later.

Clara just shook her head at him and buried herself in her work. One of her predictions about Michael was correct though. The man rushed through the entrance of the store not an hour later.

He stared at John with suspicion. "Miss Morehouse, I would like to speak to you, please. Alone."

Mr. Butler opened his mouth to protest, but Clara just leveled him with a glare. She could handle Michael on her own.

"I don't think that it's appropriate for us to be meeting without a chaperone, Mr. Emmers."

Michael clenched his fists. "May I speak to you outside, then?"

Clara sighed. She might as well get this over with. She promised herself that she wouldn't lie to get rid of Michael. And she would do her best not to be rude. But for all that, she was determined to make herself clear, once and for all. She did not want to marry him or anyone right now. She wanted to take care of her family. He would just have to accept that.

"Fine, I will talk to you out front."

"Stay where we can see you, please," Eliza chimed in, and Michael leveled her with a look that made Clara want to punch him.

She followed Michael outside and saw that her sisters and Mr. Butler were standing in the window, watching. She didn't need their help, but it was nice to know that she wasn't alone.

John gritted his teeth when he heard the raised voices outside the store. He couldn't quite make out what Clara and Mr. Emmers were saying, but it clearly wasn't pleasant. Others in the street had stopped to stare at them.

Clara stood her ground though. He couldn't help but admire her, and was glad that for once the fire in her eyes wasn't aimed at him.

Michael said something angry in a low voice, grabbing Clara's arms. John started marching to the door, but her sisters stopped him.

"She will only be mad at you if you interfere," Eliza said. "She can handle him."

Sure enough, Clara knocked Michael's hands off her arms, but then the man said something that made her pale. She replied, and Mr. Emmers just glared at her before stomping off.

Clara came back into the store, a sad look on her face.

"What happened? What did he say?" Hannah and Eliza hurried over to their sister to give her a comforting hug.

"He knows."

John crossed to the women. "Knows what? About you running the store?"

Clara nodded. "Yes, and that our father is ill. I guess he bribed our maid, Ruth, to get the information."

Eliza just shrugged. "So what if he knows?"

Clara gave her sister a tremulous smile. "If he tells everyone that we are running the store instead of Papa, people won't want to come here anymore."

Eliza dismissed her concerns. "People have been coming here for years. They come for our supplies, not to see Papa."

"They come because the Morehouse family has been trustworthy all these years," Clara explained. "When they find out we've been lying…we will lose a lot of customers. Not to mention the ones who think that women have no place in business."

John wanted to punch something. "So, what did he say—that you had to accept his offer of marriage or he would share your secret with the town?"

Clara nodded. "That is almost exactly what he said. He gave me a few days to decide."

Everything within John urged him to storm over to the Emmerses' mansion and take care of this personally. Michael Emmers was a weakling and was no match for John physically if the man challenged him to a fight. Or, he could use his negotiating skills to get the man to change his mind. He could fix this for them.

"Let me go talk to him, please. I can make sure you never have to deal with him again," John said, but he already knew what her answer would be.

Clara just smiled at him. "Thank you, Mr. Butler, but this is my problem and I'm going to fix it on my own."

Her sisters looked worried.

"You're not going to marry him, are you?" Hannah

asked. The very thought of that curdled John's blood. He told himself that it was just disgust at the idea of someone as wonderful as Clara marrying a fool like Emmers and not due to jealousy over her marrying at all.

Remember your five-year plan, he told himself.

"I don't want to marry him, but it would secure a future for our family business," Clara said. "I'm sure he would never allow me to work, but he could run the store himself or hire someone to until our father is back on his feet."

Yes, John really did want to punch something.

Apparently, Eliza had similar thoughts. She slammed her hand down on the counter. "That is so ridiculous."

"Eliza!" Clara looked taken aback at her sister's anger.

"I'm sorry, sister. I know you have made a lot of sacrifices for our family, but I'm not going to let you throw yourself at the altar of marriage to a hideous man like that. If we lose the business, we lose the business."

Eliza was rapidly becoming one of John's favorite people.

"She's right. You cannot marry him," he told Clara, who gave him a disgruntled look.

"Did I ask for your opinion?" The woman's eyes were filled with fire.

"No, you didn't. But you've spent enough time with me to know that I'm going to give it anyway. Who cares what the community thinks or what that man thinks? You are skilled at running this business."

He smiled at Clara, and some of her anger seemed to dim. "Thank you."

John nodded. "Besides, you are one of the bravest women I've ever met. You're not going to let a weakling man like that be your husband."

She arched an eyebrow at him. "Oh really? And what kind of man do I need?"

Five-year plan. Five-year plan.

"Someone who will appreciate you and let you be yourself," John told her.

Clara smiled at him. "I don't need anyone other than my family, but thank you for that. And thanks for encouraging me to be brave. Most people would urge me to marry the richest man in town."

Though he was happy that he had made her smile again, John wished he could do more for her. He hoped that he never ran into Michael Emmers on the street. He could not answer for his actions if he did.

Needing to cool his temper, John took a break from the Morehouse store to complete another errand. He headed over to the blacksmith's shop, where the man in charge had not one but two apprentices. He had been watching the business for a few days and had seen that the older blacksmith-in-training was skilled enough for his own forge.

"Are you here for another horseshoe, Mr. Butler?" Benjamin was seventeen years old, and eager to help every patron that came to the smithy. John had been by to observe him all week, hence his newly purchased collection of horseshoes.

John just chuckled at the boy's question, enjoying the heat in the smithy compared to the cool January temperatures outside. "I think I will be set on those for a while. The head of my next wagon train going out West will be grateful for the supplies though."

Just as they had all week, Ben's eyes lit up at the mention of the venture. "When do you think your next train will leave?"

John sat down on a bench. "That depends on a few things, I guess."

"Like what?"

"My brother and I are starting up a brand-new town, so we not only need materials and settlers but people to help build that town."

Ben listened with eager ears as he went back to work. "What kind of people?"

John hid his smile; the boy was so earnest. His hard-working and kind spirit would do well in their new community. "Well, people like you."

Ben nearly dropped his hammer at the words. "Like me?"

John stood up and walked up to Ben. "I have a confession to make. I didn't really come in here every day this week because I needed horseshoes. I need a blacksmith in this new town, and I'm hoping you will come and take the position."

Ben's eyes widened. He carefully put down his hammer and walked to sit on the bench, looking dumbstruck.

"Me…be the blacksmith? But I'm just an apprentice."

John smiled. "Didn't Mr. Johnson say that you were ready to move on but that he didn't have the money to hire you on as a full blacksmith?"

"You heard that?"

John nodded. "I know you will probably be looking for another place to settle soon, so why not an adventure out West? Unless you have family here…"

Ben just shook his head. "I lost my family when I was a boy, and the Johnsons took me in. But I'm not really their kin, so I don't think they want me to be another mouth they have to feed forever."

John felt for the boy. It had been just him and his

brother alone in the world when they were young adults, but at least they'd had each other.

"It sounds like this is a great opportunity for you."

Ben's shoulders slumped. "It would be... But I can't."

John raised an eyebrow. Not the response that he had been expecting.

"Why not?"

"I need to join another blacksmith's business first. I don't make much money and haven't saved up enough for my own equipment."

"We can help with that," John said, smiling as the boy's countenance lifted. "In exchange for a percentage of the money you earn from your business for the first year or two, we can finance your equipment and journey west—and also give you some land to use and build your workshop when you arrive. We can work it into the contract."

Benjamin beamed at this news. "That's... I mean, I can't believe..."

John just clapped the young man on the back. "We are just glad to have you." Then, knowing that he had to make sure the honest reputation of the Butler Brothers was maintained on this venture, John added, "But before you sign any contract, I want you to have Mr. Johnson read it over, as well. Just to make sure you feel that everything is fair."

Benjamin reached out and shook his hand. "You're a good man, Mr. Butler."

John just smiled. "So are you, lad. Now you had better get back to work before Mr. Johnson comes out to holler at you. I will be around in a couple of days with the papers for you to look over and sign. We probably won't have everything settled and be ready to move out for another few months."

He said goodbye to the boy and walked his way to the other side of town. One more business off his checklist; his brother would be pleased. He'd received a missive from Adam a few days ago, urging John to get things settled soon. Adam had already headed out with a wagon train full of supplies and a few workers to start building. His letter stated that they had staked their claim for the location of the new settlement and filed all the necessary paperwork. It would be much farther west than the last stopping point of current wagon train routes, but pioneers were aching to explore new territories and settle down on unclaimed land.

This is it. This is our home, Adam wrote in his letter. The Butler Brothers had built five towns, and this would be their last. It would be strange to be settled in one place. That was something they'd never really experienced with their father, who'd been constantly driven by wanderlust, always eager to pick up everything after a few years and stake a claim elsewhere. The two boys had used their experience when they were grown to help lead wagon trains west and assist settlers in starting new lives.

Once they'd gathered enough money, they'd financed their first town and staked their own claim. That community, a small watering hole that provided a welcome respite to weary travelers about two weeks into their wagon train journey, had made them a hefty profit. So they built another, farther down the trail. And then another.

But the Butler brothers longed for something they had never had—a home. They had made a promise to each other that this venture would be their last. They would put down roots and live in their new community.

They just had to build it first. And now that he was

spending every day with the Morehouse daughters, he was one step closer to convincing them that the Butlers' new town could be their home too.

Chapter Five

Adjusting to John Butler's presence in their store was easier than Clara had expected. He did all the heavy lifting for them, and her sisters loved him. All the ladies in the town who stopped by to see him work seemed to appreciate the new scenery, as well.

"I know you love giving me all the big supplies to lift, but you do realize I'm here to learn the store business," he teased her on his third day there.

He did have a point. And the sooner she taught him how to do things, the sooner he would be out of their lives. So, she dove with fervor into showing him how to keep the books.

"Pay attention," she scolded him when he groaned at every new ledger Clara brought forth.

John pushed them back and stood up. "I think I've gotten the idea, and my brother can mostly handle the books. And hopefully whatever family we find to open the store won't be completely inexperienced."

Clara leveled a stare at him. "Why are you here, then?" She called his bluff, wondering if he would keep up the pretense of trying to learn the business, when he really just wanted to convince her to move the family.

Surprisingly, he did not back down. "I don't need to learn about the financial aspect, I need to know how you prepare the crates for the wagon train. And what kind of supplies we should have on hand for new settlers. I want to make sure we have everything we need for the people who will rely on us."

She narrowed her eyes at him. "Why didn't you say that before?"

John shrugged. "You didn't ask."

Clara studied him for a moment. Even though she knew this was all a ploy, there was something sincere in his tone when he talked about being there for his community. She wondered if he really did want to know these things or if he was just using his charm on her.

Either way, she didn't have an argument as to why she shouldn't show him. Of course, she did make him pick the heaviest container from the shelf to lift down and open. It was only fair.

"This is one of our crates for longer journeys, if someone is going all the way to Oregon or California. We usually recommend purchasing several of them. Some with food items and others with necessary supplies," she explained.

John started picking items out of the box—this one contained food. "It's amazing how much you were able to fit in one crate."

Clara beamed with pride. "We put in more now, since I started packing them. You would be amazed at how much you can fit if you only plan it right."

Her heart clenched at the memory of her mother watching while Clara packed and unpacked the crates, trying to come up with the exactly perfect plan.

Only you could do something like this, my darling girl, Mama had said.

Clara wiped a tear from her eye but not before John looked at her with concern. "Are you all right?"

She ignored the question, embarrassed that he'd caught her in a moment of weakness. Clara turned and grabbed the supply list she used to stock the crates.

"In this one, we have tea, coffee, flour, sugar, beans, hardtack, rice, pepper and some dried fruit. Enough to last several months, but most people try not to open these until their fresh ingredients run out," Clara explained.

John tried to restock the container in the same way she had arranged everything, but was failing miserably, making her laugh.

"How were you able to do this?" His frustration was evident in his voice, and his hair, which had been brushed back neatly when he came in, was now ruffled and hanging in his face as he stooped over the crate. It made an endearing sight, if one was interested in that sort of thing.

Which she was not. *Focus on the work*, Clara told herself.

"It took a lot of practice. But I will let you pack one every day until you leave, if you think that will help," Clara said.

She hid a grin when he looked slightly afraid at that plan, but she knew that he would be here every day to do it. John Butler was not the type of man who backed down from anything.

Clara pulled a smaller crate from the shelf, this one with an easy-to-open lid. "Now, in this one, we keep a lot of the everyday items that might be needed on the trail, such as cooking utensils, a cast-iron skillet, tin plates and cups, eating utensils, matches…"

She pulled out every item as she listed it, laying them

out on the counter in a row. John had pulled a pad out of his back pocket and was taking notes.

"And this is one item that most people forget but we always pack for our customers—a mending kit." Clara held it up excitedly to him.

John smiled at her exuberance and wrote it on his list. "That's smart thinking, because people don't bring too many clothes and the trail is hard on them. Their other sewing supplies might be packed away where it would be hard to easily retrieve."

Clara nodded. "That's what my father told me. I'm assuming now that he got that little bit of information from you and your stories about life on the journey."

Her father had told her last night that John stopped in whenever he was in town to talk about his experiences in the West. Clara wondered why she had not crossed paths with him before, but he must have visited when she was still in school or on days she wasn't in the shop when she was older. Not that it mattered. Soon he would be heading out of Independence, and it would be a long time before they saw him again. It was strange that after only a few days in his company, she was sad at that idea.

Clara forced herself to focus again on the topic at hand.

"But I can only tell you about what we prepare people with for the journey itself. The missing piece will be what sort of supplies you want to have at your store in the West. Since you won't be stocking them for the wagon train but to start their new homes."

John surveyed the items in front of him. "I imagine a lot of the same things that are in the food crate. Until they can get their farms going, they are going to need nonperishable supplies. But maybe with the dishes, utensils, and such, you can add nice things—like some-one would want in their permanent home?"

Clara nodded at that and thought of the possibilities. What would a family want in their new dwelling, once it was built?

"Linens. People don't spare much room for linens in their wagons when they're heading to the West, but a wife is going to want to hang curtains, make a table-cloth, blankets and more when she finally enters her new home," Clara exclaimed excitedly. "You're going to want to make sure whoever is opening your store has a good supply of fabric."

John studied the textile shelves, which were getting low in supply lately. They would have to restock once again. She made a note to tell Hannah.

"This is a large town compared to what we will have. Do you think half this stock will do?"

She walked over to the fabric counter and pulled out a book from underneath. "Probably more than half. People will still need to make clothes and things for the home. You may even need to keep more of certain ma-terials in stock for special occasions since you won't be able to special order anything quickly."

He still looked very confused, and she took pity on him.

"How about this—when you find a new person to set up a store, they can place their fabric orders through us, and we will keep fully stocked with the vendor so we can satisfy those requests as quickly as possible. That way, you know you will have someone you trust handling it. Our shelves are low now because Mama was the one who filled them and my sister just started restocking, but we will fill them immediately so we can help."

John's shoulders slumped in relief. "That would be wonderful. In fact, I'm wondering if your business can just be my middleman, or middlewoman, and help us restock supplies to send to the store every time a wagon train is heading our way."

Clara was surprised that he was considering a possibility that didn't include their family traveling westward. It was progress, and the least she could do was be accommodating so that he would give up his silly notion of them moving. Besides, it would be really good for their bottom line to have an ongoing relationship with his town's store.

"That sounds like a wonderful plan. My sisters and I will start working on a recommended inventory list for you tomorrow," she said happily.

John tucked his notepad back into his pocket. "But this doesn't mean I'm finished learning how things are done around here. I need to know, just in case."

Clara almost scoffed at that. So, he wasn't giving up on trying to win over her approval. "Fine, but I won't change my mind about the West."

He just laughed and went back to trying to repack the large crate in the perfect way Clara had. Try all he could, she knew it would take him a long time. That was fine by her. She'd found that it was nice to have someone to talk to in the evening while she was stuck restocking the store.

John adjusted his tie and brushed the dust off his suit the best that he could. He would be attending church this morning. It had been some time since he'd had the opportunity. While they were finding their land, he and Adam had been forced to worship God on their own, under the sky. That didn't make it any less meaningful, but still, it would be nice to sit with other believers and hear preaching from the Bible for once. Independence now boasted two churches, another hastily built to keep up with the town's growth in the past few years.

John approached the older establishment, knowing that the Morehouse family would be attending that one. Arthur had sent him a note this morning, inviting him to sit with his daughters during service. It was so kind that he could hardly say no. John was so used to doing things on his own during these trips away from his brother. It was nice to have someone welcome him into their family while he was here.

He might have been a little too excited about the idea, because he was one of the first to arrive at the church building, quite a while before services started. He didn't dare sit down, not wanting to offend anyone by taking their usual place. Even though people didn't own pews here, years of tradition typically indicated where people would sit.

"Mr. Butler, it's good to see you again." The quiet voice of Hannah Morehouse came from behind him. He turned to see the three young ladies and their housekeeper standing there in their Sunday best.

"Good morning, ladies. It's good to see you, as well. I thought your father would be joining us? He sent me a note inviting me."

Clara gave him a sad look and shook her head, which he knew meant that the patriarch could not bring himself to leave the house yet. John sent her an encouraging smile.

"Maybe next week. Shall we?"

He held out his arm to the eldest Miss Morehouse, and she stared at it for a moment before taking it so John could lead them into the church. He suppressed his smile when he heard the two youngest Morehouse girls giggling behind him. If anything, he had definitely won those two over.

Their housekeeper, Betty, apparently had no patience for their nonsense and barreled past them toward a bench near the front of the church. John stopped next to the pew and waited politely for the other two Morehouse sisters to sit down. Clara ended up next to him. She was looking in every direction but at him.

"Are you back to ignoring me, Miss Morehouse? I had hoped we were well beyond that. After the past few days in the store, I thought we were on our way to becoming friends," he teased.

Clara finally met his eyes and gave him a slight smile. "I will admit, you are more tolerable than expected. But I'm curious as to why our father invited you to come sit with our family. The others will find it strange to have an unwed man sit with three unmarried ladies, even if their housekeeper is here to chaperone," she explained.

John hadn't even considered what his presence might do to her reputation. "I can move to another pew, then…"

She laid a hand on his arm to stop him from rising. "That's all right. You're here now, so if there was any damage to be done, it already has been. Besides, there is also a benefit to your scandalous presence in our pew." Clara nodded her head to a pew that was on the opposite side of the church, where Michael Emmers was glaring at them.

"Oh, he does not look happy," John said, not even trying to hide his grin as he waved at the man.

Clara giggled—the first such sound he had ever

heard from her—but then attempted to scold him. "Stop, you are only going to make him angrier."

"Is that a bad thing?"

The two of them considered it before both bursting into laughter, causing many eyes in the church to turn to them and a few older attendees to make shushing noises.

"You two behave or I will have to separate you," Betty said from the other side of the pew, which only made them want to giggle more.

John couldn't remember having a better time in church. When the services started, the companionship of Clara next to him and the voices of the community joined in song put him in an even more lighthearted mood. Was this what it felt like to belong somewhere? John never had, so he didn't know the feeling.

The minister, Reverend Bolton, delivered a sermon that not only taught the Bible but showed people how to apply it to their daily lives. John hoped that the minister he was taking west to their new town would be the same.

That reminded him that he needed to have a conversation with Reverend Bolton. After the service, he introduced himself to the man and thanked him for the sermon.

"I've seen you here from time to time when you've been in town in the past, and of course I've heard of you and your brother, but it's nice to finally meet you, young man. Hopefully, we will be seeing more of you in the future," the reverend said.

John apologized for not introducing himself sooner. "And I'm even more sorry to tell you that I need to ask you a favor so quickly after our first meeting. Do you think we could chat for a few minutes after you are done here?"

He was aware of the long line of people waiting to say their greetings to the minister. The man nodded and invited him for lunch at the parsonage with him and his wife. Never one to turn down a free meal, John agreed.

He caught up to the Morehouse sisters as they were nearing the sidewalk to begin their walk home. "Thank you for letting me sit with you today, ladies."

Clara just nodded, but Eliza stepped forward with a twinkle in her eyes.

"Betty put a roast in the oven this morning. Would you like to come over for our Sunday meal?"

John felt instant regret that he had agreed to eat with the reverend and his wife. He longed to spend more time with the Morehouse family. Something about being with them made him very happy. With regret, he declined—but despite his excuse, the two younger Morehouse daughters were not taking no for an answer.

"Well, you will just have to come to supper, then, since you are occupied for lunch," Hannah said and Eliza nodded.

John glanced at Clara, who maintained her stoic expression throughout the entire exchange. He wished he knew what she was thinking. She either was all smiles and laughter or looked at him like he was the most annoying creature on the planet. He never knew exactly where he stood with her, and he knew that Arthur would want a report soon about his progress on the push to move to the West. Clearly, he needed to continue to spend more time with her.

"I guess I will be well-fed today, then," he teased as he agreed to supper.

His first big meal of the day, at the parsonage, was a pleasant affair. Reverend Butler and his wife begged for stories of life in the West. They'd had quite a few young people from their community leave for a new life in the past few years, and they longed for more information about what it was like.

"That's actually why I wanted to meet with you," John said after Mrs. Bolton handed him a piece of pie. "I have a young man that is interested in becoming the minister in our new town, but he needs a place to stay in Independence for a while, before we are ready to leave."

Mrs. Bolton sat down across from him excitedly. "Oh! He can have our son's room. Our boy is off to college, and it has been so lonely and quiet around here."

The reverend laughed at his wife's excitement. "I guess I don't even need to offer my say in the matter. See? The Good Lord has provided someone to fill that hole in your heart just a little bit, my love."

John saw the two exchange an affectionate smile and his heart clenched. Would he ever have anything like that? Would his wanderlust take over and never allow him to settle down for a long time, as it had with his father—or would his new town finally be his home so he could find someone to grow old with?

He didn't realize until this moment, seeing the reverend and his wife so in love after all of these years, just how much he wanted that.

"Thank you for taking him in. He is a very pleasant young man. You won't regret it," John said, his voice gruff.

The elder couple broke eye contact to turn back to him and smile. "I would hope he's pleasant if he's a man of God," Mrs. Bolton teased. "Or he would be out of a job very quickly. He isn't married?"

John shook his head. "No, but I heard there are plenty who are willing to volunteer for the job."

The Reverend squeezed his wife's hand. "Well, I

can't say that it is an easy job without a good partner by your side, but maybe someone will come along for the young man once he's settled."

For me too, I hope, John thought as he took another bite of pie.

Chapter Six

Clara waited eagerly for John to arrive in the store before it opened a few days later. She lifted her new crate onto the counter, hoping that it would catch his eye when he came in the door. Despite her earlier objections to his presence, Clara had grown quite used to having him around and sharing things about the business with him.

For once, it was nice to have someone outside her family respect her actions and opinions and not think she was just a little girl playing at being a businessman. Even her family teased her rather more than she thought she warranted. Her sisters were out making the early morning deliveries, so they wouldn't be around to roll their eyes at her when she went on and on about another new idea.

The door chimed as John entered the store, and he stopped short when she smiled at him.

"What? Do I have flour on my face or something?" she asked when he continued to stare at her.

John just shook his head in response. "No, it's just that you seem in a pretty good mood today. It took me by surprise."

She glared at him, her jovial attitude vanishing. "Are you saying that I'm not normally a pleasant person?"

"Oh, you are always pleasant, but sometimes you have an extra fire in your eyes that makes me approach with caution," he teased.

Normally, she would argue with him more, because it was becoming her favorite pastime, but she was too excited to show him what she had done. And they had only about an hour before the store was going to open to customers for the day.

"Come, look. I got the idea for a new crate last night and I came in early to work on it."

John stared in confusion at the things gathered on the counter. Clara laughed when she realized how strange it must look. There was a folded canvas tarp, a pile of sticks, a satchel with wadded up newspapers and matches.

"No, it's not trash, I promise. It's a rainy-day kit!"

John picked up the tarp and looked at her questioningly. She held up the rope that went with it. "So, you can put this tarp up between wagons to create a dry place to eat and cook if you are stuck in a rainstorm for days on end."

He lifted the sticks. "And these are to build a little fire if all the available wood is wet?"

She nodded and held up the satchel of newspaper scraps. "And this is for kindling, in case it's hard to get that fire started."

During their shared Sunday supper, Clara had listened to John's story about how on one trip, they had been held up for nearly a week because a storm had resulted in wagons getting stuck in the mud. Everyone was so wet and miserable by the end of it because they'd not been able to have a cup of coffee or any warm food. It had severely hurt morale.

"But do you think everyone is going to make room on their wagons for it?" John looked pleased with her idea, but she knew that he would think about the practical aspects of it. It was one of the things she had grown to like about him.

"They will when I tell them about all the storms you got stuck in," she said proudly.

John started packing the rainy-day items into the small crate she had made, smiling as he did so. "Leave it to you to take the worst part of the wagon train adventure and find a way to capitalize on it."

"Well, I am a very serious businesswoman," she said, half teasing.

Then John did something that completely shocked her—he grabbed a handful of flour from the bin and tossed it at her. "A very serious businesswoman who now really does have flour on her face."

He stared at her, grinning. Clara knew he was waiting to see what she would do next. She had two options here. She could yell at him and kick him out of the store or she could get revenge.

Clara was a serious businesswoman, but she also wasn't one to let go of a challenge. Against her better judgment, she reached for a handful of flour and shoved it back in his face.

He coughed, and a cloud of white floated in the air around him. She burst out into laughter. "I can't believe you just did that," he said.

"I can't believe *you* started it. All your time here has never indicated that you would be such a troublemaker."

John stepped a little closer, his hand on the flour

barrel. "I don't think you have any idea of just what a troublemaker I am."

Oh, this was going to be bad, she thought. *This was going to be very bad*. "Don't you even think about it, Mr. Butler!"

But he did—grabbing a handful and flinging it at her. She, of course, retaliated and this continued until they were both covered with flour and so was the floor. Clara couldn't help but laugh at the sight of him looking like a snowman.

"I have to tell you, Miss Morehouse, I never suspected you had this much fun in you. I thought you were strictly business all the time."

"I'll have you know I can be very fun, but also practical." She surveyed the havoc they had made and groaned. "We need to clean up this mess before the store opens."

They both started laughing again as they grabbed dusters to brush off any wayward flour that had landed on items on the shelves, then tackled the floor.

"I can hardly believe I did this either, to be honest. I haven't laughed this much since, well, since Mama got sick," Clara said as she started sweeping the flour into a pile at the center of the room. Thinking of her mother wasn't as difficult as it had been a few weeks ago, but the loss still hurt deeply.

"I'm glad I could at least bring a smile to your face, along with the flour on it, as well," John teased, adding some powder to her pile with his broom. Clara ran her fingers on her face and saw a cloud of white fill the air.

"Oh! How bad is it?"

John wiped a hand over his face and produced his own cloud. "Take a look at me, and you have your answer. It's bad. Let's get this cleaned up, and then we can take turns cleaning ourselves up."

The flour in the air tickled Clara's nose, and she let out the sneeze she couldn't hold in any longer. Another burst of flour came off her face, and some landed right back in her eyes.

"I can't see!" She kept her eyes closed, but she could feel John coming closer before his thumbs rubbed gently over her eyelids.

"Hold still, I'll get the worst of it."

The calmness of his voice and the softness of his touch on her face made Clara feel both comfortable and nervous at the same time, if such a thing were possible.

"All right, try opening them now."

Clara blinked her eyes, and John came into focus. She shifted uncomfortably when she realized how close he was to her face and he took a hurried step back.

"Much better, thank you," Clara said, her voice just above a whisper.

They grabbed their brooms and went back to work in silence until John started sweeping around the counter. He paused and pointed to a row of notches on the door frame to the back room. "What's this?"

Clara crossed to him and ran her fingers along the notches, remembering when each one was made. "These are our height measurements, as we grew up. Here's mine, the ones that say *CM*, and there's Hannah's and Eliza's. We've been working in this store since we could walk."

As she traced the lines, Clara realized this was another reason she couldn't just sell the store and move the family west. She could not leave their family's history behind. She couldn't leave Mama behind.

Caught up in her memories, she kept talking, almost

forgetting that Mr. Butler was even there. "We would beg Mama to measure us every month, to see how tall we'd grown. But she said that would ruin the surprise. She made us wait until our birthday every year to add a new notch."

She saw a faint stain of white in one of the notches and laughed. "Eliza stole some chalk from school one day so we could measure on our own. It took a week for Mama to notice, because the white lines just got thicker and thicker when we measured every day and didn't do much growing. She made us scrub them off."

When John reached out and touched one of the smaller notches of Clara's, she finally remembered that he was standing next to her. She shook herself out of her reverie and saw a single tear going down John's face. Clara wouldn't have noticed, except it made a track in the flour coating on his cheek.

"Are you all right?"

He didn't say anything, just nodded and went back to his sweeping. Clara didn't know what had affected him so but didn't want to push.

In the back room of the store, John took one of the clean rags and started brushing the powder off his face and out of his brown hair. While the flour war with Clara had been fun, they needed to look presentable before the store opened for the day.

He couldn't help chuckling as he brushed away the mess, impressed by how much Clara had gotten on him. He wouldn't have thought her capable of it. For his part, he hadn't done anything like that since he was a small child.

Despite the distraction of their little battle, the notches on the wall that showed their growth as children had brought him back to reality, reminding him of what he had never had.

Had his parents marked their heights on walls? Maybe, but they were never in one place long enough to make more than a few scores. And now the markers of his existence as a child were on someone else's walls.

Did people see those notches and wonder what child had been that height many years ago? Did other children mark their own passages of time over his? Or did the new owners of those homes simply whitewash all the old measurements away—erasing them as if he and his brother had never been there?

This is why it was so important for him to find a place and settle down before he could get married and start a family. If he ever had children, he wanted them to know the stability of growing up in one place, with a community that made them feel like they belonged. He prayed for that every day.

"Are you almost done?" Clara asked from the doorway. "My sisters will be here soon and I would prefer not to be covered with flour when they arrive."

John had to laugh at the sight of her still coated in flour. He reached out and handed her a towel. "Here, you need this more than me."

He turned to go back out to the front to give her privacy to clean up, but she stopped him.

"Mr. Butler, I hope you don't mind my asking again—but are you all right? You seemed...sad earlier."

He felt himself flush a little in embarrassment that she had seen him cry, even though it was only one tear. "Oh, it's nothing, just a little melancholy about moving around so much and not having a place like this to call home."

Clara paused in brushing the flour off her skirt to

give him a pitying look. "That must have been hard, but some parts of starting a life in a new land must have been exciting."

She was just trying to make him feel better—he knew that for sure, because Clara Morehouse thought that the pioneer life was a bad risk and not exciting at all. But her saying that, whether she meant it or not, still opened a door for him. Now might be a good time to promote a different notion—she had asked after all.

"Yes, there were a lot of good things about it. Every time we built a new home, my father had learned from his mistakes in the past and the structure got better and stronger."

He thought back to the first lean-to his father had constructed and how pieces of the clay he'd used to hold it together had dripped on their heads during a rainstorm. John told Clara that story and it made her laugh.

"Well, I'm glad his building skills improved!" She started pulling pins out of her hair and asked him to turn around while she got the flour out of her hair. "You don't have to leave. Just turn your back."

He wished he could see her unbound raven-black hair. He would guess it was quite the sight, even when it was whitened a bit by flour.

"Tell me more about what it was like to start out fresh on a new piece of land," she said.

John explained that while they'd longed to explore at first, their father had always put them to work gathering supplies for building their home. There was livestock to care for, new fields to plow, furniture to construct.

"But when we finally were given time to ourselves, Adam and I would explore every place we could find within a half-day's walking distance. He's three years older and didn't want me trailing along after him everywhere, but eventually he'd give in. We would jump in every creek, roll down every hill, catch every frog. We were covered in dirt every night when we came home."

Clara laughed, a sweet sound that John had come to enjoy immensely. "I'm sure your mama hated doing your laundry after all that adventure."

When she was there, he thought, pushing back the anger that always bubbled to the surface at the thought of her. No matter how many years passed, he couldn't let go of the memories of his mother abandoning her family when he was young.

"She hated a lot of things," John said out loud before he could stop himself. His voice dripped with bitterness, and even though he couldn't see Clara's expression, he could guess it was probably shocked.

"I'm sorry your childhood wasn't filled with joy," she said softly. "All children should have some joy."

John thought about laughing on the riverbeds while fishing with his brother, climbing trees and learning to ride a horse. "There was joy—plenty of it, largely thanks to my brother. Don't you worry on my part, Miss Morehouse."

She cleared her throat and stepped to his side, her hair tidy again, with barely any flour evident.

"That was fast."

Clara shook out her skirts one more time and grinned when some powder came off. "It wasn't as thorough as I hoped it would be, but it will do. Can you see any noticeable flour on me?"

John took a moment to study her, glad for permission to look at her. While there could never be anything romantic between him and Miss Morehouse, she was a lovely person. Looking at a beautiful person was good for the soul, he told himself.

"I don't see any flour except a little under your ear, just there," he said and pointed.

She quickly removed the flour, just in time to hear the bell above the door jingle. The two of them rushed out of the back room to see the other Morehouse sisters standing there.

Eliza gave them a smirk as they hurried about the business of opening the store. "And just what were you two doing back there?"

"We were just finishing up the books from yesterday," Clara explained, but Eliza still looked suspicious.

"Why is it so dusty in here?" Hannah asked, and John couldn't help but exchange a grin with Clara. They had stirred up some of the flour into the air when they were sweeping, it seemed.

"Oh, we must have stirred something up while we were pulling supplies down from the shelves." John picked up the brooms and feather dusters that they had used earlier and hurried them into the back room.

"Uh, why are there sticks and old newspapers on the counter?" As she said the words, Eliza picked up one of the old papers. "And this is my favorite column by the famous adventurer out West! You aren't throwing this away, are you?"

Clara explained the purpose of the rainy-day box to her sisters, and Eliza lovingly held the piece of newspaper to her chest, declaring they would never use her favorite writer's words as kindling. John went quickly back to work, studying the list of heavy lifting that the ladies had planned for him today.

"I'm going to have a broken back when all this is over," he complained.

Clara quirked an eyebrow at him. "Whining again? I

thought you said you wanted to be here. You can leave at any time."

"Trying to get rid of me again? I thought we got somewhere today and could call ourselves friends, Miss Morehouse."

Eliza leaned forward eagerly at that. "Oh, what happened today?"

Clara gave her sister a quelling look before turning back to John. "I wouldn't say 'friends' yet, Mr. Butler. How about we call us 'friendly acquaintances' for now?"

Well, it was better than 'enemies,' he thought. It would do—for now, as she'd said.

"All right, but I will be your friend by the end of the week, I promise."

Eliza looked between him and her sister. "Don't make promises that are too hard to keep. Clara is the most stubborn creature alive. If you turn it into a challenge, then she won't be your friend if you are the last person on earth."

Clara didn't protest her sister's words, but John noticed some fire flash in her eyes. She didn't like being told what she would or would not do.

Yes, he and Clara Morehouse would be friends. If he couldn't get the family to move out West, at least he would have something worthwhile out of all of this.

Chapter Seven

The week went by swiftly after The Flour Incident, as they were calling it. John came into the store every day and worked, while charming the Morehouse sisters with his stories.

Clara's heart started to melt toward the man, thanks to his kind words about her bravery and business skills. Plus he made an excellent companion. At the end of every business day, he would sit next to her and they would go over the books from that datc's sales and note anything of interest for a new store out West.

Clara had to admit that it was nice to have someone to share the load with. Her sisters helped around the shop, but they didn't care about the overall plans for making a business successful the way Mr. Butler did.

"I think we are officially starting to become friends, despite your objections," he said to her one day as they were walking home from the store after closing. He was on his way to spend some time with her father.

"Oh really? Why do you think that?"

He chuckled. "We spend most of our time in each other's company, and I will admit it—I have fun when I'm with you. Don't you feel the same?"

Clara thought about it for a moment. It was true that she enjoyed his companionship more each day. If some of his other business kept him away for a couple of hours, she started to miss him.

"I suppose. But that doesn't change how I feel about going," Clara told him sternly.

He grinned at her. "I didn't think so. You are the hardest sell I've ever met, but I *will* sell you, nonetheless."

Clara gave a huff at that. "Oh really? I heard you and father talking about how you were going to charm me into being excited about the West. It's not working. My practical sense is still firmly in place."

John narrowed his eyes at her. "I knew you were listening outside the door."

She smiled. "Of course I was. I wasn't about to let you two men decide everything without getting my say, was I?"

When they entered the Morehouse home, they were surprised to see the housekeeper running around and handing out orders excitedly to the maid.

"What's going on, Betty?"

She paused for a second to breathe heavily. "It's your father. He's decided to come downstairs, so we have to get the drawing room ready for him."

Clara gasped. Her father was leaving his room? She looked at Mr. Butler with wide eyes.

"It's happening sooner than I expected," Mr. Butler said with a smile. "I predicted it would be several more days."

Clara shook her head at him. "I thought this might never happen at all."

Mr. Butler gave her a smile and reached out to

squeeze her hand. "I'm glad it is. He needs to be a part of his family again."

She studied the man who had come into her life not long ago but who had already done so much for all of them. Mr. Butler and her father were divided in age by many years, but they were truly friends.

"Thank you, Mr. Butler, for encouraging my father to start healing. For bringing life back into him."

Mr. Butler gave her a smile. "John, if you will. We spend far too much time together to continue being so formal."

Clara blushed at that but nodded. "Well, then, please call me Clara."

He smiled at her. "I would love to, Clara. Before I go into the drawing room to sit with your father, I want to ask you something."

She was distracted for a moment by the sound of him saying her given name. It wasn't the first time he had used it, but for some reason, when it passed his lips this time, it sounded softer than from anyone she'd heard it from before.

"Can I have an hour of your time?" His question pulled her from her reverie.

She chuckled. "You just had more than an hour of my time. A whole day, to be exact."

John shifted on his feet nervously. "Yes, but… Look, I know you are adamantly against my venture, but I'm wondering if you might give me a second chance to present it to you. In person, this time, and not in a letter."

Clara considered his words. She was still adamant that it would be unwise for the family to pick up and move their lives right now. Moreover, her encounter with Michael had made her more determined to make their business a success right here in town, just to show him that he had no control over her life. Still, John had been such a help to their family, the least she could do was hear him out.

"One hour. Tomorrow, after the store closes. And I'm still saying no."

He grinned. "Oh, you think that now. But I'm one of the greatest salesmen you will ever meet."

With a wink, he turned and entered the drawing room. Clara knew that he would not be able to convince her, so she didn't have to worry.

As she walked up the stairs, she heard her sisters giggling in their room. She entered to see them brushing each other's hair and gossiping, and for a moment, Clara could remember how life had been like this every day before Mama got sick.

Laughter was back in the Morehouse home, and she hadn't realized how much she had missed it.

"There you are! We were just talking about you," Hannah said as she hopped off the bed and yanked Clara through the door and into the room.

Eliza reached out and pulled her down onto a seat before starting to take her hair from its bun.

"What are you doing?" She protested as both her sisters recklessly yanked out all her hairpins, sending her raven locks spilling around her face.

"We're going to dress your hair for supper, and for once, you are going to look like a normal girl your age and not an old society widow who has nothing but bitterness in her life," Eliza teased.

"I'm not a widow! Nor am I old. I'm only twenty-one." Her disgruntled voice shook as she tried to pull away from her sisters.

"We know. So why do you always try to look like

you're ninety years old?" Eliza got the last pin out of her hair and threw it onto the floor.

Clara just shrugged. She hadn't been doing it intentionally, it was just easier to work when her hair was held tightly away from her face.

"Why now?" Both sisters exchanged a look. She narrowed her eyes at them. "What are you up to?"

Hannah just shook her head. "We're not 'up to' anything. We just thought you might like a little change."

Eliza grabbed a brush and started running it through Clara's hair. "For no reason at all," she said.

Clara was suspicious of their motives, but it felt really nice to have someone brush her hair. It had been a long time since anybody else had done it for her. She decided just to enjoy it.

"So, Hannah said you two were talking about me before I came in—what about?"

Eliza smiled. "We were talking about how you made the right decision in turning Michael Emmers down and how we are proud of you."

Clara's breath caught at that. "I'd have expected you to ask me to reconsider. My marrying him could open a lot of doors for the two of you, and you would be taken care of. And he wouldn't spread gossip about Papa's condition all over town and hurt the business."

Hannah waved the idea away. "If you've taught me anything as my older sister, it's that I don't need anyone to take care of me."

Eliza nodded. "You are always worried about making us happy, but that doesn't mean that we don't also want you to be happy."

Clara wiped a tear from her eye, not attempting to hide that she was touched by their words. "But it's my job as the eldest to care for you."

Eliza rolled her eyes at that and tackled a tangle in Clara's hair with vigor. "We will care for you too."

Not long after, Clara looked at herself in the mirror and saw a woman she hadn't seen in a long time. Her hair was still pinned up in the front, but the back was worn loose and relaxed. Gentle curls spilled over her shoulders.

"You look lovely. I'm sure Mr. Butler will agree."

Clara sputtered at this. "What? Is that why you did this? So I could look nice for Mr. Butler?"

Hannah blinked innocently. "Well, he is here for supper. Shouldn't we all look nice for a guest?"

Eliza nodded, an innocent expression on her face that was almost certainly insincere. "Yes, it would be rude not to."

Clara scowled at her sisters. "I see what you're doing and it is not going to work. Mr. Butler and I are just friends. I have no interest in anyone romantically for now."

Hannah gave her a sad look. "But you don't have much time with him. He will be leaving for the West in a few months, and who knows when we will see him again?"

Clara's heart clenched at the thought. In just a matter of days, Mr. Butler had become such an integral part of their lives. The thought of him being gone filled her with sadness.

"We will just have to see him again when he travels back East to recruit for another venture," she reassured her sisters (and perhaps herself).

Eliza just shook her head. "No, he said this would be his last one. He's going to settle in this town. We may never see him again if he's serious about settling in his new town for good."

Clara remembered John mentioning his plans to put down roots and to find a wife, if he stayed for five years. He and his brother already collected rents from several businesses in their five previous towns, and revenue from this new one would only add to their wealth. This meant they could settle anywhere they wanted. She wondered if he could really last for that long in one location or if he did have a wanderlust. It wasn't any of her business though.

"Well, then, you can maintain your friendship with him through letters. There is really no need to carry on so."

Both sisters looked at her sadly. "What about *your* friendship with him? Aren't you going to miss him?" Hannah, ever the romantic, looked devastated by the idea of Clara and John parting ways with each other.

Clara reflected on her thoughts from earlier. She did not need a man in her life, but she liked having John Butler in it. "Yes, I will miss him, I suppose. He's become a good friend."

Again, her sisters exchanged a look.

"Friends. That's it. And that's an improvement from what I first thought of him, anyway. So stop your scheming, you two."

They giggled, and Clara knew this would not be the last time she heard of such things.

John sat in the parlor with Arthur Morehouse, but his mind was elsewhere. More pointedly, with the woman who was probably upstairs thinking of more ways she could deny his proposal to move the family out West.

She'd been so adamant against it, he could scarcely believe Clara had agreed to the meeting.

"I think she's softening to the idea," Arthur said,

pulling him from his thoughts. "You are putting cracks in her armor."

John smiled at his friend. "I doubt it. Although your other daughters are enthusiastic about the idea."

He took a sip of his tea as Arthur talked about his plans. John was happy to see the older man speaking with such excitement and vigor. Eliza and Hannah were also thrilled about the thought of a new quest. Arthur knew Eliza would be an easy sell, because she longed for adventure and a life outside Independence.

Truth be told, he had initially thought Hannah would be tougher because she wasn't the type that longed for new horizons. But she was eager for a change after all their family had been through, and had asked him quietly one day if there might be a need for a schoolteacher in his new town.

"I'm almost done with my studies, and I have top marks. I thought maybe I could be a teacher, if the town needs one." Hannah looked at him with such hopeful eyes that he could do nothing but nod.

"There will probably be only a few families with school-age children when our town starts, but I imagine we will grow over time. A schoolteacher is a fine idea." He was in favor of anything that meant that the Morehouses would be going with him instead of him having to leave them behind.

The entire Morehouse family had firmly entrenched themselves in John's heart, which was a strange and new feeling for him. For years, it had been only him and his brother.

But the Morehouses were starting to seem like family to him, as well. *Is this what putting down roots feels like?*

"You seem distracted tonight, John," Arthur said, and he felt immediate regret.

"I'm sorry. Here you made all this effort to finally come downstairs and I'm ignoring you."

Arthur gave him a smile. "It's all right. I'm grateful for the motivation—and for the company, as well, even if the conversation isn't lively. What were you thinking about, if I may ask?"

"Just how much I've enjoyed spending time with your family. I will miss you all when it's time for me to go west."

Arthur studied him for a moment, and it took everything in John not to shift under the older man's scrutiny.

"We don't know for sure that we won't be coming with you," he finally said.

"Your eldest daughter is never going to agree."

Arthur leaned forward in his chair, meeting John's eyes.

"You don't know that. I have faith in you, son. I thought you said she agreed to have a meeting with you about it?"

John felt the weight of Arthur's belief in him pressing heavily on his shoulders. He feared letting down his friend—and all the other Morehouses. Excepting Clara, they all wanted to go, and yet they were firm about staying unless it was a unanimous decision. If Clara wasn't willing, none of them were moving. He couldn't help but admire the loyalty she had earned from her loved ones, not to mention the close-knit bond of the Morehouse family.

"Yes, she will meet with me. But she is adamant that it is just out of gratitude for me helping you out of your melancholy."

Arthur nodded. "Well, you did. And we all feel grateful. But perhaps we should really use her feelings on this matter for our benefit. I will come up with another plan."

John hid his smile behind his teacup. Arthur did love a good plan.

Betty called them in to supper, and John was thrilled when Arthur said he would be eating in the dining room for the first time in well over a month. "Trust me, my boy. I know what I'm doing," he said under his breath as his daughters entered the dining room.

The ladies chattered excitedly about their father's return to the dining room, but John's attention was on the eldest Miss Morehouse. He had frozen in step when the lady entered the room.

Gone was the practical and proper hairstyle that he was used to seeing. Her raven locks fell gently on her shoulders. John had thought she was lovely before but seeing her like this now… She was beautiful.

Smart, brave, fun, beautiful, kind… Clara was all of these things in one.

Remember your five-year plan, his inward voice told him. But keeping that plan in mind was becoming more difficult each day that he spent with Clara.

"It's so wonderful to see you down here, Papa," Clara said, her voice more cheerful than John had ever heard it.

I want more of this. I want to make her happy, he thought. His more practical self was screaming at him to not think of such things, but he couldn't help it. Surely he could still be just friends with her and want to make her happy. Yes, that was what he was feeling.

Finally, he forced his feet to move and he approached the table to pull out Clara's seat for her. She gave him a grateful look and sat down without missing a beat in the conversation.

Arthur's plan became evident relatively quickly as he played into his daughters' excitement about him being downstairs.

"All this talk of the West has given me a new lease on life. I can't wait until we start getting ready to go." He smiled at John and winked.

"Papa," Clara hissed, and the room fell silent.

Arthur raised up his hands in surrender. "I know, dearest daughter, you will make the final decision. But forgive an old man for dreaming about the one thing that has made me happy in weeks."

Oh, he's really going to try to convince her through guilt. John hid a grin when he saw the fire that sparked in Clara's eyes. Maybe Mr. Morehouse didn't know his daughter as well as he thought. John was sure she would see right through her father and his plans. And the idea that he was trying to manipulate her would make her dig in her heels even further.

His meeting with her tomorrow was going to be more difficult than he had originally hoped. John made his excuses and left the family early in the evening. He needed to get home and make a plan of attack to convince Clara.

When he arrived at his hotel, the clerk at the desk waved frantically at him before he reached the stairs. A message had been left for him from the man he had asked to discreetly gather information about Michael Emmers. Despite Clara's insistence that she could handle her problems herself, John had still felt driven to do a little quiet investigating. The rejected suitor was threatening the Morehouses' livelihood if he revealed Clara's secrets, so the least he could do to protect his friends was to see if there was any leverage to be had over the man.

John read the message, and his entire body coiled with tension. He crumpled the letter and stomped up the stairs—all thoughts of his presentation to Clara forgotten. Instead, he was imagining his fist landing squarely on Mr. Emmers's jaw.

Chapter Eight

Clara went to the store early the next morning. She had agreed to meet with John at the end of the day, so she needed to get some of her paperwork done ahead of time.

She still was against the notion of agreeing to John's scheme. This town was the place that held all the memories of her mother, and she didn't want to even think about all the work and planning it would take to get them all ready to travel. But last night, after everyone went to sleep, Clara had lain in her bed and thought about what would happen when John left.

She and her sisters would miss him—she didn't hesitate to admit that. But what about her father? If he didn't have the westward adventure to think about, would he retreat back into his shell of grief? Would all the progress he had made be lost?

Clara hated making business decisions based on emotion, but she couldn't stop thinking about it. There were other advantages, as well. Being able to start fresh in a new community would be a boon if Michael revealed the news that the ladies of the Morehouse family were really the ones running the business. If they stayed, she wasn't sure what kind of backlash would occur. She had some friends here who she believed would stay loyal to the store, but many customers would be lost. In a new town, no one would blink an eye at Clara for managing a store if that's what she had always done in their memories.

But who knew if they would even make it out West? Tragedy happened on wagon trains every time. John had told them as much himself. And what if their father had a relapse and they had already committed to this new life? What if the town the Butler Brothers built was not a success? There were so many things that went into creating a new community, and any one of them could go wrong.

"I'm not willing to risk my family's future on it. They can be mad at me all they want," she murmured as she turned her attention to the store's ledgers. She focused on her work until she was distracted by a knock on the window. She looked up to see Michael standing there.

She sighed. "I'm not in the mood for this today," she said, but she got up and unlocked the door anyway.

"Mr. Emmers, I wish I could say that it was nice to see you."

Michael gave her a patronizing smile. "Clara, I'm sorry to disturb you at this early hour. I had to know if you had reconsidered my offer of marriage. Today was the deadline that I gave you. I just wanted to get your official agreement before I stopped by the church to make the arrangements."

Clara scowled at both his use of her given name and his presumption that she would give in to his demands.

"Those arrangements will not be necessary. I will not be marrying you," Clara said.

His smug smile didn't even waver. "We went over this, darling. You *will* be my wife, or I'll tell the community that your father can't even get out of bed. No one is going to trust your family to stock their homes if you can't keep your own house in order. There is not much choice in this."

Clara sighed. She wished that she had not come into the store alone this morning. While her sisters wouldn't be able to strong-arm Michael out of the store, at least she would have witnesses to his behavior if needed.

"I spoke with my family, and they are not willing to sacrifice my happiness to save the store. Besides, our family has a well-established reputation in this community. I refuse to believe that one little issue is going to tear the whole thing down."

Michael stepped closer to her. "I could make you very happy, Clara."

She stepped back, looking for something to use to keep him away if he continued to advance.

"I don't think you could. I will risk our business struggling as opposed to accepting the prospect of a lifetime with you. Besides, my father is on the mend, so your claims will appear unfounded in the community."

Michael scoffed at this, and he stepped closer again. Clara reached for a broomstick that was in the corner.

"My family *is* this community," Michael retorted. "Everyone will believe what I tell them. And I will tell them that not only do you run this store without supervision but that you spend quite a bit of time alone with male customers. And who knows what you get up to with Mr. Butler after hours?"

She gasped. "You would lie to ruin my reputation just because I won't marry you? You could have any girl in town. Why won't you leave me alone?"

He shrugged. "You're the only person who has ever told me no. And I will get a yes out of you, eventually." He reached out and grabbed her arm, tightly. Clara reacted out of instinct, bringing the broomstick down on his head, hard.

Michael fell to the ground, howling in pain.

"You could have killed me!"

She rolled her eyes at him. "Oh, stop your whining, it is just a bump. You should know better than to touch a lady without her permission."

Michael scowled at her as he climbed to his feet, holding his head. "You're no lady. You're a harridan."

He made to step toward her again, but Clara raised the broomstick and he stopped. The doorbell jingled, and she turned to see Mr. Butler standing there, looking stunned.

"I planned to come and discuss something about Mr. Emmers with you, but I see he has beaten me here." Clara was more than relieved that John had arrived. She would have smacked Michael again if she had to, but she was hoping it wouldn't come to that. Maybe now that someone else was there, Michael would show more wariness about imposing himself on her.

"Thank you, Mr. Butler, I mean, John. Mr. Emmers is just leaving."

Michael narrowed his eyes when she called John by his given name and made to protest, but she brandished the broom again.

"I thought you might need my help with him, but judging from the large bump on the side of his head, it seems you have things well in hand," John said, covering his mouth so Michael wouldn't see that he was smiling. Clara fought the urge to grin back at him.

Michael looked between the two of them, and even

though his head must be paining him greatly, he still made one last effort to change her mind.

"Clara, please. Think of all I have to offer you as my wife. This man, he may be a friend of the family, but he has nothing but a plot of land in the middle of the wilderness that may or may not become a town someday."

She would admire his persistence, if it weren't directed at her.

Clara was about to reject him again when John intervened. "You don't have much to offer her either, it turns out."

Michael turned and glared at him. "What do you mean? I'm from one of the wealthiest families in the city."

John just shook his head. "Yes, your family is wealthy, but when you threatened that fortune with your gambling debts, they cut you off. Not socially but financially. That's the real reason for your determination to marry Miss Morehouse, isn't it? It's not a response to her unquestionable beauty, but because you need the income from the store."

Clara tried to concentrate on what he said after his remark about her appearance, but it was hard to focus as he kept talking, now directing his words to Clara. "My source said he was bragging to one of his debtors at the saloon that he already had a buyer lined up for the store for after the two of you were wed."

Clara's blood boiled. "What? He couldn't sell the store! It's ours!"

Michael seethed while John nodded. "He told his friends that he had a plan to make you stay at home after you were married. He would convince your father to let him run the store, and then he would sell it before you all knew what was happening."

Michael schooled his emotions and turned on his charm. "Darling Clara, this man is lying because he's jealous that I can give you a better life than he can. Who are you going to believe—me, who you've known most of your life, or him, who wanders in and out of your life as his whims take him?"

Clara looked between the two. Michael, so duplicitous from the beginning. John, so straightforward, even when he was trying to change her mind about the West.

"Him. I believe him," she said, pointing to Mr. Butler.

Michael's fist clenched. "You will regret that you didn't accept my offer of marriage, Clara. I told you what would happen. And I will keep my word."

He stormed out of the store, slamming the door behind him.

Clara exchanged a look with John before they both burst out laughing. Michael's threats were not funny, but the tantrum he had just thrown and the fact that she had felled him with a broomstick were definitely hilarious.

"I'm sorry that I didn't arrive sooner. I could have saved you from having to brandish that very dangerous weapon," John teased.

She clutched it tighter. "Just don't get too pushy in your presentation today, or I may have to use it on you."

John just laughed as he helped her clean up some of the stock Michael had knocked over. Something was nagging at Clara.

"How did you learn all that about Michael's gambling debt?"

He looked sheepish. "I know that you didn't want my interference, but I had an associate do a little bit of background research on the man. Just in case you needed it, of course."

Clara wanted to be angry at his presumption, but instead, she was grateful. "At least now I won't have any guilt or remorse about turning him down."

John stopped organizing the shelf. "You would have felt guilty about not marrying him?"

She shook her head. "No, I definitely have no desire to be his wife. But I might have felt guilty about passing on the opportunity to make sure my sisters would be well cared for."

Clara now knew that she had made the best choice in turning Michael down. All of his promises to make sure her family was provided for had been nothing but lies. Financially, the man couldn't even take care of himself.

"I wasn't lying the other day when I said you were brave, you know? You're taking this entire Emmers encounter in stride. It's very admirable," John said with awe in his voice.

She blushed a little at his words. She liked that he did not run in the other direction when he encountered a strong woman.

"Maybe I'm crying on the inside," she teased.

John chuckled. "So you are tough on the outside, soft on the inside. I like it."

Clara didn't know about being completely soft, but she was definitely softening to John Butler. She found that she was actually looking forward to his presentation today.

Her sisters arrived, and Clara couldn't help but notice their wide eyes when they saw the disarray in the store after her encounter with Michael.

"What happened here?" Eliza asked as they cleaned up the last of the mess.

Clara grinned. "We had a rodent."

John laughed, a deep chuckle that came from his belly. "A very large rodent that we threw out of here."

The younger sisters exchanged a confused look, which only made Clara and John laugh more. The morning may have started out rotten, but things felt much better now.

John was nervous all day for his upcoming meeting with Clara after the store closed. They had reached a new level in their friendship during their shared experience with Michael Emmers this morning, but their conversation later today would shift things once again. If she changed her mind about leaving, they would be able to spend more time together not only preparing the store to be moved but on the journey to the new town, as well.

She could be part of your five-year plan if she lives nearby.

John had a moment of panic, wondering where that thought had come from. For the past few weeks, he had put Clara Morehouse firmly in the friendship category, despite her beauty and the way he felt lighter when he was around her. But if the family were to go, too, could he finally open himself up to the possibility of something more with her? Would she be willing to wait the five years he needed as part of his plan?

But then there was the other possibility—that she would stand firm in her conviction that a move to the West was a foolish idea. Would John have the strength to ride away from her when the wagon train rolled out?

His heart ached at the prospect of leaving behind the family he had found here, but he brushed those feelings aside and pushed himself into work for the rest of the day. He would think about that problem when the time came.

John had just received a letter from his brother. Adam had sent it when he'd journeyed the several weeks' ride to the closest settlement to gather some supplies for their new claim. He'd dropped the letter at the army fort en route, and from there, it had wound its way along to Independence to give John an update. The town was ready to be built. The workers they had hired were felling logs to prepare to start the first structures. A lumber mill would obviously be the first thing erected, so they would have what they needed to construct the rest.

Adam was eager to have his brother back. *I hope you are ready to leave in a few months' time, with all the people and supplies we need. Things are progressing on this end, and I hope you are doing your part in Independence,* the elder Butler wrote.

John regretted that he had indeed neglected some of his work during his time spent with the Morehouse family, but he could not claim the interludes had been wasted. On the contrary, Arthur had been a great help to him. He knew Independence better than anybody, having lived here since before the town's recent growth. Arthur had told him who might be good recruits for his new town.

"The Gray boy—he's just coming home from medical school this month. He had hoped to replace our doctor, but another young man already beat him to it. If you go and visit him before he makes any plans, he might be willing to move out West."

John took the older man's advice, and he had an appointment to call on the Gray family tomorrow. He was sure the young man's mother would not like to hear about the possibility of her son leaving. But the lad might be keen on starting a new adventure.

First, though, he had to use all his sales experience to charm the eldest Morehouse sister into signing on to the new town for herself and her family.

Unfortunately, he didn't get the chance to make his presentation, because just as the store was about to close, Eliza rushed in. She had gone to deliver an order to the hotel, and her eyes were wide when she returned.

"He did it. I can't believe he did it."

The other Morehouse girls looked confused, but John knew exactly what must have happened.

"Michael Emmers made some trouble," he said and Eliza turned to him with tears in her eyes, nodding.

"So what? We can handle the loss of a few customers who don't want to do business with a woman," Clara said, raising her chin high in the air. He saw right through her bravado to the fear hidden underneath. He itched to reach for her, but he knew that would not be appropriate.

"It's worse than that. Michael...he's made up lies about you. About your virtue and the way you do business."

Clara closed her eyes and sat down with a groan. She may not have believed that Michael would take his threats that far, but John had known that the vile rodent would indeed stoop so low.

"Clara...you've been part of this town for so long people are going to know that you would never do anything improper," Hannah tried to comfort.

Eliza let out a strained sound from her throat, and Clara opened her eyes and gave her sister a sad look. "What is it?"

Eliza sat down by Clara and put her arm around

her shoulders as if to brace her for the words to come. "Three people stopped me on the way back from the hotel, canceling their grocery deliveries. They said they didn't think the rumors were true but didn't want their business reputations sullied by ours. We have a lot of families that will be loyal and continue to shop here, but losing the merchants in town that buy their supplies from us will be a huge loss. Especially the hotel and the restaurant."

A lone tear slipped down Clara's cheek, and John knew that she was about to break. She looked around the store, panicked. She was not one to cry in public, let alone show that she was anything less than a strong businesswoman, but everyone had their breaking point.

"Eliza, Hannah, do you think you two could man the store by yourselves for a while?" He pulled Clara's hand until she was in a standing position next to him. All three Morehouse girls looked at him in surprise.

"Don't you think we should close for the day now?" Hannah said it in a conspiratorial whisper, as if the townspeople could hear them. John just shook his head.

"No, we have to stay open. If we close, that would mean that Emmers wins," John said, and Clara looked at him with grateful eyes. "Your sister just needs a couple of hours to gather herself."

The younger Morehouse sisters looked at Clara, who was standing there, calm and stoic as ever. Her clenched fist and the tear trail down her face were the only indications that she was holding in some big emotions.

Thankfully, Eliza and Hannah knew their sister well enough to agree to his plan, and soon he was rushing Clara out of the store. She didn't say anything on the whole walk home, just keeping her eyes on the sidewalk so she didn't have to meet the gaze of every nosy person that passed.

John did, however. He met the gaze of every single person who might think less of her. He gave them fiery stares that had them all hang their heads in shame as they walked by. She deserved so much more than their doubt and scrutiny now.

When they entered the home, Clara started walking toward the stairs, probably to retreat to her room. He heard her choke on a sob and grabbed her hand.

He couldn't take it anymore. Politeness was forgotten. He pulled Clara into his arms for a comforting hug.

Chapter Nine

Clara melted against John, taking comfort from crying against his broad chest. She had been so strong for so long. And now she just couldn't do it anymore.

John did not seem bothered that her tears were staining his shirt. He just gently rubbed circles onto her back as she cried. Betty came in to see what the fuss was all about, and she took one look at Clara's condition before bestowing on her a gentle smile.

"Come now, dear. Why don't you and Mr. Butler go sit in the drawing room? I will fix you a cup of tea. I've always thought tea can help make anything feel better."

Clara wanted to thank the woman who had been part of her life since she was a little girl, but all that came out was a hiccup. John came to her aid once again.

"That would be lovely. Thank you, Betty."

He kept one of his arms around Clara's shoulders as he led her to the drawing room. On any other day, she would be able to process the feeling of his nearness, but she was too bereft to even think about it now.

She'd failed. She was a business failure. Something like this would never happen to her father. Maybe women really weren't meant to be in trade after all.

No, that wasn't true. She excelled at running the store. It was just stupid men like Michael Emmers who had to go around ruining it all.

"It's fascinating to watch you process things. Your face just went from sad to angry in about ten seconds," John teased. He sat down on the settee and gently pulled her beside him. Normally, she would be against someone leading her around like this. But today, she welcomed letting him take command, lifting the burden off her shoulders.

"I *am* angry. This is not my fault," she said firmly.

He looked at her in surprise. "Of course it's not your fault."

She studied the man next to her, grateful that he had been there today.

"I felt like it was for a little while there. That I was a failure."

He frowned at her. "Nobody is perfect, but I would choose you as the least likely person to ever be a failure. Ever. This is all on Emmers."

Clara blinked at the rage that showed in his eyes. He wasn't even part of their family, but he cared for them like he was. He was the complete opposite of Michael Emmers. Without thinking, Clara leaned forward and pressed her lips against his.

She felt John freeze for a moment before kissing her back. His lips were so different from hers, more solid and dry from his years in the sun on his journeys to the West and back. But they were also softer than she'd expected.

Clara sighed contentedly against him, before the world invaded her happy space when John stood and gently backed away from her.

"Whoa, uh, Clara, we should stop and think about this," he said, his eyes wide and his breath heavy.

Her heart sank as she realized what she had done.

"I'm sorry, I don't know what happened. You've just been so kind and I was upset and…"

John reached out and pulled her into his arms again for another hug. "That's precisely why we should not be doing this right now. You're upset, and I don't want to take advantage of you and your emotions."

Clara stood up.

"Still, I apologize for forcing myself on you like that. I shouldn't have done so. Thank you for putting a stop to it."

John let out a groan and ran his fingers through his hair.

"You have no idea how hard it was to stop."

Clara's heart raced. "Really?"

"You are one of the most beautiful women I've ever seen, Clara."

Her heart sunk. Of course. He had just kissed her back because she was a beautiful girl that was throwing herself at him. What man wouldn't? But when he realized what was happening, he'd pulled away, not wanting to ruin their friendship.

"Please say we can remain friends after this, John. I couldn't bear to lose another one today," Clara said, thinking of all the scornful looks she had received on the streets.

John looked at her in surprise. "Of course you won't lose my friendship!"

Clara sighed and sat back down. She didn't know why she had kissed him. She didn't have time to start a relationship, let alone with a man who would be leaving town permanently in just a few months. Clara had a business to run and a family to support. She couldn't just go around kissing the first man she found appealing.

Hopefully, she and John could put this in the past. But she knew she would struggle to forgive herself for behaving so inappropriately. "Maybe I'm no better than the things they are saying about me. I just went and kissed you without warning."

John's jaw clenched. "Clara Morehouse, you are a lot of things, but none of them come even close to those foul rumors Michael is spreading about you."

She leaned back in her chair and closed her eyes. "What are we going to do? How am I going to tell Papa about what people are saying? About the canceled orders?"

"We aren't going to tell him anything yet. We will find a way out of this, I promise."

Honestly, Clara was surprised he wasn't using this as an excuse as to why she should pack up everything and move the establishment. It would save her reputation, unless the rumors followed her.

"Well, you may get your wish. We may have to close the store," she said sadly.

John scowled at her. "Do you think I wanted any of this to happen? Honestly, Emmers should count his blessings that this is not a Butler Brothers' town, or he would be kicked out of it in a heartbeat."

John stood up and started pacing the room. She knew him well enough now to know that this was his way of trying to come up with a plan.

"You can't close the business. It would mean that Emmers still gets to ruin your life. We can't allow that."

Clara nodded. "The worst part is, you know he and his family will be right up front at church this week, as if nothing happened. As if he didn't lie and gossip and behave horribly just because I dared to reject him."

It sounded to her as if John growled during his pacing. "I cannot stand people like that."

They remained silent for a few minutes, each of them lost in their thoughts. Suddenly, John stopped pacing. "What if we continued the pretense that we hinted at before and announce our engagement?"

It took Clara a moment to digest his words. Engagement? That was a big jump from their first kiss—which was a complete mistake that they were never going to mention again. Now he thought they should be engaged? "What are you talking about?"

John grinned excitedly and puffed up with pride at having come up with a solution. "It would be a fake engagement, of course. Just to get the wagging tongues to settle down for a while."

Clara's mind raced at the suggestion. "What? Why would we do something like that?"

John sat down next to her on the settee. "It would explain why I've been at the shop so much in the past few weeks. Learning the business to take over from my future father-in-law. I have enough respectability in the community from my business dealings to bolster your reputation, and it would be a real opposition to Michael's claims."

Clara bristled at the idea that people would believe John's affirmation of her character over her own defense. Sometimes being a woman had severe disadvantages.

Still, there were many things that did not make sense with this plan of his. "And what about when you leave to go west? People would realize our engagement was a ruse and the rumors would just spring up again."

He grinned at her. "You could end our betrothal very publicly, making it evident that I was in the wrong. Or if you'd rather not display our troubles, I could say that after I establish the new town, I plan to come back here and settle down with you and work the store. A few months after I'm gone, you could say that we decided to end our engagement because I wanted to stay in the West instead."

This was all too much for Clara. This morning she was preparing to open the doors to the store for another successful day of sales, and now she was contemplating a public, dramatic squabble with a fake fiancé.

"Both ideas would make you look like a cad to everyone here. Why would you let me ruin your own reputation like that? This plan seems like quite the burden on your part," Clara said.

John reached over and grabbed her hand. "Because I want to, and for once, someone should be doing something nice for you. You are usually the one who helps people."

Clara fought back tears. It had been so long since someone had considered her needs above their own that she didn't know how to react. She looked down at their joined hands. His were so solid around hers, but she also knew that he respected her own strength.

She had found a true friend in John Butler. They'd worked so well together over the past few weeks. Their bond was reflected in the way he treated her by supporting her endeavors instead of trying to crush them. It was in the way he cared for her family. It was in the way he made her feel—like she wasn't alone.

John was someone she could talk to about things that interested her, and she hadn't had that in a very long time. Sure, she had her sisters and father, but in her determination to run the business, Clara had pulled away from many of her friends. Most of them were busy settling down and making their own families while Clara was supporting hers.

For all her protests about not needing a man, she desperately needed *this* one in her life, even if it was not in the romantic sense. She would miss him when he left, she realized.

But he was departing soon and she wasn't going with him…or could she? Clara had been so adamant about not heading to the West, but leaving would save her family from having to listen to foul rumors and watching their business fall apart. Clara had never thought of herself as a runner when things got tough, however. No, that wasn't a true option.

"Are you all right?" John asked. The myriad of emotions from the thoughts racing through her mind must have shown on her face.

Clara forced herself to push them aside until a time when she could process them alone.

"Yes, I'm just thinking over a few things, I guess. No, I don't think we should go with a public breaking up of the betrothal. It's a kind offer, John. But I would never do that to you."

John scowled at her. "Shouldn't I be the one to decide what I want to do with my own reputation?"

Clara just laughed. "If I don't get to decide about mine, you don't get to decide about yours. Tell people we are engaged all you want, Mr. Butler, but I will not be ending the betrothal. If you name me as your future bride, you will be stuck with me."

She knew he wouldn't call her bluff. He had a five-year plan. He had said as much.

John seemed to freeze at her words. Here it was. He

was going to give up this foolhardy plan to pretend to be betrothed.

But she should have realized he would only dig in his heels even deeper.

"Fine, then. Let's go pick out a ring."

John didn't know why the words came out of his mouth, but he was desperate to help Clara through this situation. He found himself not as panicked as he would have expected to be upon uttering them. He just told Clara Morehouse they should get engaged. Immediately.

And he didn't regret it.

His potential betrothed, however, was still recovering from the idea that she might have a ring on her finger by the end of the day. Clara gaped at him after his announcement. "What? Now?"

He grinned at her. "Why waste time and let those nasty rumors continue to spread?"

To be sure, the circumstances were not what he'd imagined he'd experience when he found someone to propose to, but that didn't mean all his plans had to change. The five-year scheme could still work. In fact, this might help him avoid romantic advances in the future because he could tell matchmaking mamas that he had a fiancée waiting for him back East. Unless she found someone else to marry in the meantime.

"We wouldn't have to break it off right away, so that can ease your worry about making me look bad. We can stay engaged for as long as you want, or until you find someone you want to truly pledge your future to."

He couldn't tell if Clara was really listening to him. She just sat there blinking at him, her mouth hanging open.

"Clara, are you listening to me?"

She nodded mutely.

"It could work," he insisted. "And come to think of it, with this fake betrothal, it wouldn't be too outlandish for me to take a wagon train west and leave you behind until I build us a decent home. Not all women want the settler's lifestyle."

John's mind flashed to his mother, tears streaming down her face as she packed her carpetbag and walked away from her family, her homestead. "You'd be surprised how many women don't like it."

Clara finally came back to herself. "But what about when you never returned? How would I explain your absence?"

"We can exchange letters for a while, and then I could stop writing, and people would think I had abandoned you," John said. He frowned. He had said he was willing to separate from Clara after a fake engagement, but refusing to return to her would indeed need an explanation.

"I'll say it again. We would be besmirching your honor. And I don't want to do that." Clara frowned at him.

He chuckled at this. "You seem awfully concerned about my honor. I will be miles and miles away out West. Why do I care what the people here in Independence might think of me?"

Clara sighed. "I care. You are a good man. It would hurt me to hear people talking about you otherwise."

He grinned. She liked him. He liked her in the role of his biggest defender, liked knowing that she cared enough to want to safeguard his reputation. Funny, he felt the need to defend her too.

"Why is my honor more important than yours?"

She scowled at him. "Because yours has nothing to

do with mine. Michael got me into this mess. Me, not you. And I need to figure my own way out of it."

He ground his teeth. Stubborn woman. He both admired and was aggravated by that trait in her.

"Why won't you let me help you?"

Clara leveled him with a look. "John, you are a wonderful friend for making such a generous offer and for being so kind when I practically flung myself at you earlier, but I cannot pretend to be engaged to you."

John's heart clenched. Why was her statement so disappointing? "Why not? It is the perfect solution."

She reached out and grabbed his hand. "I cannot escape one proposal by jumping right into another engagement. Even if it is fake."

He ran his fingers through his hair in frustration. Why wouldn't she let him do this for her? Why was she refusing to even consider it? It might not be a perfect plan at the moment, but they could find a way to make things work; he knew they could.

"Clara, I…"

He didn't know how to convey his feelings on the subject. He wanted to do all he could to be of assistance to the Morehouses—and Clara in particular. To help her. But she was proving to be just as stubborn about this as she was about leaving Missouri.

"It's okay, John. I'm not going to let you bind yourself to me. You will go and settle in your town, settle for five years and marry a fine woman you find out there. I will still be here, running the store."

She would have no business to run if they didn't go with an extreme plan to save her reputation. He didn't know what else Michael Emmers would do to increase the pressure on her and what further damage he might cause to her business and reputation. "Please reconsider. It's the only way."

Clara pondered his words, but she looked torn. "You don't think we can come up with a different solution?"

John shook his head. Maybe in order for this engagement to take place, he needed to do things properly. So, he dropped to one knee.

Chapter Ten

Clara wished she could reach down and pull John off his knee, but the man proved to be just as stubborn as her. She had half a mind to agree to his silly plan just to get him to shut up about it. "Please get up."

He shook his head. "No, I'm not going to give up until I've asked formally and you've rejected me formally. Only then can I be certain that you're taking this seriously and not dismissing it out of hand."

How could this man be so adamant that this was the only course of action? While it might solve a lot of problems for her and her family, she couldn't help feeling that there had to be another way. "You don't have to do this."

John reached out and grabbed her hand. "Clara Morehouse…"

She tried to pull her hand back, but he held it tight. "John…"

"Will you do me the honor of pretending that someday you will be my wife?" He grinned when he said it, and Clara couldn't stop the snort of laughter that escaped her lips.

It was in that moment Clara began to allow the slight

possibility this could work. She and John were friends, so spending more time with him and pretending to be betrothed wouldn't be unpleasant. She studied him for a moment. While there was mirth in his eyes, he had a hopeful expression.

Clara's heart melted. How could she say no to such a genuinely kind gesture from a friend? But she had a level head and did not like being forced to make rash decisions.

"Can you give me some time to think about it?"

John nodded and got back to his feet. "That's more promising than the fervent rejection you gave me earlier."

What they needed was time and distance to sort all of this out. So much had happened today, and she was exhausted.

"I think you should go," Clara said softly, standing up and starting toward the door.

"Clara," John said, his voice taking on a tender tone. "Why is the idea of being my fiancé so repulsive to you?"

She tried to ignore how warm their connected hands made her feel. "It's not repulsive, not at all."

John tugged her closer so that she was inches apart from him. He studied her face. "I know you despised me at first, but I'd like to think we've gotten past that."

It seemed so long ago that the sight of John Butler made her want to turn in the other direction. A lot had changed since then. "Of course we have. You are one of my dearest friends."

And that was why she would not burden him with a fiancée whom he didn't love except as a friend, no matter how much he wanted to assist her family.

"Your life doesn't have to change with this engagement. It will only help you, not hinder you. Clara, you know I will never make you stop running your business like Michael would. You know I would never ask you to change who you are," John pleaded.

She nodded. Yes, she did know he would never do those things. She thought of his dreams of a new town and his standing as a good man who people would follow anywhere. This was why she would never put him in a position where he would have to sacrifice his reputation to save hers.

But he was so insistent about it. "How about we think about it for a few more days, but if anyone brings up the scandal about us…"

Clara sighed. She could tell someone they were engaged if asked outright why John spent so many hours in her store. But hopefully, this would blow over without her being questioned by anyone. "All right, if we have to."

John gave her a sad smile and promised it would be okay. "I'll go buy you a ring tomorrow, just in case."

The thought of wearing an engagement ring as a symbol of her false commitment to someone she wasn't truly going to wed was too much for Clara to even think about right now. This was not how her life was supposed to go. She said her goodbyes to John and hurried out of the room.

She held her tears inside as she ran up the stairs and into her bedroom. Once she was alone, she grabbed her pillow and let out loud sobs into it. Everything that had happened today came rushing out of her in streaks of tears running down her cheeks. The looks of scorn on the faces of people she had grown up with. People who she had always believed loved her and respected her. But had she ever fully had their regard? She had turned down several requests to court her throughout the years, and a few families had proven to be quick to judge her ever since. And the older she got without showing interest in romance, the less people here understood her. The rapid spread of this latest rumor was only additional proof of that growing divide.

Besides their rejections, she had the embarrassment of kissing John and then his proposal. She had accepted, reluctantly, hoping they would never have to tell anyone.

It was too much for her to think about.

When she was a little girl, she had dreamed of her first kiss and someone proposing to her. But not like this. Never like this.

While Clara's initial rejection of his proposal, piled on top of the other events of the day, should have put John in a perpetually bad mood, he was feeling surprisingly light as he left her home.

He wanted to confront Emmers and get him to retract his claims against Clara, but John knew it would be of no use. Still, he had found a way to help her. They could be an engaged couple to the public, and it would provide her with a reason for why he was spending so much time with her family—particularly time alone with her in the store.

He felt a tiny bit of guilt that he'd pressured her into following his plan. But it was worth it to know that he was protecting her, even though he had to manipulate her somewhat to get her to agree. He had seen firsthand how stubborn Clara was and knew that it was hard for her to accept help. He knew her initial refusal was out of some misplaced reasoning that it would be a burden for him to be engaged to her. It was not at all. The idea of being an unofficial member of the Morehouse family was appealing to him, even though it was just in pretense.

John was already formulating the plans in his mind. First, he would buy her a ring today. Then, once he had it on her finger, they would tell her family. He would leave it up to Clara if she wanted to let the others in on the plan or not. Finally, they would subtly announce their engagement by attending church together once again, with her wearing the band and John sitting by her side.

When he left for the West, she would still be wearing his ring. They would "break up" via letter sometime in the future—at a moment of her choosing. He intended to let Clara be engaged to him for as long as she needed. He had five years to spare per his plan after all.

All of this meant that even when he left, John would still be able to maintain a friendship with Clara whenever letters were possible. He had grown accustomed to talking to her nearly every day, and letters wouldn't be the same, but they would be something at least.

Part of him still hoped he could convince the Morehouse family to go too, but he knew Clara still thought this wasn't a very good business decision. He hoped he had not used up all his persuasion power on her to convince her of the fake engagement.

He wished Clara could smash Michael Emmers over the head with a broomstick once again, just for causing John so many complications.

John was just turning the corner toward his hotel when a fist crashed into his face. Then one in his stomach. Two men jumped him before he even had the chance to realize what was happening, much less try to defend himself. John swung and connected with one man's jaw, but the other came behind him and slammed his fist into John's lower back. The pain sent him to his knees.

"This is for taking away what belonged to Emmers."

John clenched his fist. *So that's what this was about.* "She doesn't belong to anyone, least of all Michael Emmers."

The men landed another round of blows on him, one of them breaking his nose. He fell over onto the sidewalk, spitting blood.

"Hey, you stay away from him," a voice yelled from across the street. Young Benjamin, the blacksmith, came to his rescue. John's attackers apparently didn't want anyone to see their faces, so they had raced away by the time Ben arrived by John's side.

"Are you all right, Mr. Butler?"

Benjamin helped him to his feet. "No, this day just keeps getting worse by the minute. I'm not all right."

John's head began to spin, and his vision blurred after he stood. He wobbled a bit, reaching out to grab Benjamin's arm so he wouldn't topple over.

The young man looked at him with concern. "I think you might have hit your head on the sidewalk with that last blow, Mr. Butler. Let's get you to the doc."

John just nodded and leaned on the young man's shoulders as they walked slowly through town. Each step he took ratcheted up his pain, and his head began to feel foggy. But he could focus only on what he was supposed to be doing instead of limping his way through Independence.

"I'm supposed to be buying a ring right now."

Benjamin gave him a confused look. "A ring?"

John shook his head, wincing at the pain as he did so. "I asked her to marry me. She needs a ring. She can't go around being engaged without a ring. That would defeat the purpose of everything."

His words were slurred, he could hear it himself, but through his pain he could think only of Clara.

Benjamin patted him gently on the shoulder. "I don't know much about love, and I don't know how much of this you will be remembering tomorrow, but I have a feeling that whoever you proposed to won't care about the ring when she hears about what happened to you."

John mumbled "It's not about love. It's about the ring. It's very important."

He didn't think Benjamin heard him as he steered him toward the doctor's office. "Who are you buying a ring for, Mr. Butler?"

John heard the question, and he tried to process how he should answer it as he sat down on the doctor's table. Now was definitely not the time he and Clara planned to announce their fake engagement to the town. Benjamin wasn't even asking out of true curiosity. John knew the lad was trying to distract him from the pain of having his injuries examined. He barely felt it when the doctor jabbed him with a needle and said, "Something for the pain."

John didn't have time for this. Clara had barely agreed to his plan, and more rumors were spreading around the town and hurting the Morehouse business with each wag of the tongue. He started to get off the table, and the two men pushed him back.

"Where do you think you're going, Mr. Butler?" the doctor asked, holding on to his arm with a vise grip.

"I have to go buy Clara a ring. I promised her it would fix it. Just this one thing, and it will be all right." His words were slurring, but surely he could handle the purchase of one ring.

The doctor chuckled. "You can do your shopping later, son. First, I need to set your nose, and after that, you have to get some rest. I'll give you something and you can sleep off the night here."

Benjamin studied his face. "Is it broken?"

The doctor nodded. "It is, but I don't think it's the first broken nose he's had and judging from his lifestyle wandering the world, it won't be his last."

John sat up to object. "No! I'm done wandering! Just one more and I'm done! Think she will be there for me in five years?"

"Who?" The doctor asked, making John wince as he examined his other wounds.

John's head was really starting to feel heavy now. He was having a hard time keeping his eyes open. "The woman I'm going to marry after my five-year plan."

Benjamin laughed. "Well, you can start to test that by making her wait until morning to get that ring you want to buy her."

They thought Clara was the woman he was going to marry in five years. He didn't have the energy to explain the whole thing to them. But the reminder of his proposal had him trying to muster the energy to get going. "No, I have to get the ring now. I promised."

The doctor sighed and guided him back. "You don't want to show up at her door with a bloody nose. Let it heal a bit, and you won't frighten her as much."

John wanted to object, but his eyes started to drift closed in spite of himself.

John's last thought before he saw black was that he really needed to buy a ring that matched the color of her eyes.

Chapter Eleven

Clara was sound asleep when her sisters came home after closing the store for the night. They must have been completely taken aback by this, as she never went to bed before them. She had intended to hound them for the sales results from the day, but her exhaustion was just too much.

In the morning, however, Clara felt a little better. Things were still terrible, and she didn't know the state of her friendship, engagement or whatever with John, but she had gotten plenty of rest. Still, she wasn't one to sit around moping. She needed to come up with a plan.

Her sisters, however, had a different idea. They bounced into her room full of chatter and bearing a breakfast tray.

"You are never going to believe everything that happened yesterday after you fell asleep!"

Eliza was practically jumping up and down with excitement. Hannah just nodded and grinned.

"Judging from your expressions, I don't have to brace myself for bad news. What happened?"

Eliza plopped down on the bed next to her and stole an apple slice from her tray. "Father got wind of what

Michael did. Of what was going around town about you."

Clara paled. *Oh no.* She had hoped to spare her father from this information for two reasons. First, obviously no daughter wanted their father to hear untoward stories about her, whether they were true or not. Second, she didn't want him to think she couldn't handle things on her own.

She'd made him a promise that everything would be handled while he rested. Now she felt like she had broken that promise.

"And you're never going to believe what he did!" Hannah was positively giddy. Clara couldn't remember the last time she had seen her sister like that.

"He wrote a strongly worded letter to the Emmers family?"

Eliza shook her head excitedly. "No, even better. He left the house!"

Clara dropped the piece of toast she had been nibbling on. "He what?"

Hannah grinned. "Yes, he left the house. First, he visited every business that had canceled their order yesterday. Made them all feel ashamed for believing such foul things about you."

Clara looked doubtful. "But why would they believe father over Michael Emmers?"

Eliza just shrugged. "They all have known him longer than Michael, since Papa opened the store before Michael was even born, and most know he is much nicer—more trustworthy, as well."

Clara couldn't disagree with that. "And then what did Father do? Did he come home and collapse in bed after all that excitement?"

She imagined the toll of spending even an hour

around people after avoiding them for so long would be quite heavy.

"No, he came by the store!"

Clara froze at that, shock mingling with disappointment. She had wanted to be there when her father first saw the store after his recovery. She had wanted to explain all the changes they had made and show off their hard work proudly. "What did he say?"

Eliza pulled her in for a hug. "Of course he said that he was pleased with you and everything looked wonderful."

Hannah agreed. "He said that he had known you could do it, but seeing it in person was a balm to his heart."

Clara wiped a tear from her eye. She hadn't known just how much she had needed her father's validation. Now that she had it, though, she couldn't help but be filled with joy. She had helped maintain the store's success, even through the most difficult of times.

"I'm sorry that he had to go out and fix my mess with Michael though," Clara said glumly.

Eliza gave her a guilty look. "It's my fault. When you didn't come back to the store, I ran home over lunch to see what had happened. Betty said you were asleep. Father overheard and wanted to know what was going on."

Clara nodded. "I was just so exhausted after everything. I cried all over John until I could barely keep my eyes open."

Her two sisters exchanged a look. "How long did John stay with you?"

Clara sighed. She did not want to get into this with them. "About an hour. He was so sweet and kind. And he offered many…unique suggestions on how he wanted to handle the Emmers situation."

Her sisters, thankfully, did not press her further on what those suggestions were. Hannah just nodded and gave a happy sigh. "He's such a nice man. You should marry him instead of Michael."

Clara scowled. "I'm not marrying Michael. I'm not marrying anyone."

Now that her father had fixed some of the mess caused by Michael, Clara supposed that the fake engagement with John wasn't even necessary anymore. She wondered why that realization didn't give her an immediate sense of relief.

Eliza shook her finger at her. "But you like John. You are just too stubborn to admit it."

"I'm not!" Clara's voice reached an octave that she was not quite familiar with. "That is to say, I like him just fine. Are you happy? We are just friends. Besides, if there were anything romantic between us, it's not like we could do anything about it. We live two very different lives."

Eliza just rolled her eyes. "That is because you are insisting on not giving in when it comes to moving west. If we did, you could be with John."

"I don't want to 'be' anything with John, other than his friend." This whole conversation was getting ludicrous. She wasn't going to uproot her entire family just so she could spend more time with a friend.

But there was also that kiss. Though it was a mistake, she couldn't erase it from her mind…

"What are you thinking about?" Hannah asked, her voice filled with excitement.

Clara panicked, wondering how much her face had revealed of her train of thought. She definitely could not tell them what had happened in the drawing room yesterday. They would read too much into it.

"What? Nothing. I'm thinking about my breakfast."

Both sisters snickered at her obvious lie.

Eliza crossed her arms, staring Clara down. "You are not. You got this wistful look on your face. Like you were remembering the best thing in the world."

Clara scowled. "Well, I do really like pancakes."

The three of them burst into laughter. It felt good to giggle with two of her favorite people after the day she'd had yesterday. Clara was so thankful that no matter what happened in life, she would always have her sisters.

"Don't you think for a moment we are going to let you change the subject on us. What had you all wistful a few moments ago?" Eliza wasn't going to let it go. Clara gave up. Even if they misinterpreted her relationship with John, it would be nice to have friendly ears to share the details with.

Clara got up and closed the door. She didn't want Betty—or worse, their father—to overhear.

"All right, I will tell you, but you cannot tell anyone."

Both of her sisters nodded and sat excitedly on the edge of the bed.

"I kissed John. Yesterday. Downstairs." Though she was speaking in fragmented sentences because she had apparently forgotten how to talk when it came to this situation, her sisters got the message. Both of them screeched in delight and launched themselves on her with hugs and a barrage of questions.

"What was it like?" Hannah asked eagerly. "Was it romantic?"

Clara shook her head. "Not at all. I was sobbing and he was being nice. So, I kissed him on an impulse and regretted it immediately."

Eliza's eyes narrowed at this. "Why would you regret

it? You kissed him, so clearly some part of you wanted it. And you like John. We all do."

Clara sighed. "Yes, we've established that I like John, but that's as far as it will go. You know how I feel about romance—especially since I took over the store. It's not for me. I don't have time for it with all my responsibilities."

Her sisters objected and started arguing about how she and John would be perfect together. How could she ever convince them that she had no intention of ever falling in love with anyone, including John?

As they continued to pepper her with questions, Clara rubbed her temples. It was going to be a long morning, and an even longer day at the store.

John groaned as he woke up in an unfamiliar room. Acclimating to new settings was something he was accustomed to, having traveled so much in his lifetime, but it still took him a few minutes to remember where he was and why he was here.

"Ah, welcome back to the world, Mr. Butler. You took quite a blow to the nose, and a few of your ribs are bruised too," the doctor said as he entered the room.

"What time is it?" His head hurt; his nose hurt; his ribs hurt. John figured the only part of him that didn't have an ache was probably his pinky toe on his right foot. That had somehow survived the brawl last night.

"Just past noon." The doctor made quick work of rechecking his nose. "I think you will heal nicely. I suspect you are in a lot of pain right now, but it should go away in a week's time, with the bruising."

John groaned. He had so much work to do to get ready for the next wagon train; he could not afford to take off for a week. "Can I still work?"

The doctor chuckled but nodded. "Yes, although you may wish you weren't. Just don't get into any more brawls before you're fully healed."

John couldn't help but agree. The attack by Michael Emmers's lackeys, probably paid for by credit or promise of payment once Clara married him, could possibly be a one-time thing. But he would still take precautions to make sure he was never alone out in public until he was fully healed. It also wouldn't hurt to involve the authorities if it came down to it.

"I don't think your young lady would appreciate you showing up with even more bruising when you rush over there to declare your love."

John startled at the doctor's words. Clara. His proposal. It all came back to him at once. How much did the doctor know? He couldn't remember what he'd done or said after the fight last night. He didn't bother to correct the doctor about their feelings, because if they were going to convince the community that their engagement was real, they would have to pretend they were very much in love.

"How did I get here?"

The doc gave him a concerned look. "You don't remember?"

John just shook his head, and the elder man started feeling his head for lumps. "Nothing too damaged up here—it must be that your brain is still cloudy from the pain medications. Young Benjamin brought you here, after your fight."

John made a mental note to buy the man a gift in thanks for saving him and bringing him to help. "Did I...do anything embarrassing?"

The doctor laughed. "Nothing I haven't seen much of before, son. You did a lot of talking about how you had to buy that Morehouse girl a ring, and we had to hold you down so you didn't run off and do it right then."

It was all coming back to John now, very slowly. Thankfully, he hadn't let slip the truth about their engagement. And he was grateful, as well, that Doc and Benjamin had kept him away from Clara. She would have been terrified if a bloodied man practically out of his mind had showed up at her doorway, even if he brought the most beautiful ring in the world. Not that he could have even purchased a band in the condition he was in.

"I'm sorry I was talking nonsense last night. I was injured and also still excited about my betrothal." It wasn't a full lie, because he *had* been excited that Clara had finally accepted his fake engagement plan. The doctor just smiled at him.

"That's all right, son. Now that you're in your right mind, why don't you sit here and tell me all about it? Or are you still going to rush out and buy that ring today and give it to her looking like this?"

John grinned at the doctor and stood up, unsteady on his feet. "I promised her a ring yesterday, and I didn't make it. I need to get over there and put it on her finger before she changes her mind."

Who knew what further damage had been done to the Morehouse business while he was unconscious? Now that the assault in the street had shown him how low Emmers would go, there was no telling what else he might do to Clara.

The doctor helped him put on his coat and shoes. John tried to concentrate on putting his plan in motion to ensure that Clara was safe from Emmers.

The doctor sighed as he walked John to the door.

"Well, if you insist on going, Mr. Butler, I have two pieces of advice for you."

John nodded, and the doctor continued.

"First, you should probably go take a bath. You do not smell as fresh as a daisy. Official proposals are best done when the young woman doesn't want to wretch upon being in the same room with you."

John nodded, conceding that it was sound advice. He supposed he could go to his hotel to bathe first. He had already slept away the morning, and Clara was probably already at the store. What difference would another hour or so make?

"And what's the second piece of advice?"

The doctor's expression turned serious. "I heard you ramble about a five-year plan last night, and I think you should reconsider it."

John just shook his head at the doctor. "It's a well-thought-out and sound plan."

The doctor clapped him on the shoulder and then immediately looked apologetic for making John gasp in pain. "Sorry, Mr. Butler. Listen, when it comes to romance, well-thought-out and sound plans never succeed."

John was confused. If a plan was sound, how could it fail? "Never?"

Doc shook his head. "Love causes you to make impulsive and sometimes wonderful decisions. But only if you are willing to open yourself up to it. Besides, you can't expect that girl to wait around for you that long."

It made some sense. John had seen many people make foolish decisions for love. But the doctor was mistaken when he assumed it was Clara he was talking about when it came to his five-year-plan. By the time he had settled in his new town for that long and was ready to take a wife, his engagement with her would be long over.

First, though, he needed to go buy that ring so it could at least begin.

Chapter Twelve

"So please repeat that again. You both kissed. He proposed a fake engagement to you, you turned him down but then finally agreed?"

Both sisters were staring at her in shock. She had repeated this story to them several times while they were working together in the store. Clara wondered when they would tire of it.

"And I thought *we* had a busy afternoon." Eliza said it as a joke, but recounting the whole incident did not fill Clara with humor.

"How was it? How was the kiss?" Hannah asked again. Of course, her younger sister, who had read every tale of romance she could get her hands on, wanted to know how the kiss was.

"It was...nice."

"Just nice?" Eliza really was not letting her get away with lies today.

Clara sighed. "Yes, fine, it was absolutely wonderful. But it meant nothing."

Her two sisters' eyes still glowed with excitement.

Hannah gave her a wistful look. "Why did you reject his idea of a fake proposal at first? It sounds like the perfect solution."

Clara wrung her hands in frustration. "I will tell you what I told him. I'm not going to escape one betrothal by jumping into another. And besides, John is far too willing to sully his reputation just to save our family. I won't let him do it."

Eliza tilted her head in confusion. "I don't understand. Didn't you confess to me not a week ago that you were willing to consider Michael Emmers out of a misguided notion that you had to in order to protect us?"

Clara nodded, glad that her sisters had talked her out of that plan.

"So why would you be willing to marry that dreadful man to save our family and not become betrothed to one you actually like for the exact same reason, especially when it's just for pretense?"

Her sister did have a point, but she didn't want to explain her reasons.

"It doesn't matter now anyway. Papa fixed everything with our customers. We can go on with life as normal—no engagement required." Indeed, the store had maintained a steady stream of visitors this morning, each of them looking apologetic as they purchased their items from Clara. It was almost as if the incident with Michael had never happened.

Almost. She knew that this would always be in the back of people's minds whenever they looked at her.

Eliza narrowed her eyes. "I think you aren't telling us the real reason you hesitated." Clara tried to ignore her sister's pestering, keeping her nose in the daily ledger. She hoped they would be able to recover from yesterday's loss of sales.

Eliza marched over and pulled the book out of her hands. "Eliza, I'm working," Clara protested.

But her sister was not about to give up. "You have feelings for him, and you're afraid of this fake engagement because you think it will be too hard to end it when it's time."

Clara glared at her sister. "I do not have any feelings other than friendship for him."

"You're wrong, you know," Hannah chimed in.

"About what?" She tried to get her ledger out of Eliza's hands, but to no avail.

"You don't have to worry about the fake engagement leading to your heart breaking when it's over. Because I think the sentiment you have is mutual, so you won't need to break up."

Clara rolled her eyes at Hannah, grabbing her ledger out of Eliza's hand so that she could get back to work. "This isn't one of your fairy-tale books, Hannah. It was a business proposal, nothing more."

Eliza snickered. "Oh yes, because we always seal business proposals with a kiss around here."

Clara scowled at her sister. "Can you just let it go?"

Both sisters shook their heads. "No, we just want you to be happy," Eliza insisted. "This notion that you can't run a business and also be in love is silly. And you don't see the way you look at each other when the other person's back is turned."

Clara did a quick inventory of all the time she'd spent with John. Did she act differently around him? She didn't think so. Her sisters were just too romantically inclined and always believed they'd found evidence of love where it didn't exist.

"I don't look at him in any particular way at all," she protested.

Her sisters laughed at that. "You haven't smiled much since Mama died. But you smile at him," Hannah said.

That couldn't be true, she thought. "I've smiled."

Eliza just patted her on the shoulders. "It's okay if you don't believe us yet, someday you will. We're just glad that you've found a man who makes you happy. Even if he's just your friend."

She said the last sentence in a sarcastic tone, but Eliza had softened it with a tender expression that reminded Clara so much of their mother that it made her burst into tears. She stifled a sob and sat down on her chair. "What is wrong with me? I never cry and now I've done it twice in as many days."

Hannah slung her arm around her sister's shoulders. "You've had a busy and complicated couple of days. Give yourself a moment or two to be upset about it."

Clara cried harder. "But I'm normally not like this."

Eliza came to her other side. "Maybe now that Papa's doing better, you're finally letting everything you've been holding inside this whole time out a little bit? Because you don't have to be strong anymore?"

Clara stiffened at her words. She knew that she was still resilient, even though she was in a puddle of tears right now. But the thought of giving up some of the responsibility she had shouldered for so long made her feel both relieved and sad. She did like running the store after all. She liked the independence she felt, and the sense of accomplishment. Her father wouldn't take it all away from her, but it wouldn't be the same when she was no longer the one in charge.

When she finally dried her tears, her sisters still sat beside her to offer her more comfort if needed. Eliza, however, seemed to think that maybe this moment of her weakness was the time to bring up a subject of contention between them.

"Do you think, now that Papa is well and things may start getting better, that you might reconsider the family moving west? After everything going on, maybe it might be a good time to start over somewhere else."

She shook her head. "I can't uproot everyone and take such a huge business risk over a little setback in our social status and enterprise."

Hannah sighed. "But what about John? Are you just going to let him leave when it's time for the wagon train to roll out?"

Clara didn't want to think about that day. She would miss John, as he had become an important part of their lives in the past couple of weeks. And she would never forget the sacrifice that he had been willing to make to his reputation in order to save their family. He was a good man, and his leaving would make a hole in their lives.

"John and I are not really engaged, so there is no reason for him to stay any longer or for me to go with him. That wasn't part of the plan anyway. When he's gone, I'm sure we can keep in touch through letters from time to time. And he will visit us, I'm sure, whenever he has to come to the city for business."

Eliza shook her head in frustration. "That doesn't seem like enough. He's like family now. You know how much Papa loves him."

It was true that John was practically a Morehouse by now, but their brief engagement wasn't real, and he had a life to lead somewhere else. He would be missed, but she was also determined not to let her emotions steer her to make such large, impractical decisions for their family.

"You need to tell him how you feel," Hannah urged. "That you love him."

Clara slammed her ledger closed. "I am not in love with John. I'm not in love with anyone. Can't you let it be?" Now that this business with Michael Emmers was settled by her father, she just wanted to get back to focusing on her work.

"You both are being stubborn." Eliza chuckled. "I don't think you should write him off completely."

Clara sighed. "I have work to do to keep this family business running. Nothing will come between me and doing what it takes to ensure your futures. And no man, whether he be friend or foe."

Hannah squeezed her hand. "You deserve to be happy. You've taken care of us long enough. Besides, we can take care of ourselves."

She shook her head. Her sisters had no idea the amount of work she put into keeping the store and household running ever since Mama got sick. Things would fall apart without her—and if she let even the smallest thing drop, she couldn't trust anyone else to pick up the slack. Sure, John had tried to help her in the Emmers situation, but for the most part, she did everything on her own.

Thinking of John reminded her that she hadn't seen him yet today, even to tell him that their fake engagement was off. Maybe he had changed his mind after all and was hiding so he wouldn't have to break the news. Clara frowned. That wasn't like him at all.

"I think my friendship with John might not be as strong as you believe. After all, he never showed up with the ring he promised, and he's avoiding work today."

The two sisters shared a knowing look that Clara

recognized immediately as them hiding something. "What?"

They hesitated before Hannah spoke. "We didn't exactly tell you *everything* that happened yesterday."

Their nervousness made Clara worried. "What is it?"

Hannah was ringing her hands.

"We heard it from the paper boy this morning. John was beaten up after he left our house, and he had to spend the night at Doc's."

Panic surged through Clara.

"What? Why didn't you tell me earlier? Is he all right? Do I need to go to him? Who did this?"

The sisters were about to answer when John himself appeared outside their store window, looking in. Their eyes met, and he smiled nervously. His shoulders slumped as if he was relieved when she returned his smile. Maybe their friendship was still intact after all, she thought.

But just as John was about to open the door to come in, a messenger ran up to him and pulled him away. They did not see him again the rest of the afternoon.

Clara hoped he would pay her a visit this evening, or she would have to hunt him down and get the full story of his injuries from the man himself.

"I don't understand why this couldn't have been delayed. There's a short conversation I needed to have with a friend first," John told the messenger boy who he was following to the Morehouse residence.

"He said right away, sir. He specifically said it had to be *before* you went into the store today. I'd been waiting here for you for two hours."

The boy looked a little annoyed at the delay. John couldn't help but chuckle.

"I apologize, young sir, for keeping you waiting." He had spent his morning following the doctor's advice. His bath had made him feel slightly better, but the delay in his conversation with Clara had only increased his anxiety. At least he had finally gotten the ring. That had taken longer than he'd hoped, as well.

When he finally reached the store, he'd been blocked from entering by this young messenger, who told him he was needed by Mr. Morehouse right away.

"What's your name, boy?" He held out his hand to shake.

The boy looked at him in surprise, but then shook it solemnly. "Henry, sir."

"It's nice to meet you, Henry. Your parents must be very proud of you, working like this."

The boy gave him a sad smile. "It's just me and my dad now, and my baby sister. Mom died last year."

His heart broke for the boy. He hadn't had a mother for most of his growing up either.

"I think you are doing an excellent job helping to care for your family. You remind me a lot of my big brother."

The boy's eyes widened. "The other Butler brother?"

John nodded. "Yes, that's right. He got his start in business, just like you—running errands. Being a help wherever he could. I think you've got a bright future."

The boy grinned at this news, and John gave one last wistful look at Clara before following Henry to the Morehouse home.

"What does your father do for a living, Henry?"

The boy told him that the family had lost their farm last year because of a series of events. Bad weather ruined crops. Their cattle were stolen. Their barn burned down.

"Father tried to keep things going after mother died,

really he did. But it's hard to do it all alone and care for children."

John nodded. He knew that part of the story all too well, thinking back to the days when his father would be out in the fields all day and his brother had to step in as a parent to John. Adam had taught himself to use the stove so they could at least eat something.

"So, what does he do now?"

Henry explained that his father now worked in the livery, caring for horses. "He's good at it, and he loves the animals, but…"

"He would rather be doing something else?" John said, finishing the boy's sentence.

The boy gave his sad agreement. John felt for him, knowing his parent was unhappy and not able to do anything about it. He had been there before. John wiped the image of his own father's sad eyes out of his mind.

He pulled a coin out of his pocket and handed it to Henry. "But Mr. Morehouse already paid me," the boy protested.

"I'm paying you extra, as an apology for the wait. And I will try to stop by and visit your father later. I think I may have a few ideas on how we can help bring his smile back."

Henry's eyes widened. "Really?"

John nodded, thanked the lad and sent him on his way. John patted his front pocket where the ring was hidden. Hopefully, it would be on Clara's finger by the end of the day.

Not talking to her this morning left things strangely unsettled between them. When he saw her through the shop's window, she'd had tears in her eyes.

Because of him?

Because of that fool, Emmers?

Both of them had made her life complicated yesterday, although John's reasons were much nicer than Michael's. But maybe she needed a break from that sort of drama today. Before he could find out why she was crying or slide the ring on her finger, he had to talk to Mr. Morehouse first.

He raised his hand to ring the bell, but the door swung open before he could. Betty was standing there, giving him a matronly glare that could make anyone run away in terror. Good thing John was made of sterner stuff.

"There you are. He's been waiting for hours," she said with an angry tone. He had always thought of Betty as a sweet woman, but there was fire under that sweetness. And it warmed him to know it came from protectiveness for the Morehouse family.

He waved a hand over the injuries on his face. "I apologize. I'm moving slowly today because of all of this."

Betty surveyed his bruises and her eyes softened as she gave him a pitying look. "Well, then, why don't you go on in and talk with him, and I'll see if I can make you a nice cup of that tea that I always give the girls when they aren't feeling their best."

Thankful to be on her good side again, John hurried inside. He walked tentatively toward the drawing room. What did Mr. Morehouse need to see him about? Did he know that his daughter had kissed John in this very room just a day ago? Was he aware that John had proposed to her? He hadn't asked permission to propose to Arthur's daughter before sharing his plan with Clara, and maybe he should have. It had been a spur-of-the-moment decision.

When he entered the drawing room, he was delighted

to see his friend fully dressed for the day, a far cry from the Arthur Morehouse who had refused to leave his bed a few weeks ago.

"John! Come in! Sorry for the rush to get you over here, but we need to have a serious conversation about my daughter. Please, have a seat."

John didn't know whether to be nervous or terrified. So he settled on both.

Chapter Thirteen

Though her father's visits had quieted the roar of rumors that Michael Emmers had started, he had not been able to silence them completely. The morning was busy in the store, but business dried up again after lunch.

Clara went over the books again with a sigh. They could not maintain for long if revenue remained at this level.

"I hope that sales will rebound within the next few days—but if they don't, the business could be seriously impacted. If worse comes to worst, we may need to start thinking about selling the store," she told her father that night after supper. "I'm really sorry, Papa. I know you tried to fix things for me yesterday, but I let you down. I couldn't make the business work."

He smiled at her and patted her hand. "I don't think you should give up after a slow day."

Clara knew he was patronizing her. "It's more than that. This scandal has reminded people that they have other options when it comes to stores to patronize. Our most loyal customers are staying, but the other suppliers in town are doing their best to capitalize on our distraction, particularly when it comes to pursuing the people coming in for the wagon train. You can visit some of them tomorrow, but I don't know if it will be enough. And the wagon train after that is the Butler Brothers'... and I haven't seen John all day. I fear that our relationship, both in friendship and business, may be damaged."

Her father just laughed. "Don't worry about Mr. Butler. Your friendship with him is intact. I had him come for a visit with me instead of going in to the store today."

Clara gasped at her father's words. Did he know what had transpired between her and John?

"Did he...? Do you...?"

Father chuckled again, and invited her to sit down on the chair across from him. Her sisters were reading by the fire, pretending not to listen to the conversation.

"Did he tell me that he offered his hand in marriage to you? Yes, he did."

Clara didn't know what to say. Her father was a friend of John's and probably would approve of the match. But she got the impression that John hadn't told him the full details of their fake betrothal, and her father thought it was real. She didn't want to disappoint him.

"I hesitated to accept him," she said carefully. "You can probably guess why he asked. I didn't want to become engaged to him just because he wants to save us from the Michael Emmers situation."

Surprisingly, her father nodded in agreement.

"A sound reason. You should marry for love, nothing less."

Clara was relieved that she didn't have one of those fathers who pressured their daughters to marry to increase their social standing or to get them out of their house.

"I will probably never wed. I want our business to be a success—that is my first priority. And with our latest setbacks, I'm not sure we can do that here. I know you are confident we will recover, Papa, but I've been going through the numbers all day. We've been dealing with increasing competition for a while now. Damage to our bottom line at this point could be enough to pull us under. We might be better off selling the business and starting off fresh somewhere else."

There was a twinkle in her father's eyes, which made Clara very nervous.

"Somewhere else like the new Butler Brothers' town?"

Clara wanted to grind her teeth. She hated that the men in her life were getting their way, especially because of the actions of Michael.

"I'm not sure that particular location is a good idea," she hedged. "Shouldn't we start over in a town that isn't so far away, where it won't be so much harder to access the supplies we need?"

Her father leveled a stern stare at her. "Any towns closer by will already have plenty of their own established stores. We would do best by setting ourselves up where there isn't one yet. Why are you being so stubborn about this?"

Clara searched for answers. The Butler Brothers' offer would be a good thing for them right now, but there was still so much uncertainty. They were already going to have to decide what to do with their store— would a risk in a brand-new town be safe enough for them?

"We can't afford to go there," she argued.

Her father gave her a grim smile. "We can't afford to stay either."

Then, there was the matter of his emotional well-being on the long and difficult journey. That wasn't something to ignore. "Papa, you are just now getting downstairs and out more often. Do you really think you will be ready for a wagon train in a few months?"

But he was not to be swayed. "I will be ready."

Clara had never heard such sincerity in his voice. He really wanted this. It was almost enough to make her say yes, just to make him happy.

"Papa…"

He held up his hand. "Taking your complicated… friendship for Mr. Butler out of the equation, let me explain why I believe we should take him up on his offer."

Clara sighed and sat down, finally ready to listen. It was her family's future too, so they deserved to have a say.

"You girls are the most important thing to me, and I feel it would be to your benefit if we can start over somewhere—fresh. I think it's a wonderful idea."

Clara shook her head, the weight of leaving her childhood home pressing in on her. "But Papa, Mama lived here with us. Why would we abandon her home?"

Father gave her a sad look. "Without the store, how would we support ourselves in this big house?"

She knew that he was right, but it was so hard to let go.

"Your mother loved this house, but she wouldn't want us to live in it like a coffin. I've let myself get trapped in my grief. We need to go somewhere away and make new memories. Your mother will go with us, in our hearts," Father said.

Clara could feel tears forming in her eyes. He was right, of course. While this place brought up many happy memories for them, it also served as a constant reminder of what they had lost.

Clara turned to her sisters. "What do you think?"

They had been silent for the whole conversation, and they deserved a chance to offer an opinion. "You would be giving up everything you know."

Eliza opened her mouth to speak, but Clara interrupted her. "Not to mention the grueling journey to get there. You will have to walk all day, getting blisters on your feet. We would all sleep in cramped wagons, surrounded by untold dangers." Clara knew she was rambling, but she desperately wanted to get her point across to her sisters.

Eliza was biting her lip, visibly holding in a laugh and tapping her foot while waiting for Clara to finish.

"Can I speak now?"

Clara nodded, forcing herself to remain quiet.

"You know I'm always up for an adventure. Going out West sounds exciting—even with the discomforts of life on the wagon train. Think of how many people we will meet." Eliza was shifting her feet excitedly as she said it, so Clara knew she was holding herself in check to keep from bouncing around the room with glee.

"And Mr. Butler said that they might have use for me as a teacher. I've wanted to be one for so long," Hannah said, jumping in.

Clara looked between her two sisters. It seemed like they had already done quite a bit of dreaming about their life in a new frontier. "But what about husbands? If you do find one out West, who's to say they will let you pursue adventure or teaching, as each of you want?"

Hannah shook her head. "We have no reason to think that the men here would be any more supportive than the men there. Should we marry, that is always a question that will have to be asked. If we don't care for the answer, then perhaps we won't marry at all. There is more to life than finding a husband. Besides, I was reading in the newspaper the other day that there are more men there than women, so if I do want to find one—they are readily available."

Eliza grinned and nodded. "They will be begging us to be their wives."

They had a point. She knew of one very good man indeed who would be out West, but she had ruined her chances with him.

"Would I still get to run the store?" She turned to her father eagerly. That was the one issue she still had with the idea. She had longed to run the business herself and didn't want to lose the opportunity by leaving Independence.

Her father nodded.

"I will help with the move and get you set up, but you will be completely in charge. You can put me to work whenever you want once we are there."

Clara's shoulders slumped in relief. Three pairs of eyes looked at her eagerly.

"So, are we decided?" Eliza asked.

Clara nodded, and the rest of the Morehouse family cheered.

"We will accept the Butlers' offer—if it is still good," Clara said. "But it will be for the business proposal, not marriage."

Her sisters groaned, but her father just nodded.

"Maybe you will change your mind when you get out West, but it is best to say yes to a proposal because you want to, not because you have to," he said."

Clara knew that there wouldn't be another proposal coming from Mr. Butler. There would be no need, now that their plans would remove the Michael Emmers situation completely from consideration. He would be free to settle unencumbered for his five-year plan and someday find a woman to propose to out of love and not just for pretense.

Meanwhile, Clara would be free to start their new store and run it in a brand-new town. The idea had scared her before, but now that she was opening herself up to the possibilities, her excitement grew. She would be able to establish a business from the ground up, putting her own ideas into it. "Do you think I've ruined our chances of the deal? I turned him down several times. Maybe he's started to consider someone else for the project."

Her father gave her a reassuring smile. "No, remember that I spoke with him today? I think he will be very happy to hear from you."

Clara wanted to ask more about the meeting, but the family sprang into action. Hannah went to fetch a piece of paper so Clara could write John a note. Father went to send for his solicitor to request a meeting tomorrow so he could start the process of putting the store and their home up for sale. Eliza went to break the news to Betty, who had been with the family for so long. They would have to leave her behind unless they could convince her to join them. Their maid had been let go when they learned she'd sold information to Emmers.

Clara thought briefly of Betty on the wagon train and had to laugh. The woman was more of a lady than any of them. She would not enjoy the adventure of the journey. Still, she hoped Betty would come. They loved her like family.

After Hannah returned with her stationery, Clara pondered what she should write to John. Although it was very forward of her to invite a man who wasn't her husband out for supper at the hotel restaurant, she figured that it might be easier to have the conversation in a public place.

Clara was determined to keep things professional with John from now on. If they were alone in a private setting like her home, she might be tempted to kiss him once more. And that was something that absolutely, definitively could not happen again.

John was wallowing; there was no other word for it. He had no desire to do any sort of business at the moment, and he knew that if his brother were here, there would be stern words for him.

Pretty much like the lecture he had received in the Morehouse drawing room earlier today. Arthur Morehouse had indeed heard about the beating he had received from Emmers's goons and the kiss shared between John and his daughter. Apparently, Betty had walked in and seen them kissing. He promised the man that he intended to marry Clara, and that he had, in fact, offered his hand—repeatedly—and that she had tentatively agreed. There was no need to tell Arthur that the engagement was in name only and would be called off someday before a wedding could take place.

"I took care of the immediate problems from the Michael Emmers situation, but the rumors will persist," the older man told John.

"That's why I offered to marry her."

The old man chuckled and leaned forward, a twinkle in his eye.

"Is that the only reason you told her that you wanted to marry her?"

John knew what the man was getting at, but he didn't know how to answer. The idea of not putting the ring on her finger bothered him a little, though he didn't know why. He could just return it and get his money back. Or better yet, tuck it away for his future wife.

"Clara is aware of all the reasons I proposed to her."

Arthur's eyes lit up with delight. "So, you told her that you love her?"

John didn't correct the man, letting him believe what he wanted to. He wished that he and Clara had had a conversation about how much to tell her family. Arthur was obviously thrilled and told him he had been secretly hoping that the two would fall in love and he'd gain John as a son-in-law. John hated that he would disappoint his friend someday when the engagement was over.

Arthur leaned forward, a thoughtful look on his face. "But the only problem is that she is determined to stay here and you need to go."

John nodded, suddenly hating this pretense with his friend. He should confess everything now, but he wanted to talk to Clara first.

"I'm still convinced that going west is what is best for Clara—for all of us. She would positively shine as a businesswoman in a new land."

John couldn't help but agree. He had come to Independence to recruit Arthur Morehouse to open a store in his new town, but now he wanted the determination and expertise that only Clara could provide.

He hated the idea, however, that Clara would think that he was using their false engagement as a manipulation to make her father even more determined to move them.

"I think you should let me worry about convincing her," John told his friend, but the gleam in the older man's eye told him that his request would be ignored.

As the day progressed after his meeting with Arthur, he started to doubt that convincing her would be possible. Clara was firmly against relocating. He would have to leave here in a few months' time without her.

John was pacing his hotel room in frustration, trying to figure out what he could do. There was a knock on the door, and he opened it to see Henry standing there, note in hand.

"Message for you, sir."

John smiled at the boy, taking the envelope. "Thanks, Henry," he said. He remembered the conversation he'd had earlier with the bright young man. "Can you ask your father if I can pay him a visit in the morning? I have something to discuss with him."

Henry grinned and agreed, running off to deliver that message, as well. John looked at the envelope that had been handed to him. His heartbeat sped up when he recognized Clara's handwriting.

She was inviting him to supper at the hotel! John nearly fell over from his shock and excitement. First, their friendship was indeed not over if she wanted to meet with him. The kiss and proposal had not pushed her away. Second, she must have something important to say to him—too important to be conveyed in a note. Either she had changed her mind on his proposal or her father had convinced her to move to the West.

Either way, he was having supper with the prettiest woman in town, and he needed to look his best. He went down to the hotel lobby to send a message back to Clara agreeing to the supper.

Once back in his room, he laid out his best suit—the one he used to impress investors. John hoped his best suit would work in his favor tonight.

Chapter Fourteen

Clara was nervous about her supper with John. She didn't know why. She had spent so much time with him in recent weeks that it should be easy for the two of them to be together without any tension or awkwardness. But she was now trying to be a different person with him. Formal, no emotion involved.

That plan almost went out the window when the man in question strolled around the corner of the hotel lobby and into the restaurant. He didn't see her at first, so she had time to study him. He wore a suit, like the one he'd had on when they first spoke, only a bit nicer. Over the past few weeks, he had dressed less formally for his time in the store, oftentimes with his shirtsleeves rolled up for ease of motion while doing all the hauling and lifting she and her sisters required of him. He was handsome no matter what he wore, but he was almost breathtaking now.

The suit clung to his form nicely, and he had brushed his hair back out of his face, so his eyes were the first thing you noticed about him. He surveyed the room, looking for her.

Only when he found her and grinned (which made

her traitorous stomach do flips) did she notice the bruising on his face and his swollen nose.

How was she supposed to be professional when her friend was so injured? She stood up when he walked over to her and fussed over his nose, which he seemed to enjoy.

"Clara," he said in a soft voice. "It's so good to see you. It's been forever."

She scowled at him. "We last saw each other yesterday, and you were in much better shape."

He grinned, and it was infuriating that he was making light of his injuries. "I will be fine. Emmers just wanted to thank me for stealing his fiancée."

Clara wanted to object that she had never been Michael's fiancée, but she decided to leave it alone. John was mostly fine, despite how terrible his injuries looked. She had to get back to her plan of being professional with him instead of personal. She wanted to put their kiss and the fake engagement behind them. She dropped her hands from his face and stepped back.

"Thank you for coming, Mr. Butler. Especially at such a short notice. Will you please sit down?"

John's grin dimmed a bit at her formality, but he just nodded and took a seat. "John. My name is John, Clara. I think we agreed to drop that propriety a long time ago."

Clara just shook her head. "I have to discuss business with you. In light of that, I think it's best we keep things professional."

He leaned across the table and took her hand. "We have some unprofessional things to talk about too, Clara."

Clara mustered all her resolve and stared him straight

in the eye. "Be that as it may, Mr. Butler, I think we need to proceed professionally."

She pulled her hand from his, immediately feeling the loss of their connection.

He hardened his jaw (and she tried not to notice how strong his jawline was) and nodded stiffly. "Very well, Miss Morehouse. Let's carry on with your business."

Though she had implemented the formality, it still hurt to hear John address her so distantly. She yearned to take it all back and embrace the closeness of their friendship once again. Clara told herself to stay strong.

"My family and I have decided to accept your proposal. Not—" she started when he opened his mouth to interject "—not the marriage proposal but your business proposal. We want to sell our store and open one out West with the Butler Brothers, in your new town."

John's eyes widened with surprise, and she forced herself to keep her emotions in check. This was just professional.

"Really? You are coming?"

She nodded. "My father will be meeting with his solicitor about putting the store and our house up for sale. So long as they both sell, and they should as there have been plenty of interested parties in the past, we should have the money to fund our trip and we will bring much of our stock with us."

John smiled at her and reached across the table for her hand once more. This time, she pulled hers away quickly before they could connect. He looked at her with concern.

"Are you all right?"

Clara knew that she had to put up the wall between them, but it was difficult with him looking at her with those sad eyes.

"I'm fine, Mr. Butler. I wanted to let you know that you are no longer on the hook for the marriage proposal you made yesterday, as this decision will remove the problems that Michael Emmers created for my family."

John leaned forward, a gleam of something—annoyance, hope…perhaps affection—reflected in his eyes. "Are you sure that's really a good idea? Calling it off while you're still in town?"

She frowned. He was not making this any easier on her. Clara had agreed to his plan to resettle. Why was he still pushing this fake engagement? "What? Why would that be necessary?"

"After I was assaulted in the street yesterday, I'm thinking that we haven't heard the last of Michael Emmers. Who knows what he will do next, especially if he hears you will be leaving and out of his grasp soon."

John managed to snag her hand this time, and a shiver ran down Clara's spine when she felt his thumb rub the inside of her palm.

"I think it's best that we just focus on the business. I don't have time for any betrothals, real or otherwise," she whispered.

He looked at her with sad eyes. "Clara, please let me help you. Use the protection of my ring until it's time for us to leave. It will make me feel better."

Clara knew that he was probably correct to think that Michael wouldn't stop until they left, but that was what she was concerned about. "What if by putting on that ring, I make things worse for you? You were already beaten. What if he escalates? My father, my sisters… we could all be in danger."

John nodded, reached in his pocket and pulled out a ring. He fiddled with it, gathering his thoughts. "Michael Emmers is a dangerous man—but he was a threat to me yesterday, when no one had any idea you and I had discussed becoming engaged. If he intends to harm me, I don't think the presence or absence of a ring on your finger will stop him. As for your family, if we're engaged, I'll be in a better position to provide some protection. Frankly, I think we have little to lose and a good deal to gain. If we are 'officially' engaged, and it's announced that we are moving to the West—it will help with the community. Your building will sell faster if there isn't any scandal attached. And once you leave, our engagement will protect you on the journey. Those on the wagon train who are traveling from Independence won't look at you as harshly. They're going to be your future customers in the new town we're building. I want them to have every reason to think well of you."

Clara blinked. She hadn't thought about that. Could she bear the ongoing pressure of rumors swirling about her relationship with the man who was in charge of the new town where most of them would settle? "But that would mean we would have to keep pretending while we were on the wagon train."

John nodded, still playing with the ring in his fingers. She wished she could see it, but he wasn't handing it over yet. "Yes, but I'm willing to, if you are."

"But our breakup would be even worse when we got to the new town. Your reputation there would be a lot more to lose."

John waved that argument away. "My reputation can take it there more than it could here in Independence. As one of the town founders it would be hard for the citizens to run me out of it."

Clara thought this all seemed far more complicated than she had imagined. She hadn't anticipated that agreeing to move west would bring more problems when it came to the rumors from Emmers. But she wanted her father and sisters to have the wonderful lives they had dreamed of in the new town, and she would do what she had to in order to ensure it.

"All right, we can continue our betrothal," she finally agreed.

John beamed, his shoulders slumping in relief as he reached across the table and took her hand. This time, she allowed it. He slowly slid the ring over her finger. The gold band glided on as a perfect fit, and it had a beautiful emerald in it. "I thought it matched your eyes," John said softly as she gazed down at it.

It was lovely, the kind of jeweled circlet girls dreamed of getting from their fiancé someday. But it didn't feel right. Not under these circumstances. "You didn't have to go to all this trouble, especially when our betrothal is not real."

John just shrugged and leaned back in his seat. "You deserve a nice ring, whether our engagement is permanent or not. If we want to make sure people believe we are in love, wouldn't it make sense that I give you an expensive one?"

That made sense, but it still felt like too much for Clara. "Maybe you can hold on to it someday for your real bride. After you've settled in your town for five years."

The thought of someone else wearing the beautiful band made Clara a little sad, if only because she had been so touched that he'd bought it for her. She knew that she wasn't destined to be someone's wife—she couldn't be married while running a store, and her business was far too important to her to give up—so this may be the only opportunity she had to wear a ring on her finger.

"That ring is just for you. Even if...when...our engagement ends, I wouldn't think of taking it back. You can keep it as a remembrance, or you can sell it. Either way, it's yours. No matter what happens, we're friends, right? You can take this ring as a promise that I will always be there to support you if you need it."

Clara made a promise to herself that she would find a way to return it after the engagement ended, whether he wanted her to or not. John was looking at her with such tenderness in his eyes, that it made Clara shift nervously in her seat. She didn't have time for romance, and maybe she didn't have time for friendships either if they made her feel this unsettled and confused.

"I, uh, Mr. Butler, we have to keep things professional. We have a busy year in front of us and don't have time for much else."

John gave her a sad smile. "I know we will be busy, but I hope I'm still welcome in your home. Both with you and your family."

She almost laughed at that. Her sisters and father would be very upset if he wasn't around. "Of course you are. Besides, it would appear very strange if my fiancé never spent time with me. I just think we need to only bring up the engagement when we have to. I don't want a big fuss when we have to prepare for our trip."

He frowned, but nodded in agreement. "All right, if that's what you want."

A small part of Clara wished she could be the same as all her friends who had proudly showed off their engagement rings all over town and planned their weddings and future homes with excitement. But this betrothal wasn't real, and she had a lot of work to do if her family was going to be ready to go in a month's time.

She just nodded and started to stand up.

"Thank you for meeting with me, Mr. Butler. I'm sure you have plenty of work to do. I will let you know when there is news of the store's sale and what will be needed from you to help facilitate our move west."

He reached out toward her. "Clara, please, sit down. We haven't even eaten yet."

Instead of giving in to the plea in his voice, Clara practically ran from the restaurant. The more time she spent with John, the more distracted she got from her business and responsibilities toward her family.

As she walked home, the ring on her finger weighed heavily on her. For better or worse, she was betrothed to John Butler.

The packing and planning for the trip to the West suddenly didn't seem like the hardest thing ahead of her. How on earth would they be able to keep up this pretense for months?

After she had gone, John went up to his room, still thinking about their too-brief meeting. This supper had not gone how he had expected. But at least his ring was now on her finger. John was pleased that it fit her so perfectly, and it did indeed match her eyes.

And yet everything that had happened put a damper on the friendship that had been growing between them. While Clara had disliked him when they first met, she had grown to care for him in the past few weeks. There was a wariness in her eyes today after she put her professional walls up between them.

At first, all he had wanted was for the Morehouse family to go west. Now that he had gotten his wish, however, it didn't feel right to him. His only satisfaction in the situation came from the knowledge that the journey would give them more time to bring their friendship back to normal, and he would be able to spend time with their whole family. He looked forward to more advice from Arthur, and he loved the excitement in Eliza's and Hannah's eyes when they talked about their future plans. And Clara, well, he loved talking to her about business and just about anything else. Maybe he was just lonely, after all these months away from his brother, and not really having anyone else in the world but him.

Being around Clara made him feel more driven and happy than he had been in a very long time. He was glad he wouldn't be leaving her behind when he headed west.

Exhausted from the emotion of the day and from his injuries, John fell into an uneasy sleep.

The next morning, he was determined to not think about Clara and focus on the business at hand. Now that the Morehouses had agreed, they had just about all the people required to start their new town.

John's first order of business was to send a letter to his brother to let him know that the men they had hired to help with the town's construction could start the initial buildings in earnest.

His second stop of the day was to visit young Henry's father at the livery. The man was expecting him but curious as to the reason for the visit.

"We don't have much need for a livery yet as the town is so small. But I could give you work in town to help with the building, if you and your children wanted to stake a claim and start a new farm nearby. It would be a chance to start over," John explained.

Henry's father, who was also named Henry Smith but insisted on being called Hank, listened eagerly to his idea, but at the end of the offer, his shoulders slumped.

"I can't afford to buy a wagon or the supplies needed

to take me and my young'uns. We can't go, Mr. Butler. I'm sorry."

John already had a solution, however.

"I have several wagons going west loaded with supplies that my brother and I will need for the town, and I need drivers. I would be willing to pay for your food and some extra money for wages if you would be one of them."

Hank's eyes lit with excitement, still shadowed with some doubt. "But what about Henry and the baby?"

The lad was hardworking and eager, and John was sure that there could be something for him to do on the way. Besides, there were plenty of people who could help look after the children while his father was driving. He explained all of this to Hank.

"Why are you being so kind to us?" These days, it sometimes felt like every man was for himself, so John understood the man's hesitation.

"I was raised by a single father for a long time, and we wouldn't have made it if kind people along the way hadn't lent a helping hand. Now it's my turn to return the favor."

John thought of all the women who had made sure they had plenty to eat and all the holes in their clothes were patched. All the men who helped his father put together a new barn on his homestead or repair a wagon wheel that broke.

"Our town will survive only if we all work together, and that starts now."

Hank seemed taken aback by his words, but he was also clearly touched by what he'd heard. He agreed to the move immediately. "That sounds like the kind of place where I would like my children to grow up."

John bid good day to the man after telling him they

would meet next week to arrange the details of the trip. He felt a renewed excitement for his mission following his conversation with Hank. This was exactly why he and his brother were doing this.

They had grown up without a permanent home, and they wanted to provide a place where others could stay and prosper. The people who had lent their father aid had inspired in the brothers the drive to create a similar sense of community for others. Their town would be a haven for people who wanted to belong, and a safe starting point for the adventurous ones who were building their homes in unpopulated areas.

And when they needed somewhere to go for supplies, rest and conversation, when life on their homesteads got hard, the community the Butler Brothers built would be there for them. This was his dream. And it was part of the reason he had implemented the five-year plan in the first place. He didn't need a wife right now—he had work to do.

Chapter Fifteen

Clara surveyed the store the next day, just before opening. She and her sisters had agreed to keep the store in business for one more week. They would fulfill all their orders and give the regulars they had left an opportunity to set up accounts with another merchant so there would be no interruption of service.

For those who would be traveling on the wagon train with them, Clara wanted to make sure they filled all those orders, as well. There were still plenty of crates to be sold, and it was good business to establish now in the minds of their future customers that the Morehouse family could meet their needs. That trust would be invaluable in the new town.

It all added up to a heavy workload, though, because she and her sisters had to operate the store, start organizing the inventory they were taking, pack their house, and try to sell their building and home all at the same time.

The burden seemed nearly impossible to Clara, but she rolled her sleeves and got to work.

She was eager to get out of the house, because she couldn't handle all the excitement over the ring on her finger. Her sisters knew the truth about the arrangement with John, but no matter what Clara said, they were convinced that there was more than friendship between the two of them. They were thrilled that the engagement was still on.

They could not stop talking about it.

And her father was even worse. Not wanting to lie to him for months, Clara had confessed everything. She hated to spoil his happiness at their betrothal but wanted to be honest.

He had just laughed and said, "We'll see about that."

He seemed to be wishing for something that wasn't there. Though she and John were good friends and he was a welcome part of the family, there was nothing more between them.

Eliza and Hannah interrupted her thoughts when they entered the store. They stood next to Clara as she took in all the shelves completely full of stock. Not to mention all the shipments in the back from their suppliers that still hadn't been opened.

"How are we going to package up all this inventory when we are still selling it this week?" Eliza asked.

Hannah looked just as overwhelmed. Clara knew she needed to give them a plan, quickly.

"We're not going to seriously start packing until after we close next week. But for now, we aren't going to add any new stock to the shelves if things start to sell off."

That would save them from unpacking and then re-packing things.

Clara opened the store to their customers for the day. While business was steady, it was still considerably lower than it had been before the Michael Emmers scandal. "I don't think we all need to be here right now," Clara decided. "Do you think one of you could go around and start informing our regulars of our closing date and take their final orders?"

Eliza sat down on a stool behind the counter. "Why don't you go? You've been in the store working on the books for several hours already. I'm sure you could use some fresh air. We just got here."

Hannah nodded in agreement, and Clara decided not to argue. She did feel the need to clear her head after staring down the daunting mountain of work in front of them. She left the store just as a group of customers arrived, but her sisters waved her off. "We can handle it. Go," Hannah said.

Clara took her time strolling through town and stopping in on her clients. She would miss Independence when she was in the West. She had lived here her entire life, and she had no idea what it would be like to reside somewhere else. What would it feel like to stroll down a main street that wasn't as familiar to her as the back of her hand?

Her visits took longer than she'd expected because many of her customers noticed the ring on her finger, and then she was trapped in endless conversations about it.

"I knew he had come calling to your house, but I didn't realize Mr. Butler was officially courting you," Mrs. Anderson said.

Clara smiled shyly and nodded, keeping to the story she had established. "Yes, well, we kept quiet about our intentions. It still seems so soon after my mother…"

This statement always stopped people from prying further, because nothing made someone more uncomfortable than discussing grief.

"Understandable dear. You have a wonderful young man. And handsome too."

Clara couldn't argue with either of those things. John was a good man, indeed, and she had to admit that he was very fine-looking.

The next customer she visited, the whole conversation basically repeated itself. Clara imagined that by lunchtime, word of the engagement would have spread throughout town.

She was about to go back to the store when something strange caught her eye. She passed by the livery and saw someone bailing hay. What made her stop and stare was that it was John Butler.

He had shed his business suit and was in normal work clothes. Sweat was dripping down his neck and he had smudges of dirt on his face.

"What are you doing?"

John stopped bailing and turned to her. His eyes lit up. "Well, good morning to you, Miss Morehouse."

She let out a small laugh. "Good morning to you too, Mr. Butler."

He leaned against the wall, taking a long drink from a cup of water that had been sitting nearby. "I know you said you wanted to keep things as professional as possible last night, but it seems strange to me that a betrothed couple supposedly in love wouldn't be on a first-name basis."

She supposed he was right, but taking down some of the professional barriers she had carefully erected between them somehow made things feel dangerously real to her. Even though this engagement certainly was not. "I suppose you're right. People already know about us." He arched an eyebrow at that. "I thought you weren't going to tell anyone unless they asked?"

Clara waved her hand with the ring on it. "People are asking a lot about this."

John smiled when he saw it on her finger. "The way this town works, I'm surprised I didn't hear about it before you even crossed the street."

Clara doubted that someone would have cause to run and share the news at the livery. "What are you doing working here today?"

John grabbed a handkerchief out of his pocket and wiped the sweat off his brow. He offered Clara the only seat nearby, a small stool, but she shook her head. He sat down, heaving a relieved sigh as he did.

"It's been a long time since I mucked a stall. It's exhausting."

He took another drink of water. "The man who normally works here is going west with us. He needed to take his children to go say goodbye to their grandparents, and they live several hours away. I volunteered to cover his shift."

Clara looked around at all the work that needed to be done. "You are willing to do all this so his offspring could see their grandparents?"

John shrugged. "Those children are the only thing the grandparents have left of his late wife, so he wanted to make sure they had a proper goodbye before heading west."

Clara's eyes widened. This was why the Butler Brothers were so successful in building new towns—they legitimately cared about the people who lived in them. "It's not common for someone who wears business attire most days to switch to work clothes."

He laughed at that. "You'll see that it is a little bit different in the West. If you want to succeed, you're going to have to get a little dirty sometimes."

She thought of all the hard work her parents had put into building their store. Maybe things weren't so different here either. "I was going to have you come and lift some heavy crates, but now I know you will be too tired."

His eyes gleamed with mischief. "Oh, I can never shirk my duties to do all the hardest chores at the Morehouse General Store. But maybe I can come by tomorrow."

She knew that he would, because he valued everyone going on this trip west. And because he was their friend. If they needed help, John would be there. It was just the kind of man he was. "I suppose that will be all right. And we'll try to make sure we do some of the hard stuff this time instead of leaving it all for you."

He nodded. "I imagine you will be delivering some supply crates to your customers toward the end of the week too. I'll help with that. I just can't on Saturday because I'll be here again."

She arched an eyebrow at that. "You're going to help another day too?"

John nodded. "Mr. Smith has to have a day to start packing up their belongings. The owner of this establishment has new help coming in, but not until around the time we are leaving."

The man would work himself to death, Clara thought. "We can help with the children, my sisters and I. If he needs it. Hannah would probably enjoy the chance to practice her teaching skills."

John's eyes widened in surprise. "You would do that?"

Clara was not used to young children, except in passing in the store, when they were usually under the close supervision of their mothers, but she could do anything she set her mind to. "Isn't that the purpose of the new town we're going to live in—to support one another?"

The look he gave her was filled with so much appreciation, Clara smiled at him.

"Thank you," he said, his voice soft. He looked tired, and it was no wonder, if he was taking on all the manual labor of his friends in Independence.

"Have you eaten?" she asked. "I was just heading over to the hotel to get their supply order for the week. I can bring you back a sandwich or something, if you want."

John stood, ready to get back to work. "That would be wonderful, thank you. But I don't want to inconvenience you."

Of course this man who inconveniences himself for others says something like that, she thought.

"It's no trouble at all. I'll see you in about a half hour or maybe longer if the people in the hotel start asking about this ring."

He laughed, and she hurried to meet her next customer. Clara's mind stayed preoccupied the entire time with the businessman who was currently mucking out horse stalls.

John's back was aching, but he supposed it was his own fault for skipping this kind of task for such a long time. Mucking out stalls should come as second nature to him, as it had been one of his chores growing up, but he was entirely out of practice and the work had been much harder than he'd recalled. Seeing Clara was one of the few things that had brightened his day.

And she was coming back. He set himself a personal goal to get these stalls done by the time she returned so he could sit and enjoy lunch with her.

True to her word, Clara returned an hour later, carrying a sandwich for him. "You got caught up in a conversation about the ring, didn't you?" he teased as he pulled an empty crate over for seating and gave her the stool.

She nodded, rolling her eyes. "If I have to have one more conversation about wedding plans today, I'm throwing this ring at you and leaving town."

He laughed. "Well, you're already leaving town in a few months. You might as well hold on to the ring for now."

Clara nodded and took a bite of her own sandwich. John took a moment to study her. She looked tired, as well. "How are the preparations going for the move?"

Clara groaned. "There is so much to do, and we have to still serve our existing customers while thinking about our journey. I don't know how we'll get it all done."

Clara rarely showed any sign of uncertainty when it came to running her business, so John knew that she was either so overcome that it just came pouring out of her or their friendship had hit a level of trust that made it easier for her to open up to him. He hoped it was the latter.

"You'll get it done. You have your father and sisters to help. Not to mention Betty," John said. "And I'll lend a hand whenever I can."

Her brows furrowed at that. "You have more than enough to do without worrying about us. We'll be ready when the time comes."

The determination in her voice reminded him of the Clara Morehouse he'd first met, who had refused to even consider moving west. Once she had her mind set on something, it was very difficult to change it. But not impossible.

"Still, I'm here if you need me."

She smiled. "Thank you. However, just because we

don't require your help doesn't mean you should be a stranger around our house."

John hadn't visited the Morehouse home for tea or a meal at all yesterday.

"You should try to come to supper, at least once or twice a week. My father would miss you if you didn't. And my sisters too."

He grinned at her. "Just them? Wouldn't *you* miss me too, Miss Morehouse?"

She rolled her eyes. "I've seen you. I'm looking right at you now."

John let out a loud laugh. This was a lovely reprieve from the hard work he had done all day. "Well, I promise to try to stop in sometime in the next few days."

Clara smiled in return. "Good. You have a standing invitation. We are betrothed after all, and it would seem strange if you did not call on us once in a while."

John's smile slipped a little. Had she invited him only because she wanted to keep up the engagement ruse? He didn't know why that was so disappointing, since this whole fake betrothal was his idea.

Regardless of her reasons, he still wanted to spend time with the Morehouse family. "I could use a meal or two outside my hotel's dining room."

He could also use some time talking to people who weren't just business associates. John missed his brother, and spending time with the Morehouse family made him feel less lonely. "I'll be there," he promised.

Clara perked up at this, and he thought that maybe it wasn't just about the pretense for her. Maybe she enjoyed his company, as well. "Good, perhaps for supper tomorrow?"

He nodded. "It's a deal."

They chatted about the new town in the West for the

rest of their meal, and too quickly, it was over. Clara gathered up the remnants of their food and stood to go. "I should probably get back. I trust my sisters to run the store, but they probably think I abandoned them with all the work we have to do."

He chuckled. "No one who knows you would believe that about you for a minute."

She promised to bring him lunch again the next time he was working, and hurried back to her store.

Her visit had been a nice break in his day—and he finished his work with a smile on his face.

Chapter Sixteen

The next few weeks passed by for Clara in a busy flurry of activity. Their father had received several offers for the store and a few for their home and was working with the solicitor to finalize all the details of the sales.

Eliza and Hannah had been put in charge of packing up their house, with Betty supervising. Betty had been the biggest surprise of them all, declaring she wouldn't let her babies travel all the way to the West without her. Clara told her that they couldn't afford to pay her the same salary, and with limited structures in the new town at first, they wouldn't have a permanent home for a while, let alone need a housekeeper.

The older woman waved off their objections, saying that as long as they could put a roof of some sort over her head and provide food she could use to make their meals, she was going.

"I don't have any family left except for you girls," she explained, and they all engulfed her in a hug. Of course she could go with them.

The Morehouse family would be taking an unprecedented four wagons with them on the wagon train.

Three of them would be filled with inventory for their new store and one would be packed to the brim with the family's personal items. But four wagons were hardly infinite in the space they provided. Plus, room needed to be made in each one for the family and their drivers to sleep or take shelter during a rainstorm. That meant some hard decisions had to be made about what would travel with them and what would be left behind.

It was hard to let go of some of the things that belonged to their mother, but they were gifted to family friends who would cherish them, as well.

"We haven't seen John around as much lately," her father observed one day. "Did you two get into a fight?"

She didn't appreciate the reminder that her father was still convinced that there was something romantic between her and John. "He's been busy getting everything ready. Just like we are," Clara explained. "But he promised to continue stopping in for supper once or twice a week."

She was surprised at just how much she missed seeing him at the store each day. Clara had been fine before John Butler came into her life, but she had grown used to working beside him every day. Now she felt his absence profoundly.

Her father gave a nod of approval at the idea of John coming for supper.

"He should at least visit for longer from time to time. We're practically family," her father grumbled as he loaded a crate.

"We aren't the only people going on this journey," Clara reminded her father. "There are others that need his help and his time much more than we do. We have plenty of hands to do all this work. Others don't have that luxury."

Indeed, there were some days that it seemed the whole town of Independence would be on the wagon train. Though they'd closed the shop last week, they had sold so many supply packets that they had nearly funded their own foodstuffs for the journey, just from those crates.

True to his word, however, John came by the very next night to share a meal with the Morehouse family. Her father drank in every detail that John shared about preparations for the trip. Hannah volunteered to help out with the children for those families who would be busy making ready, and John gratefully gave her the names of some who might need an extra pair of hands.

John stayed for a while after supper, spending time with the family in the drawing room. It was a nice break from the fast pace they'd been working the rest of the week.

He came two nights later, bearing a bouquet of flowers for her. "To keep up appearances, you know. For the betrothal."

Whether they were for their fake courtship or not, the blooms were beautiful and made Clara smile. She had not really received gifts from gentlemen in the past, so these were special, even if they were just part of the ruse. Her sisters, of course, thought it was all very romantic.

"You may be convincing the town, but you are making these two even worse," she teased John.

He, of course, thought this was funny. The next day that he was helping them pack the heavier supplies in their last crates for customers, he made a show of heaping Clara with romantic compliments whenever a customer walked in in the last few weeks it was open.

"Those fabrics are lovely, Hannah, but not as lovely

as my future wife," he said loudly one day when Mrs. Anderson was buying eggs. Her sisters burst into a fit of giggles while Clara felt her cheeks warm. She certainly didn't like all this attention. Especially when they had work to do.

The next day, he was back at the livery, and Clara was preparing to close the business for the final time. Though it was for good reason, a new adventure in the West, it was still hard to shut the door on everything her mother and father had built through the years. She sniffled as she rang up her last customer for the day.

"It's time to close, my dear. Just get it over with," her father said from behind her shoulder. After many months of not working in the store, he'd made a point to come in for its last day.

She was about to lock the entrance when Eliza rushed in with excitement. "I just met him—the wagon master!"

Clara chuckled at her sister's giddiness. Everything about this journey excited Eliza. It was as if she had come alive once they announced they were leaving.

"Oh? What's he like? As dashing as you were hoping?"

Eliza had raved about how all the riders that accompanied them on their journey would surely be handsome, rugged men who lived fascinating lives. But now as she frowned, it seemed that some of that notion had been dispelled.

"He was actually quite a grumpy man. I thought to lead a wagon train you had to at least be a pleasant person. You are required to actually talk to people sometimes to guide them, aren't you?"

Her father laughed at this. "I'm sure that John didn't hire him for his charm, but for his experience in getting people safely across the miles to their destination. You don't have to be friendly to keep people alive. Sometimes it takes just the opposite."

Both daughters gave him a curious look at that.

"What do you mean, Papa?"

Father heaved a crate onto the counter, preparing to load it with inventory.

"Well, if you needed to be told how to cross a river safely—with death for you or your family as a possibility if something goes wrong—would you rather someone who is going to be pleasant so he doesn't hurt your feelings if you are doing something wrong, or would you rather have someone that is going to yell at you until you make the safe choice?"

He had a point, Clara thought. There were many perils on the journey, and they needed someone who was hardened enough to get them through it all. Eliza, on the other hand, wasn't convinced.

"I just thought he would be able to tell me more tales about his journeys, but the man didn't have the patience to even talk to me about anything else other than what we'll need for our trip," she complained.

Clara hid her smile. It wasn't often that men weren't railroaded by Eliza's charm and exuberance, so perhaps she had finally found someone immune to her.

"Well, did you ask about our other drivers?" She needed her sister to focus on the task at hand, getting them ready for their trip.

Eliza nodded. "Yes, he recommended three men that he's used in the past. All of them trustworthy and experienced in driving teams."

Clara breathed a sigh of relief. While the three girls would from time to time be able to help their father drive the wagon that would hold their personal items, none of them had the upper-arm strength to do it for days on end. *Maybe by the end of the wagon train we will be strong enough,* she thought with amusement.

They would have enough money from the sale of their store to hire men to drive their other wagons on the journey.

"I think that's all I can do for today. Let's go home for supper and sleep. I'm starving," their father declared.

Clara couldn't argue with that as her stomach rumbled, and they all laughed. Her father had put in more hours in the store than he had since their mother started getting sick, and it was good to see him out and laughing again. Their family didn't feel like it had a shroud of gloom over it anymore.

They would always miss Mama, but they would live to the fullest, just what she would have wanted for them.

Clara called out to Betty when they arrived home. She knew supper would be a simple affair, as the kitchen was currently being used to can and prepare ahead as many food supplies as possible for their journey.

John joined them once again for supper. Betty fussed a bit about not serving their guest a fancier meal, but Clara's father just laughed. "Nonsense, we're all family here."

John's eyes brightened at his words, and Clara was glad that even though everyone in this room knew that there was no real wedding planned between her and John, he was still a welcome member of the Morehouse family.

As they settled around the dining room table, they decided they were too hungry to wait for Hannah, who had a very important meeting today. They were halfway through their meal when she hurried in holding a piece of paper.

"I passed! I finished my last examination and completed the last of my schooling, and several months early. Now I'm ready to teach any young children that we will have in our new community."

The family cheered and Clara couldn't help but feel a twinge of regret for holding off on moving them west for so long. The Morehouses were happy, and this change in their life was exactly what they needed.

It wasn't until the middle of the night when all that joy came to an end with a loud banging on the front door. Young Henry Smith was standing there, covered in soot and panting.

"They sent me to get you—your store—it's on fire!"

John woke to shouts in the middle of the night, several voices calling for people to come help with a fire. He immediately hopped out of bed and put his shoes on. Buildings in towns such as this were so close together that if one went up in flames, the rest were sure to follow if the blaze could not be stopped quickly enough.

He ran out in the street to see people rushing by, carrying buckets. He followed the crowd, and his heart stopped when he saw the source of the flames. It was the Morehouse's store, burning to a crisp. Though people were dumping water on the blaze to stop the fire's spread, it was clear that the store could not be saved.

But maybe something could survive. John rushed to join the bucket brigade, pouring loads of water one after the other on the fire. Before long, his face was flushed and his entire body was drenched in sweat and covered in soot. Every muscle in his body ached, and he wanted to go back to bed or even sit down and take a break.

But John wouldn't. He couldn't. Clara would be devastated to see all of her hard work destroyed. This store was her life. Even though it had officially closed, he knew she cared about it deeply, would be heartbroken to see it destroyed.

He heard a scream behind him and knew without turning around that the Morehouse family had arrived. They lived on the other side of town, so someone must have been sent to wake them from their slumber.

From the corner of his eye, he saw Arthur More-house join them in their efforts to put out the fire. Several weeks ago, that man had been unable to get out of bed. Now he was rolling up his sleeves to get to work.

After hours of grueling labor, the flames were finally defeated. Thankfully, the fire had not spread to the rest of the town. But the Morehouse family had little to be thankful about.

All that was left of their store was a pile of ashes and rubble.

"At least you were starting over anyway," he told Arthur, desperate to say anything to make the family feel better.

Arthur gave him a defeated look. "I don't think we can go west now, son."

Clara nodded glumly behind him. John looked between the two, confused.

"Whyever not? You were set to leave in a couple of months anyway. Now you should have even more motivation."

Clara opened her mouth to speak, but her eyes filled with tears and she turned away instead. Out of instinct, John reached out and pulled her into a hug. She cried into his chest.

Arthur watched the smoldering ruins for a moment before answering. "Our entire stock that we were going to use to open a new store was in that building, and it's gone now. And we were planning on the revenue from the sale of the building to pay our drivers. Obviously, the purchase won't go through now, and we won't even need extra drivers anyway, since we have no stock."

John scrambled for solutions. This couldn't be the end for the Morehouse family's plans.

"But the sale of the house means you will still have something," he said.

Arthur shook his head. "It won't be near enough to get a store started from scratch. I'm sorry, son, but it won't be happening."

John surveyed the damage, his heart broken for not only losing a business that would help their town but for the ones who had become family to him. Concern for their future overpowered everything else. "But what will you all do now?"

Clara finally pulled away from him and wiped the tears from her eyes. "I'm too tired to make any plans tonight. We will probably have to sell our home and stay somewhere smaller. Maybe take out a loan to start over with a new store. It will be a lot of work, but my father has done it before—and he'll have our help."

John was going to suggest that they use the loan to move west and start their business there, but he knew banks wouldn't take such a risk. The Morehouses were a safe investment, but only if they stayed in Independence.

"So it's just…over?"

Arthur nodded and patted him on the back. He thought it was pathetic that the man who had just lost everything was comforting him, but John's devastation was palpable.

His wagon train was leaving soon.

Without the Morehouse family.

Without Clara.

If Clara didn't go west with him, he didn't know when he would ever see her again. Or any of them, for that matter. And the Morehouse family had no income beyond what they earned from their store. What would become of them? He would hate to pull out of town in a few weeks, knowing that he was leaving people who were so dear to him in such dire straits. The fire had destroyed more than just a building—it had laid waste to a lot of people's futures.

And John had no idea how to fix it.

Chapter Seventeen

Clara walked through town in a daze. She didn't really know where she was going. She just needed to get out of the house for a while and enjoy some fresh air.

I can't go to the store. It's not there anymore, she thought with a shudder. Clara felt almost numb to all that had happened. She could hardly believe it had burned down at all. The financial loss was crushing, but the memories that had been encased in that store were priceless—that was what hurt the most, even though they had all made it out with their lives.

She thought about the door frame that had had notches marking their growth through the years—gone. The fabric counter where their mother had painstakingly poured over catalogs to keep up with the latest fashions for their customers—gone. The supplies they'd meticulously packed for their trip out West—gone.

"Why did you even change my heart about going if You were just going to take it away?" she asked God in a whisper, wiping a tear from her cheek.

Most people in the town gave her a wide berth as she walked, probably because no one knew what to say.

Some people in the community, however, were full

of sympathy for the Morehouse family's plight. Clara was surprised at just how many.

"That store has been in our community for so long. I don't know what we will do without it," one sweet matron told her.

Another young mother talked about how she had grown up going to the store for a piece of candy—and later, how much she had enjoyed taking her children there, as well.

"Those other stores just don't have the same familiar feeling as yours," the woman said.

Clara knew that feeling. She'd had to stop into another store this morning to buy some lunch supplies for Betty, and it was so poorly organized that she'd wanted to scream. Clara's fingers had itched to rearrange the things on the shelf. She'd had to remind herself that it wasn't her store or her responsibility.

The shopkeeper had given her the items for free, and while it irked her to have to accept charity, Clara had known that she couldn't really turn it down. She hadn't had the heart to go through the family's finances yet, but she knew that the situation was dire.

"Oh Clara, it's good to see you out and about today, after all that happened," Mrs. Bolton, the minister's wife, said as she stopped her on the street.

"I needed to clear my head," Clara explained.

The older woman asked if she could walk with her for a bit, and while Clara didn't really want the company, she was too polite to refuse.

"How's your father holding up, dear? I imagine this loss must be really taking a toll on him after losing your mother so recently and with him only just getting back up on his feet."

Clara almost halted her steps at Mrs. Bolton's words.

In all her numbness and pain about the fire, she had been focused only on how she felt. She had not even thought about her father and how he must be reeling right now.

"I don't know," she whispered, filled with shame that she had not been paying attention.

Mrs. Bolton reached out and patted her hand. "It's all right, Clara. I understand. My husband and I were planning on calling on him later this afternoon. I baked him a pie."

Clara managed to muster up a smile. "That sounds lovely."

"Pie won't solve all of your problems, but it will make things feel better, even if only for a few minutes," the older woman said. "Have you thought about what you're going to do now that the store is gone? Still planning on going west?"

Clara didn't say the sad truth that the family probably wouldn't be heading out on the wagon train now. She couldn't bring herself to say the words.

"Things are still too recent to make any big decisions at the moment" was all she said.

"Well, we will be praying for you. The entire church. We're going to have a special meeting after services on Sunday to come up with ideas on how to help you all. It probably won't be much more than providing meals for a week or so, but we want to show our love to you."

Clara bit back tears. After the time she'd had recently—with so many in the community treating her harshly after the situation with Michael, it was nice to hear.

"You didn't believe what they were saying about me…about my supposedly immoral behavior?"

The minister's wife waved her hand in the air like

it was nothing. "Of course I didn't entertain that nonsense for a moment. You are a good girl, Clara Morehouse. I've known you since you were in petticoats and sashes. You don't need to tell me that there is absolutely no truth around those rumors."

On instinct, Clara reached out and hugged the woman. "Thank you so much. You have no idea how much I needed to hear that."

Mrs. Bolton patted her back, not ending the embrace anytime soon. "That John Butler is a fine young man. We had him over for lunch once and he was an absolute delight. I'm so happy for the two of you."

Clara blushed, glad that the woman couldn't see her face. John was indeed a good man, but now there was no reason for their faked engagement to continue. She supposed she would have to give his ring back now that they weren't going with him.

Mrs. Bolton pulled away and gave Clara a concerned look. "What's wrong, dear?"

Clara sighed and shook her head. "I don't think we will continue our betrothal. We can't, not with our business in ruin. He will be heading out soon and we…"

Mrs. Bolton linked her arm through Clara's. "Well, maybe marriage to a smart young businessman might be one of the solutions to your problems."

Clara stopped walking. "I will not wed someone just to burden him with all that is going wrong for my family right now."

The older woman looked confused. "My dear, that's the way it's been done for years. Many women marry well to better the lives of those they love."

Clara wondered why she continued to have this conversation. She had been almost willing to sacrifice her happiness to marry Michael, under the mistaken belief that he would support her family, but they all knew now what a huge mistake that would have been.

"Sometimes what seems the best solution is not always the right one," Clara told the minister's wife.

She had the decency to look humble and nod. "I suppose you are right. You would have had a horrible life if you had become a member of the Emmers family, no matter how wealthy they are. Oh dear, don't tell anyone that I was speaking ill of people in our congregation."

Clara smiled reassuringly at Mrs. Bolton. "Your secret is safe with me. Now, if you don't mind, I need to get home to my family."

The older woman nodded and let go of Clara's arm. "Very well, dear. I will see you later with some pie. Think about what I said about Mr. Butler though. You should consider keeping to your engagement, not just because he would financially benefit your family but because I think he could be a fine and loving husband for you."

Clara wanted to groan at the words. She knew very well that John was a good and kind man. But the romantic relationship that the public believed the two of them shared wasn't real. It was time to end this betrothal. John was too willing to sacrifice his reputation to save hers. There was no point to it now. She should let him get back to that five-year plan of his.

Clara didn't fit into that plan at all, especially now that her family probably was not moving west. Her heart clenched at the thought of not seeing him again. Sure, he would probably visit Independence from time to time on supply runs. But who knew if the family would even stay here now that their store was gone?

She headed toward home and put a little speed in her step. Her conversation with the minister's wife had

had some benefit—it reminded her that she had to start thinking about her family's future after the fire. She had to make sure her father was doing all right emotionally, and she had to figure out how they would support themselves.

Her time of mourning was over. Now she had to get to work.

John entered the general store in the town a half day's ride away from Independence. He was looking for someone else to go west and start a new enterprise but wasn't having much success. No one was interested—and none of the merchants were at the same expertise level as the Morehouse family.

Unfortunately, this shop was more of the same. The fabric counter was entirely disorganized, and the shelves in the rest of the place were far from stocked. No, the people running this store would not do. The people in his town needed better access to supplies than he trusted these owners to provide.

A sour-looking woman stood behind the counter, counting the eggs that a mother and her children had brought in to sell.

"They're not great on customer service," he murmured under his breath, and the man sweeping in the corner looked up and leveled him with a suspicious glarc.

"Can I help you, sir, or are you just going to stand there and gawk all day?"

For a moment, John was reminded of when he had heard something similar from Clara when they first met, but it had sounded softer and nicer coming from her.

"No, I'm just looking. Sorry to bother you."

John exited the store. It was the only one in this

smaller town. He would have to visit somewhere else. He had already been to several possibilities. But truth be told, no one lived up to his expectations—none of the other shops in Independence or the other small surrounding communities. The fire in Independence had broken a lot of hearts, his own included.

John had another mission during his visit here, however, and he walked down the street toward the small church. Next to the building was a parsonage. The pastor here was young and had a wife and three children. The family had hosted Edward Daniels while he put in a few weeks of volunteer work. He had just graduated from seminary and wanted a little practical experience of serving in a church in a small town before heading west to start a new ministry in the Butler Brothers' fledgling community.

Now it was time for him to go to Independence before the next leg of his journey began. Having secured him a place to stay with the Boltons, John would drive the young minister in the carriage he had rented. He would welcome the company, to take his mind off the Morehouse fire.

"It's so good to finally meet you in person," the young minister said when John arrived and introduced himself. He and John had communicated through correspondence, so this was their first opportunity to meet face to face.

They didn't have time for tea with the other minister and his wife, because Ed was ready to go, with his bag packed by the door.

"It's not that I didn't enjoy my time here with them, I did. It's just their children are very loud," Ed said with a laugh. "I'm going to enjoy a few weeks of peace and quiet before we head out on that busy wagon train."

John assured the young man that the Boltons had no small children but warned that the lady of the house might talk his ear off.

"She's been missing her son, so you may be adopted during the time you are with them," he joked.

Edward noted that he looked forward to the mothering since he hadn't seen his own in so long. "She was none too pleased to see me pack up and head west."

John had been hearing that a lot from the men who would be going on the journey, and he couldn't help but feel a pang of envy. It had been a very long time since he'd had a mother to worry about him or Adam. Since the loss of their father, there were no loved ones wishing they would stay close.

"If you don't mind my asking, Mr. Butler, what's on your mind?"

John was taken aback that the young minister had been able to tell that something was upsetting him. He had always prided himself on keeping his emotions in check. "I was just thinking about my own mother and wondering what it would be like to have one who cared if I came or went."

Saying the words out loud was like picking at a barely healed wound, but John was nothing if not honest. Edward nodded and gave John a sympathetic look.

"There are so many people in this world who have to live without their parents. I'm sorry you lost yours."

There was something about the young man that made him want to open up about all that had happened to him as a child. But he kept a lid on those feelings, tight. John was charming and easily talked to anyone, except when it came to this one subject. Reflecting on his mother made him grip the reins of the wagon in anger. He told himself not to think about her.

"Thank you, I appreciate that," he said, modulating his tone to indicate that this topic of conversation was closed.

Edward studied him for a moment, and it took John everything not to squirm in his seat. Despite being such a young minister, he already seemed to have mastered that stare that made a man want to confess all of his sins. John had definitely made the right choice of spiritual leader for his new town.

"You know, we have a long ride back to Independence if you want to tell me whatever's making you so angry."

He really was a wise young man.

"I'm not angry," John lied.

Edward just gave him a sideways smirk and turned his attention to the passing landscape. "Fine, you don't have to talk about it if you don't feel comfortable."

John immediately felt guilty for lying to a man of God. "Look, I *am* angry about some things in my past, but I don't like to discuss them, because that just makes the anger worse."

Edward nodded in understanding. He was silent for several minutes and John thought that maybe he had let the matter drop.

"You know, sometimes if you keep anger inside you for so long, it just keeps getting bigger. If you don't want to say anything to me, I hope you find someone to open up to someday. In the meantime, I'm going to pray for you."

John felt a surge of gratitude for the young minister.

"Thank you. I find it's best not to think of it." He seldom thought about his anger toward his parents. He carefully organized his life—even created a five-year plan—to avoid the same mistakes they had made. But aside from that, he tried to think of them as little as possible. No amount of regret could change the past, so what was the point in dwelling on it?

But Edward wasn't finished with him quite yet. "As a man of God, it goes without saying that I think you need to forgive whoever made you this angry. The details are not my business, but we are all forgiven by God for our trespasses and are therefore expected to forgive those who trespass against us. The anger you are holding on to is a sign that you haven't granted that forgiveness yet."

John's hands tightened on the reins once again. What would the point be in offering forgiveness? His parents were long dead. He had been there with his father when he passed, and he and his brother had received a letter from a relative of their mother's in the city a few years ago to let them know she was gone.

"What if the person who wronged you is dead and never said they were sorry? Or never spoke to you again after they hurt you?"

Edward gave John a pitying look. He hated looks like that. He and his brother had been getting them for years, every time a near stranger had to step in to mend their clothes or provide an extra lunch for them on the school days their father had forgotten.

"Forgiveness isn't always given to people who ask for it, or even would know it's been granted. Forgiveness is not just for them—it's also for you, allowing you to let go of the power your anger has over you. That anger is hurting you by stopping you from moving on."

His problems with his parents were not stopping John from moving on. He and Adam had grown up strong and capable, had been successful in business and had started several new towns in the West that had positively impacted plenty of lives. Their childhoods had not held them back. Sure, they hadn't started their own families yet, but it was only a matter of time. He turned to see Edward looking at him expectantly.

"Thank you. I will think about it," he told the minister.

Edward gave him a smile. "That's all I can ask. And I hope you don't think I'm being too pushy so soon. Guess I'm just eager to start ministering."

The two shared a laugh, and John was relieved the tension finally left the conversation.

"Well, I think you're already pretty good at it. I can't wait to see what you do when someone really gets out of line in our new town."

Edward pulled his thick Bible out of his bag. "Why do you think I got such a big version? The better to knock some sense into thick skulls."

John grinned. He loved the young man's sense of humor. Edward would get along just fine with the rest of the community.

"Good thing I recruited a doc too, Reverend."

"Please, call me Ed," the young minister insisted, and the rest of the journey went by in peace. Later that evening, though, John found himself wondering what losing his anger toward his parents would do to his five-year plan.

Chapter Eighteen

Clara paced the parlor nervously while she waited for John to arrive. She'd decided that they should call off their engagement, and she wanted to take care of it as soon as possible. That way, John could be free from the burden of the betrothal and would be able to start focusing on his new life in the West without his commitment to the Morehouses holding him back.

Betty announced his arrival, and John hurried into the drawing room.

"Clara, how are you? I'm sorry I haven't been by since the fire. Things have been…"

She waved away his apology. "It's all right. I know all too well how much work goes into preparing for the trip. And now you probably have to find another family of merchants to replace us."

Tears threatened to form in her eyes again at that thought. Someone else would be starting the general store in the Butler Brothers' new town. All that time she had resisted moving west, and now she was disappointed that it wouldn't be happening for them after all.

"I'm not sure I'll find any. Especially not someone as perfect as you and your family."

They were far from perfect, but she did believe they would have been a good fit in the community because of their already-established friendship with John and some of the others.

"I'll pray that you find just the right people."

He sat down across from her, his eyes filled with concern. "But how are you? And tell me the truth, not just the 'I'm fine' that you probably tell everyone who asks."

She arched an eyebrow at that. "Are you accusing me of being a liar, Mr. Butler?"

He shook his head. "No, just a person who doesn't want to tell every neighbor that they are feeling awful."

He was right. She hadn't wanted to tell everyone how worried she was about where they would live or what they would do next.

"You're right. I do feel terrible. I have no idea what's going to happen to us now."

John handed her his handkerchief to wipe away the tears she hadn't realized were streaming down her cheeks. "Is there anything I can do to help you?"

She shook her head. "I'm going to sit down and go through all of our finances with Father later today. Then we will have a better idea of where we stand."

Clara hated the idea of leaving their home, but it had already sold—and they needed the funds too badly to ask the seller to reconsider. "I'll need to find us a place to live. The money from the house will keep us going for a while."

He gave her a grim smile. "If you need any more..."

She turned away, embarrassed that she was now in such a tenuous position that he felt compelled to offer her money. "We don't need you to give us anything. We'll be fine."

John nodded and sat back in his seat. "You invited me here today, so I just assumed… I was being serious though, anything you need. Let me help."

He was such a good and kind man, which was why it was best to set him free of his obligations now. "I know you are, which is one of the reasons I asked you here. The time has come to put an end to the last method you used to help me."

Taking one last look at the ring on her finger, Clara slowly slipped it off and held it out to him. He shook his head. "Clara…"

She remained firm, continuing to hold it out until he reluctantly took it. "I don't need it anymore," she insisted. There isn't a business to protect. And you're leaving soon."

He continued to look down at the ring. "I didn't want this back."

She sighed, wishing this felt easier. After all, fake engagements weren't supposed to have any emotions involved. However, the situation got trickier when it was between friends. "Thank you for helping me when I really needed it. I cannot tell you what that means to me."

John finally looked up and met her eyes. "Are you planning on rebuilding your store here or opening a new one somewhere else?"

Clara shrugged. "We haven't talked about exactly what we are going to do yet, but probably one of those two options, if we can. It's what we're good at."

John nodded and then held the ring back out to her. "Then, you are going to need this back."

She refused to take it. "I just said I didn't need it."

This time, he was the one not backing down. "When you start your new business, unless you open far away from Independence, the rumors that Emmers started will follow you."

She hadn't thought of that. They were struggling before the store burned down. Would they be able to rebuild with a dented reputation?

"We can manage," she said. "You don't have to worry about us."

He stood and started pacing the room, the ring fisted against his palm. "I do worry, Clara! You're important to me. All of you. I'm not even sure if it's safe to leave you in town with Emmers still running around. He may try something else while I'm gone. At least let me give you this small protection. It's the best I can do at the moment."

She hesitated. John sat next to her. "Please, don't make me beg you a second time for us to become betrothed, but not really."

Clara knew he was feeling helpless when it came to her family's situation. Maybe she could allow this one thing to ease his mind.

"All right, I will continue our betrothal if it's that important to you," Clara conceded. She held out her hand so he could place the ring in it, but John had another idea, he flipped her hand over and gently slid the circlet into place himself. "There, that's where it belongs."

When she first wore the ring, it had felt heavy and strange. Now her hand felt empty without it. "So we will go back to our original plan, since I'm not going west anymore. We'll exchange letters for a bit, and then they will taper off before we eventually end our betrothal from afar."

At least she would get updates via letters about the new town. That was something.

John nodded in agreement. "Thank you for letting me do something."

An hour after John left, Clara wanted to throw the ledger in front of her across the room. The family's finances were looking very grim indeed. The store was a total loss. They didn't know how the fire started, but with so many wooden crates and other flammable supplies, it was no surprise that it had gone quickly—and that nothing had been salvageable.

Clara had put so many hours into that store, helping it thrive. As a girl, she had watched her parents work diligently to build their business.

It was all gone now. Her father had been at the bank all morning, and she wondered if he would be able to get the loan they needed to restart.

Another store opening would take a lot of work, but they could do it.

"Did you look into the rooms for rent above the dressmaker?" Clara asked her sisters, desperate to take her mind off the worrying list of numbers she'd been staring at for too long.

Hannah nodded.

"It would be tight, but we could all fit. The three of us would have to share a room."

They had done so as small children, when they'd shared a nursery, and they could again.

"I'm not staying around long anyway." Eliza plopped down on the settee angrily. "I will find another way to get myself west."

Clara knew that her sister longed for adventure, but surely she wouldn't abandon them for a life of uncertainty.

"I'm going to go somewhere and take a teaching position." Hannah's voice was quiet, as if she was afraid Clara would yell at her for her news.

Not only had Clara lost her store and their plans to go west—now she was losing her sisters too.

"I know what you're thinking, and we are not abandoning you. But building the store into a business again is your dream, not ours," Eliza said as she crossed the room and put her arm around Clara.

"But how am I to do anything without you?"

Her sisters just gave her sad smiles, reassuring her that they thought she would be just fine. For the next hour, the three of them actually managed to laugh while thinking of increasingly ridiculous ways that Eliza could travel without an escort.

They were just discussing the possibility of her stowing away on the westward expedition by hiding in someone's wagon when their father arrived home. He sat down in the drawing room with a heavy sigh.

"Well, girls, we got the loan to restart the business." His voice sounded weary, and Clara felt a twinge of guilt. Was he doing all this—starting over the business—just because it was her dream?

"Papa, we don't have to do this if you don't want to. We can go somewhere with the money we get from the house and you can retire. I can work as a shopgirl somewhere to help support us." Clara didn't know if she could go back to not being in charge, but she would do anything for her family.

He brushed her words aside.

"Nonsense. You were born to run a store, and I mean to help you do it. It's what I want—far more than any retirement where I'd sit around all day, bored silly. Having a shop is the right thing to do. Even if we have to go back to the beginning. Besides, it shouldn't take us too long to get up and running. And most of our customers will return."

Still, he didn't seem enthusiastic about the plan, and it broke Clara's heart that he didn't get to live out his dream of heading west.

"Do you think we could get enough from the sale of our house to fund only two wagons? We could take turns driving rather than hiring someone, to save money," Clara suggested.

It could be a good solution for her family. If they were going to start over, she would rather they do it all together rather than separately. Without her sisters by her side, all her hard work to secure their future would be for nothing.

Her father, however, shook his head.

"We wouldn't have enough to make a good start on the stock we'd need for a store on top of the supplies for ourselves."

Clara gave it some thought. If they started small, with the basics, maybe they could build over time.

"Everything in this house that isn't a necessity, we could sell," she said. "And then use that money to buy every piece of stock that we can to make our new enterprise run."

Her father studied her for a moment. Clara knew this type of reckless, fanciful planning was not normal for her, but she was tired of her family being unhappy. She was tired of being unhappy herself.

"I don't know. It's a huge risk compared to staying here and starting over." He tried to keep a calm and rational tone, but Clara could tell that he was excited about the possibility.

Clara smiled. "Some things are worth the risk. This

family will slowly separate if we remain here. If we go west, at least we can do it together."

The sale of their home had already been arranged, so they would just need to conduct an estate sale to sell their belongings.

"If you're sure…?"

She nodded and the entire Morehouse family cheered.

"We may not be immediately successful, but we will be together," Clara said.

Hannah took that moment to remind her that she could spend more time with Mr. Butler again now that they were going to be on the wagon train again. Clara blushed when her whole family looked at her expectantly.

"John Butler and I are just friends, and that's all we will ever be." None of them believed her protestations. To make things worse, her sisters reminded her about the kiss she had shared with the businessman in that very room. She gasped, shocked that they would betray her confidence and say such things in front of their father.

"Oh, my darling girl, I already knew." He had a twinkle in his eye as he said it. "I may have been stuck in my bed for a very long time, but there is seldom anything that goes on in this house without my knowledge."

Clara sat down in shock when her father told her that Betty overheard their entire conversation, including witnessing the kiss. "So you knew…that the engagement between us wasn't real? Even before I told you?"

Her father nodded and she folded her arms and glared at him. "Why did you pretend not to know until I told you?"

Her father gave her a sad smile. "I was hoping that

the two of you would fall in love while pretending to be."

Hannah grinned at this. "I read a book about that happening once. It was so romantic."

Clara shook her head at them. "My life is not one of your romantic stories. John insists that we keep up the betrothal pretense, but he made his reasons clear—he fears that Michael Emmers might create more problems for me after the wagon train leaves. There was no talk of a romantic relationship between us. We're just friends."

Friends that had come very close to never seeing each other again. If they hadn't changed their minds about going west, he would have left in a couple months without so much as a backward glance in her direction.

"Even now that we're going on the wagon train, we'll still have to end this charade eventually. John has plans for his future that are very important to him, and so do I," Clara insisted. Starting and running her own successful business meant everything to her. And now that they were doing so without much money, the work would be harder. She would need to pour more of her time and attention into it, without distractions.

Her father lifted her chin so their gazes met, and Clara could see that the twinkle had returned to his eyes.

"Don't give up on the boy just yet. Sometimes people need a little bit of time to get things right in their heads."

Before they could discuss the matter further, they heard a knock on their front door. Betty came into the drawing room, leading the sheriff behind her.

The man bowed to the ladies before focusing his attention on their father. "I'm so sorry to bother you this late in the evening, but I needed to have a word with you about the fire at your store, Mr. Morehouse." The policeman gestured awkwardly toward the girls, and Clara knew that he was indicating they should leave.

Arthur Morehouse, however, was not the type of father that sheltered his daughters from life's cruel realities.

"It's all right. You can tell me anything you need to in front of them. But I fail to understand why the police are involved in this matter."

The sheriff took a seat when offered, and Betty handed him a cup of tea.

"We were not going to investigate at first, but Mr. Butler insisted that we ascertain whether foul play was involved."

Clara could scarcely believe her ears. Even with all he had to occupy him as the days counted down until his wagon train, John was still looking out for her family. She felt a wave of gratitude surge through her.

"And did you find anything?" Clara asked.

The sheriff was silent for a moment, likely figuring out a way to break the news gently to them. Based on his manner, Clara could already guess what he was going to say.

"Mr. Butler was correct in his assumptions. It wasn't an accident that destroyed your store—it was arson."

John walked out of another general store, dejected. There were only so many such businesses in the area, and none of the owners were interested in closing up shop here and moving west. Well, one was, but the man had an unsavory reputation. He would not be a good fit in their town.

Perhaps part of the problem was that John's heart wasn't in this quest. He knew he wasn't giving his best sales pitches, even though he knew their town needed a general store in order to thrive.

And then there was the issue of the Morehouse family. He could not get their troubles out of his mind.

Part of John considered staying in Independence longer, just to be sure that the family was back on its feet before he left. He had gone as far as getting out pen and paper to write his brother a letter declaring that he would be delayed in his return.

A guilty conscience had him throwing the missive in his fireplace. He had made a promise—not just to his brother but to all the people who were going on the journey—and he had to keep it. He and Adam had put everything they had into this venture, including funding it entirely with their own money this time, and John not following through would ruin them. Adam was good at managing the accounts and paperwork, but John was essential for establishing the community and local government for the new town. Adam didn't handle people well, so he needed John to take care of that part of their endeavors.

But leaving meant he took the risk of never seeing Clara or the rest of the Morehouse family ever again.

John brushed these thoughts aside. He needed to focus on the task at hand—finding someone to run the general store in their new town.

If things came down to it, John had learned well from Clara and could perhaps run a store himself. But that would mean he would have to busy himself buying supplies and stocking wagons, and he already had so much other work to do to get the wagon train ready to leave soon. And despite all he had learned, he couldn't fool himself into believing he would do as well as someone who had years of practice at the job. He had learned from experience that things worked better if he and his brother supervised the construction and other particulars of keeping a town operating while the experts supplied the various trades that the community required.

If you are going to have to fund all of that anyway, why can't you do it and pay the Morehouse family to come run it for you? Or offer them a loan to get the store started?

It would be a solution to many of his problems. He wouldn't have to convince a family to give up their livelihoods within a month or so and head to the West. Or worse, arrive in their new town with nothing to show for his efforts. If that happened, his brother would be very angry.

Adam should have done this part at least once. It's not as easy as it looks. I would rather be spending time alone in the wilderness like he is.

Though that wasn't really true at all. John loved talking to people, sharing his vision for the town they wanted to build. It just hurt to have found a family that would fit so perfectly in his town and know that they wouldn't be making the journey—unless he could convince them to allow him to bankroll the venture.

But would Arthur accept such an offer from him? Would Clara? They had both seemed so defeated when they discussed what would happen after the store burned down, but that had been in the immediate aftermath of the fire. Perhaps now that they'd had a few days to consider their plans, they would be open to a more unorthodox arrangement that would allow them to follow through on their plans to go west?

He had to try. John turned to the Morehouse home. Now was as good of a time as any to try to convince the family that all was not lost.

When he reached the front gate, he was surprised to see the sheriff exiting the home. "Oh, Mr. Butler! Funny to run into you here. I was just on my way to meet you."

A million possibilities ran through John's head. Was the Morehouse family hurt? Had they been robbed? Was Clara in danger?

But the sheriff was quick to explain. "I wanted to thank you for the recommendation that we investigate the Morehouse store fire. You were correct. It was arson."

John's blood boiled. He knew *exactly* who would do something like this. It was bound to be the same man who would also hire people to beat him up in the street. Who would ruin an innocent woman's reputation because she refused to marry him?

"I know who your culprit is. It's Michael Emmers."

The sheriff nodded, not looking surprised at John's accusation.

"I know—we have him in custody. His associates confessed when we questioned them, and they freely admitted that he was the one who paid them. They started the fire and they also jumped you in the street."

John was relieved that justice could now be pursued for both crimes, but he was more relieved that Emmers wouldn't have any opportunity to bother the Morehouse family again.

"He will face a trial?"

The sheriff nodded, and John agreed to testify before he left on the wagon train. He secured a promise that Emmers would not be treated lightly because of his wealthy status.

"That won't be much of a worry. His parents have shunned him. He's on his own."

While John had already known that Michael had

been disowned financially, Clara had told John that Michael's mother was still very much involved in her son's affairs, constantly attempting to push Michael and Clara together. Perhaps the fire had finally made the woman see that her son had gone too far. Though losing one's family was tragic, John couldn't bring himself to feel any sympathy for Michael. He had gotten himself in this predicament. John said goodbye to the sheriff and hurried to the front door. He had to ring the door chime and knock several times before a very stressed-looking Betty answered it.

"Mr. Butler, I'm so sorry it took so long. Truth is, I was getting ready to send a message inviting you to supper. We are just a little out of sorts at the moment."

John explained that he had seen the sheriff on the way in and heard the news.

"A terrible business," Betty whispered as she welcomed him inside and took his coat. "And Miss Clara is beside herself with guilt. She's blaming herself for this tragedy."

Of course she was. She always bore the weight of the world on her shoulders. It didn't matter if Michael had acted of his own volition. Clara would blame herself for being the cause of his decision to burn their store down.

"Are they in the drawing room?"

Betty nodded, gesturing for him to let himself in and telling him that there was no need to stand on ceremony when he was practically family.

John had always liked Betty.

The mood in the drawing room when he entered was grim. John imagined it would be difficult to learn that such a cruel loss had been inflicted on them intentionally. Clara and her sisters were sobbing softly on the settee while their father tried to comfort them.

Arthur was the first to notice him, crossing the room to shake hands.

"Thank you for asking the authorities to look into the fire. The truth doesn't make the situation any better, but it is good to know that there will be justice, at least. And he will never bother Clara again."

At the mention of her name, Clara lifted her head and her eyes met John's. His heart clenched at the tears he saw there, and he longed to cross the room and pull her into his arms. To whisper that everything would be all right. But she didn't want any comfort from him, and she certainly didn't need him to fix her problems for her.

She wanted to do everything in this world in her own way, without any help. She was everything strong and admirable—and frustrating. He was sure it would be an uphill battle to get her to accept his assistance when it came to financing the family's trip to the West. John opened his mouth to tell Arthur about the plan he had come up with this afternoon when he was interrupted by the door chiming once again.

Moments later, Betty entered the room nervously. Evidently the newcomers were not considered family and needed to be announced.

"Mr. Morehouse, I'm sorry to interrupt, but…the Emmers family is here."

The evening was starting to get very interesting, indeed.

Chapter Nineteen

Warren and Sophia Emmers were as completely opposite looking as a couple could be. While she was short and plump, and decked with bright colors from her clothing to her jewelry to her hair, he was tall and lanky, wearing a plain and sensible black suit. She flitted about with a nervous energy, while he was still and patient.

Clara briefly wondered what their home life was like. It couldn't be too pleasant, for it had produced their son Michael, who was the worst sort of person.

"What can we do for you, Mr. Emmers, Mrs. Emmers?" Her father's voice was cold. Clara knew that he'd had his fill of the Emmers family, now that the arson charges were known. "We've just been through a family tragedy, and we don't have time for visitors."

Mrs. Emmers shifted nervously in her seat, but her husband just met Arthur Morehouse's stare and held it. "Yes, well, that tragedy is why we are here."

Clara wondered if they were going to apologize for their son's behavior. Or worse, try to make excuses for it. In Clara's experience, Mrs. Emmers worshipped the ground her boy walked on. She didn't know what the father's feelings were though.

"If you are here to render an apology, you can make it and go. We don't want to see you or your son ever again." Clara couldn't help but be proud at the way her father was remaining firm. Any other family in town would be fawning over themselves to have the elite Emmerses in their parlor. But not the Morehouse family. Not now, not ever.

Sophia looked taken aback at the harsh words and frigid tone, but she had the decency to remain silent.

The Emmers patriarch let out a long-suffering sigh. "We're not just here to apologize. We are here to make restitution. Our son has made a lot of mistakes, and it isn't right that you should have to suffer for them."

Restitution? That could mean only one thing—they were going to offer some sort of financial settlement. But what would they want in exchange? Perhaps for them to not press charges against Michael.

Clara exchanged a look with John and could see that he was thinking the exact same thing. He opened his mouth to object, but her father started talking first.

"Restitution? How much? How much of a price would you put on our livelihood? On the years of our lives that we put in that place? On the shelves full of items that my wife tended? On the back room, where our daughters would play? Do you think any of that can be replaced by money?"

Mr. Emmers didn't crack under her father's stare, which Clara had to respect a little bit. He pulled out a piece of paper and handed it to her father. "I understand you were selling your store anyway and going to head west. This should cover the money you would have made from the sale, including enough to purchase new supplies, and some extra to compensate Miss Morehouse for the emotional damage wrought by my son's harassment."

He turned his eyes on her, and she shuddered at the raging shame she saw there. She almost felt sorry for the man, even though he'd raised such a horrible son.

"This is a fair sum. What are you wanting in exchange?"

Sophia opened her mouth to speak, but her husband silenced her with a glare.

"Exchange? There is no exchange. We seek only to pay our debts, and our son made one to you."

Her father handed the paper to John, and his eyes widened, likely at the amount he saw there. But he quickly recovered himself enough to speak. "Are you hoping we won't testify against your son in exchange for this money?" he asked.

The elder Emmers turned to John as if he had just noticed him in the room. Mr. Emmers shook his head. "I've rewarded my son's behavior too many times by letting him escape consequences, and look where it's gotten him. He has lost everything we've ever given him and destroyed quite a bit that was never his. Though it pains us to say it, he will be getting no help from us in his legal matters."

Mrs. Emmers looked as if she didn't agree with the plan, but she didn't hold the purse strings in the family. She leveled an icy glare at Clara. "This is all your fault. Why couldn't you just accept Michael's proposal? What's so wrong with him that you didn't want to get married?"

Everyone in the room stood up to defend her, and it made Clara burst out laughing.

Mrs. Emmers looked at her in disdain. "You would laugh at a time like this, while my son is in jail?"

Clara just shook her head at the woman. "I'm laughing because you think that Michael and I would ever have been a good match. I would never have been willing to put up with the way he probably would have treated me. My parents raised me to have too much self-respect for that. Besides, he was going to sell my store."

The older woman huffed. "*Your* store? Don't you mean your father's store? Oh yes, that's right. He gave you free rein like the harridan you are. Well, you won't be getting any offers of marriage after Michael."

John interjected. "It just so happens that she *did* get one after him. Did you not see the ring on her finger?"

This meeting was getting awkward. Thankfully, Mr. Emmers grabbed his wife's hand and pulled her to her feet so they could take their leave. "Just call on our office tomorrow and we will make arrangements to transfer the funds to you."

Clara couldn't believe how things had turned so quickly. Now they had the money to fully fund their trip again, and they could open a fully stocked store in the West. She had so much planning to do. It took all that was in her not to run out of the room to get started, but something about this meeting still wasn't sitting right with her.

"What about Mr. Butler?"

Her words froze the Emmers as they neared the door, and John looked at her with confusion.

"What about him?" Mr. Emmers sounded rather impatient and clearly did not want to stop for more business.

Clara crossed the room and stood next to John. "Doesn't he get some sort of compensation for the wounds your son inflicted on him?"

Mrs. Emmers waved her words away.

"That was just a jealous spat. It could have happened with any two men and not because of Mikey's problems."

Clara wanted to roll her eyes at her nickname for her son. No wonder he was so spoiled and childish, with a mother who overindulged him and treated him like a little boy.

"Two men fighting over a girl would have been a jealous spat. Stupid, yes, but understandable. But your son hired two goons to track Mr. Butler down in the street and beat him senseless," Clara said.

John squeezed her arm to thank her for her support, but she could tell from the way his shoulders stiffened he didn't want anything from that family.

Sure enough, he was quick to say, "It's all right. I don't need recompense."

Mr. Emmers studied the pair of them. The impatience from a moment earlier had faded, and he was looking at Clara with more respect than before.

"Miss Morehouse is correct—we do owe you something as compensation for what you experienced. Name your price."

John made to object, but she noticed that he stopped himself apparently thinking of something.

"There's a man over at the livery that could use his trip funded with a wagon and supplies. He was going to work to pay for him and his children to go west, but you could sponsor him instead."

Mr. Emmers nodded. "It will be done. I'll be thankful to have this whole mess behind us after the trial. Thank you all for your time."

The couple left in a hurry, leaving the Morehouses and John surprised in their wake.

"I can't believe what just happened!" Eliza squealed.

"We were going anyway, but now we can fully fund our trip!" Eliza and Hannah began jumping up and down in excitement.

John gave them a confused look. Clara realized she was still holding his hand and dropped it quickly.

"Wait…" he said, "you were still going west? You told me you wouldn't be able to!"

Clara hid her smile at his dumbfounded expression.

"Yes, we were planning to tell you this evening. We had decided to sell all our belongings here and go anyway. We would have needed to start our store with the bare minimum on the shelves, but we weren't about to let Michael destroy our plans."

John grinned at her, and her stomach flipped at the sight. Would she ever get used to his smile? She had better, since she was going to be seeing a lot more of him in the future.

"That's funny, because I was on my way over here to tell you that the Butler Brothers were going to start a store at our own expense and we wanted you to come run it," John explained. "I'm glad to know that we don't have to, but I wanted to make that possibility available."

Clara didn't have time to process his words, because Betty came rushing in. "All this chatter and you girls should be eating supper and getting ready for bed. We have a full day of packing tomorrow."

After their meal, everyone's expression bore sadness that the evening had to end. The ladies said their good-nights, but Clara heard her father ask John to stay a little bit longer. Oh, how she wished she could listen to what they were saying through the door.

Clara thought about John's offer all the way upstairs. He had been determined to get them to the West no matter what the cost to him and his brother. And she thought that maybe it wasn't just about saving her family.

Had she been mistaken in his motivation this entire time? Did he want them to go so she would still be in his life? Clara tossed and turned over the answers to those questions all night.

As pleased as he always was to speak to Arthur Morehouse, John wished he could go back to the hotel and start making final plans for their trip. The fact that the Morehouse family was going with him again renewed his energy for the project. And perhaps his joy was just a bit stronger at the news as it applied to a certain raven-haired eldest daughter.

Clara was going west, and he would get to see her every day.

"Now that we have things settled and are heading out, I wanted to talk to you again about your relationship with my daughter." Arthur sat down in his chair and bid John to sit, as well. John shifted nervously.

"Let me ask you a question, son. If Clara decided that she didn't want us to move out West and that we should stay in Independence—would you still want to be engaged to her?"

John froze at the question. He didn't know how to answer it without reminding Arthur that their engagement wasn't real. Even though he knew the truth, John knew that his friend hoped the situation would change. Arthur had made so many improvements from his grieving, and John didn't want to give him another reason to be sad.

"I have to go. I made a promise to my brother, and I must keep it," he explained.

Arthur nodded. "I understand, and that's honorable

of you, but my question is—would you come back someday for her?"

Five-year plan, five-year plan, five-year plan, he repeated in his head. After a moment's consideration, he decided that explaining his plan might help Arthur understand his situation a little better—and why the eventual end of his engagement to Clara was necessary.

"I made a promise to myself too. A promise that I would stay in one location for five years before getting married," he explained.

Arthur narrowed his eyes.

"And you don't think you could live in Independence for that long?"

John sighed and thought about life in Independence compared to the wild frontier of the West. Even though this wasn't a big city like New York—which almost had him running in the opposite direction whenever he visited—it still felt crowded here. Dense. And even though he and Adam hoped to see their town grow, the skies in the West were bigger. And the air was easier to breathe. And besides, the engagement between him and Clara wasn't real anyway. "I don't think so. I'm sorry. Besides, I'm not even going to consider looking for a wife until after I've settled for five years."

Arthur heaved out a frustrated sigh, and John felt guilty that he was disappointing the man he looked up to so much.

"But what if you meet someone sooner?"

His brother had asked him this same question before, and John always replied the same way. "Well, then, she will just have to wait."

Arthur leveled him with that fatherly stare that made John want to sit up straight. "Why do you think it is all right for Clara, or any other woman, to give up her life plans for half a decade when you aren't willing to give up yours?"

John sat in silence, considering his friend's words. He had been so adamant about his five-year-plan, but for the first time, he wondered if something, or someone, might change his mind. If the right woman came along and wasn't willing to wait, what would he do?

Arthur leaned back in his chair and folded his hands in his lap, looking at John thoughtfully.

"I think you had better explain your reasoning behind this five-year plan. Right now, it's awfully confusing. It seems as if you are afraid of something."

Images of his mother riding away on a carriage flooded John's memory. It was painful to think about, but Arthur deserved to know the truth. "My parents loved each other, but it wasn't enough. Father had a wanderlust. He would settle somewhere, stay a year or two and then move us to some other remote territory to stake a claim."

John remembered their father always announcing every move like it was going to be a grand adventure while their mother would look on with tight lips.

"It's a lot of work setting up a homestead and a lot of work moving. And the way my father chose to live was very isolating. Every time a town or something would start springing up and we would have neighbors, my dad would get the itch to move on again."

Arthur nodded but remained silent so John could tell the whole story.

"Mama played along at first. But eventually, it got to be too much for her. The moving, not having family friends, limited access to a doctor or school for us. One day a wagon train master was heading back after taking a group west, and she just hopped on and went back East." It was funny, because that home had not been more than a week or so west from where they were right now. The world kept growing and changing. If she had stayed put just a few years longer, the community would not have been so remote.

Arthur gasped in surprise. "And she didn't take you boys with her?"

John shook his head. "She didn't even ask if we wanted to come. She just packed her bag and left us all behind."

Their father had allowed himself to grieve for a short period of time but then had poured himself back into his work on the land. He finally was spurred into establishing a relationship with his neighbors, to help out with his sons when needed. The boys took longer to get used to living without their mother.

"We never saw her again. But a few years back, we did get a letter from a distant relative in New York notifying us that she had died," John concluded.

Arthur looked at him with pity, which was the last thing that John wanted. What had happened to him when he was young had made him stronger, and his brother too.

"I'm sorry that happened to you, son. But what does this have to do with you and your future wife? What is the five-year plan about?"

It was difficult to explain, but John decided to try. "While I was angry at my mother for leaving, I know that it wasn't all her fault. My father was never able to settle down, and it broke her. I vowed never to do that to a woman."

He didn't know for sure if he'd inherited his father's wanderlust, but John didn't want to take any risks. What if he discovered he couldn't stick somewhere? Would his wife be able to pick up and move with him over and over?

"So, your five-year plan...?"

John stood up and started pacing the room. "I want to make sure that I'm settled for good, that I'm not going to be like my father."

Arthur Morehouse remained silent for several minutes, staring at John in a way that made him very nervous. Finally, he spoke. "Well, I've always thought you to be a smart man, son, but that's one of the stupidest things I've ever heard."

John stopped pacing and stared at his friend. He had explained the plan thoroughly, hadn't he? What was so hard to understand? "Let's say, for argument's sake, that this is your daughter we are talking about."

Arthur nodded. "Yes, son, that's what I've been considering anyway."

"I would want to make sure that I won't make her miserable by uprooting her life every few years."

John sat down on the chair opposite of Arthur, hoping that he finally understood the importance of his plan, but Arthur merely chuckled.

"First of all, you know my daughter well enough to know that she doesn't give up on anything once she sets her mind to it. And that would include her marriage. Clara is not the type to leave. Even if she isn't the one you end up marrying, I would hope you would choose a wife of sterner stuff than your mother, no offense."

John didn't want his wife to ever be in that position where she would have to stay where she didn't want to be either.

Arthur continued. "And five years isn't going to prove whether you have wanderlust or whether you can settle down. Places aren't home. People are."

John froze at his friend's words. People were home? John thought of all the new places he and his brother had settled. None of them seemed too foreign because they always had each other. Could Arthur be right?

"Your father was looking for something, for sure. But he failed to settle with his people. You are not like that at all. You've been here for a few weeks, and we already consider you family. And I know there are plenty of other folks here in Independence who would go to bat for you."

John thought of young Benjamin, who had helped him when he was injured, and Henry and his father, who would also be going west.

"All of those people will be in our new town," he said more to himself than to Arthur.

And it would feel like home. That's why he had been so insistent that the Morehouses go west. They were all his family, and their house and store were comfortable to him.

"As long as you stick to the people you love, you won't feel the need to give in to wanderlust," Arthur said. "You're perfectly capable of committing to someone. Your dedication to your brother proves that for you."

An incredible peace settled over John. Home was where his people were, and soon they would all be in his new town in the West. Home was wherever the Morehouse family was, because they had welcomed him into theirs without a second thought and made him feel like he belonged.

He had much to consider.

Arthur must have seen the myriad of emotions on his face, because he leaned forward with a twinkle in his eye. "I think she will have you, if you find a way to show her that your attachment is real and that your offer of marriage is not just because you want to save her in some way. I believe she cared for you before but may not even know it herself. And she didn't think the feelings were genuine on your part—aside from friendship and perhaps some protectiveness."

Do I have real feelings for Clara? The thought sent John reeling. He had to get out of here, go on a walk and try to make some sense out of all the thoughts whirling around his mind right now. Clara was important to him, and every moment he got to spend with her felt like a breath of fresh air. But he hadn't let himself even consider the possibility of something between them, because of his five-year plan. Now everything was confusing to him.

"I'm sorry, Arthur. I have to go. I have plans to make."

Arthur nodded. "For the wagon train?"

John shook his head and turned toward the door.

"No, I think I may have to make plans for how to court my own fiancée."

Chapter Twenty

Clara closed her eyes at the sound of the grandfather clock chiming in the hall. They had arranged the sale of the piece, which had been her mother's first purchase when they built this home. The new owners would be around to pick it up later this afternoon.

"I never realized how much I love that sound until I knew we weren't going to hear it again," Hannah said wistfully as she entered her sister's room.

"I was just thinking the same thing." Clara gave her sister a comforting hug. "How's the packing going?"

Hannah scrunched up her nose. "I'm having a hard time narrowing down the books I'm going to take. I even cut out a few dresses to make more room, but I will have to leave so many behind."

Clara laughed. Her sister loved books, plus she had the added responsibility of ensuring she had all the necessary ones to educate the children in their new town.

"Did you talk to John about maybe fitting some in his wagon? They are for the school after all."

Hannah nodded glumly. "I already did. I'm trying to fit the rest in my personal bags."

Clara hid her smile. The Morehouse family had accumulated a large library throughout the years, but there was no possibility they could take all those books to the West. It was that way with a lot of their personal items. Clara herself had narrowed her wardrobe down quite a bit and kept only a few mementos of their mother.

"How's Eliza doing? She hasn't been around much today."

Hannah huffed and plopped down on Clara's bed. "Oh, you know how Eliza is. She had everything she wanted to be packed done within five minutes. She's been preparing for this journey her entire life."

That was the truth, Clara thought. Eliza was a frequent reader of a newspaper column written by an anonymous person who worked on the wagon trains. She'd soaked up every bit of information, dreaming of the day she, too, could travel west.

"Well, we can put her to work in other areas, I suppose. Betty needs a lot of help in the kitchen."

Hannah nodded and gave Clara a sly smile. "I forgot to tell you—John sent a note over saying he would join us for supper."

Clara's heart sped up at her sister's words. She was trying to keep her relationship with John as professional as possible, but it didn't help that the man was here just about every night for supper. Often her family would make themselves scarce and the two of them would be left alone together.

"Don't get too excited, he's probably just coming here to discuss the trip with Father."

Since they had committed to going west on the wagon train, their father had peppered John with question after question as to what to expect on their journey.

"Sure, he's just coming to talk to Father," Hannah scoffed. "I'm sure you have nothing to do with it."

Before she could argue with her sister, Betty called up to them to say that Mr. Butler had arrived and was waiting in the study. Clara took a moment to brush some dust off her skirt and straighten her hair.

"Are you coming?" she asked Hannah, who was giving her an amused grin.

Her younger sister shook her head. "No, I have to figure out what to do about this book situation."

It seemed the rest of her family all had important business to attend to, so she was left to greet John alone in the drawing room.

"It's good to see you, Clara," he said, handing her a bouquet of flowers. They were lovely, but she didn't know if they had any vases left after all the flowers he had brought her this week. He was really going above and beyond to keep up appearances for their betrothal pretense.

"Thank you, John. This is too kind. You do know we are trying to pack everything up, and you are adding to our collection."

He looked taken aback by the thought. "You're right. I'm so sorry! I just thought I shouldn't arrive empty-handed. You are all so kind in feeding me every night after all."

She didn't want to admit that the bright flowers were a highlight of her day.

"You know you are welcome here, anytime, with no gift required. It's the least we can do after everything."

John accepted her invitation to sit down and Clara took a moment to study him. He looked tired. Clara felt a strange longing to take care of him, to tell him to take a nap and that she could handle some of the details of the trip to ease his load.

But it wasn't her place. Since her insistence on keeping things professional, they had fallen into this strange new relationship. They did not talk much about their betrothal charade or really anything romantic at all. It was almost as if it'd never happened, except for the ring on her finger.

But still, he came here every night. He brought her flowers. They talked for the hour or so before supper, and the next day they would repeat it.

If she was a less practical girl, she might get the false notion that he was courting her in earnest. But that was a silly, passing thought. They had a journey to prepare for. He had a five-year plan, and she had a store to start. Who knows if John would even stay for that many years in their new town? Maybe he was right to worry that he'd want to move on—that he wasn't truly ready to settle down.

Clara decided to start some small talk, not wanting to sit in awkward silence anymore. "How are the preparations faring? Are we almost ready to go?"

"We will be leaving soon, whether we are ready or not," he teased. "But yes, for the most part, things are coming together. A few more families will be arriving by the end of the week, and then the group will be complete."

John had told her about many of the families who would be going with them. Some were young married couples, ready to start their new lives in a fresh country with landholdings of their own. Other, larger families, with plenty of children, had encountered hard times and scraped together the last of their savings for a chance to start over in the West. Single young men sought to build their own futures by staking a claim on a farm or a ranch.

"I met the new pastor, did I tell you?"

John shook his head. "He's a nice young man, isn't he?"

Clara almost giggled at John referring to a man who was only a few years junior than him as a 'young man,' but she knew what he meant. John's years of travels and business experience made him seem much older than the minister fresh out of seminary school.

"He's young, but he knows what he's talking about," Clara said. "He visited us right after the fire. It was so kind of him. You chose well. He will be a much-needed asset to your town."

"*Our* town," John corrected. "You're going to live there too."

Clara blushed at his words. The way he said it almost made her think that he meant *our* as in something that belonged to the both of them...together. She was trying to keep things platonic between the two of them, but moments like this made it difficult.

"Clara..." John started, but Clara changed the subject quickly.

"So, are you ready for the trial tomorrow? I thought I wouldn't be nervous to testify, but the thought of seeing Michael again turns my stomach."

All three Morehouse women had been called to testify in Michael's trial. Her sisters would attest to his threatening behavior in the shop. But Clara's testimony of all the times Michael had made overtures to her and the things he had said would be the most compelling since they would reveal the motivations behind the fire.

Some in the town still gave her scandalized looks whenever she passed. More people, however, had rushed to comfort her once word got out that Michael had been arrested. It seemed that the police being involved had finally tipped the scales on people believing that Clara was the nice one after all.

"A bunch of fakes," Hannah whispered when family after family called on them, offering sympathy. Clara somewhat agreed, but she also knew that the Emmers family was just as established in this community as hers, and the idea that Michael would do something so heinous was probably very shocking to people. But Eliza always accused her of trying to see the best in people.

"Clara?"

She realized that she'd missed everything John had said about the trial while she was deep in thought. She laughed at her rudeness. "Oh, I'm so sorry. Just wool-gathering. What did you say?"

John gave her a relieved smile. "For a minute there I thought I was boring you," he teased. "I was just saying that I will be there in the courtroom when you testify. You won't be alone."

Clara was grateful for the support. She knew the day would be hard on him too.

"I can't believe that you have to testify too, even though the men who beat you up confessed to the crime and admitted that Michael paid them."

John just shrugged. "If my testifying means that he gets put away and never bothers you again, I'm willing to do it."

His face wore such an earnest expression. *He really is a good man*, Clara thought. *Maybe someday...*

No, she put ideas of romance aside. They had so much work to do to get ready for the West. Now was not the time for distractions.

John reached out his hand toward hers, as if he was going to hold it. He opened his mouth to say something, but they were interrupted by Eliza loudly opening the door.

"Betty sent me in here to tell you that supper is ready!"

Clara followed after her sister to the dining room, both disappointed to miss what John was about to say and relieved that she didn't have to hear it when she might not be ready for it.

John was grateful for many things, one of which was that Betty would be going west with them. The woman was a phenomenal cook and could string together a mouthwatering meal seemingly out of thin air. Certainly, her pantry was quite bare in preparation for the trip.

The woman seemed grateful to have another gentleman to feed, as well, because she was always heaping second and third helpings on John's plate.

"These girls eat like little birds, picking at their food… Well, most of them," Betty said, rolling her eyes at Eliza who stuffed a whole biscuit in her mouth.

John covered his laugh by pretending to wipe his lips.

"I'm just not used to home cooking, aside from what my brother and I can rustle up on our bachelors' stove. And certainly, nothing we make has ever come close to tasting this good." John proved his point by taking another large bite of his stew.

Betty blushed with pleasure at his words, making the patriarch of the Morehouse family smile.

"I imagine you will find excuses to be a frequent guest at our home when we get to the new town," the older man teased. "Although we probably won't have much of a home at first."

"Oh, you'd be surprised how fast the buildings go up once everyone is there and lends a hand. All the people want to make the town theirs and take pride in the community they built together."

John had seen the same thing in all the other settlements he and his brother had started, but he imagined this one would have an even stronger feeling of community. First, because he and Adam would be putting permanent roots there, so they had more invested in every detail of the community. Second, this was the farthest west they had taken a wagon train, so the group on it would have longer to form a bond on their journey together.

Third, well… It was just a feeling. The people he had met, between the blacksmith, the doctor, the minister, the Morehouses and even the widower and his two children—they just felt right. He couldn't wait to see what God did with their little town.

"Well, we would be honored to have you as our first guest in our new home, whenever that will be," Arthur said. "And your brother, as well, of course."

John chuckled. "Adam will jump at the opportunity. I know he's been longing for some company."

Even though Adam was the more introverted of the two of them, even he needed people sometimes.

"How long did it take for your last town to be built?" Hannah asked, drawing John out of his thoughts.

"It takes only a few months to get the basic buildings up and running. We've been blessed to have enough people to pitch in every time. Really, a town is never finished. Look how much Independence has grown and changed through the years," John explained. "But I know Adam and some of the men he's hired have already started building a few structures, and I expect there will be at least some done by the time we arrive."

Eliza laughed. "That wasn't really an exact answer."

"There's no way of telling. Every place is different, just like its people." John smiled when he thought of the citizens of their other communities, who they'd come to know. All of them had created something out of nothing, and he couldn't wait to do it again.

"Do you miss them? The other people?"

John gave Clara a surprised look. How did she always seem to have a window into his thoughts?

"I do, but that's why it's nice that those towns have become stops along the Oregon Trail. Whenever I pass through, it's a chance to visit everyone and see how they are doing."

Some of his favorite memories were the nightly stopovers on the trail, where he would visit the town's only restaurant and everyone would update him on all the news of the community. The places they had built were not yet large, but they continued to grow as more and more people took the journey west.

"How do you know that you won't abandon the people in this new one?"

John turned to Clara at her question. Her voice was calm, but there was a challenge in her eyes.

"My brother and I promised this would be our last town. We aren't going to build any more." John kept his gaze on Clara, but she looked down at her plate.

Eliza cleared her throat. "Did you ever say that about any of your other towns?" Eliza gave him a meaningful look, and nodded her head toward Clara, indicating that the question was on her behalf.

"Not once. Never. We always knew that each one of those was only a temporary stopping point for us.

That we were filling a need for life on the trail and then would move on once the community was stable enough to continue without us."

Eliza nodded in encouragement. "So, what's different this time around?"

"Because my brother and I never had a home, and it's time we made one. When things were coming to a close in our most recent town and we were thinking about our future, Adam and I both took time to pray about what God wanted next from us."

He paused, remembering that time. He'd been nervous about sharing his permanency plans with his brother, worried that they might not want the same thing.

"We both came to the same conclusion separately—this would be it for us. Butler Valley will be our home," John told the Morehouse family, revealing the name of the new town.

"Butler Valley?"

Clara had a small smile when she said the name, and John almost breathed a sigh of relief at the sight of it.

"Yes, that's how we knew that this would be our home for sure—we put our name on it. All the other towns we've made were named after geographical features or people who invested in them. But this one, we called it Butler Valley. This is where we are going to stay."

Everyone's eyes shone with happy tears. "I think that's just lovely," Hannah said, and Clara nodded her head in agreement.

"Butler Valley, I like it," she said, reaching over to squeeze his hand.

He grasped her fingers with his, marveling at how

small yet strong they were. "Do you think it sounds good?"

Clara nodded. "It sounds like home."

And John couldn't help but agree more, especially since she would be there with him.

Chapter Twenty-One

The trial of Michael Emmers was the event of the century for the town of Independence. Everyone wanted a seat, but only those who showed up first were able to get one. Clara was thankful that John seemed to be an early riser, grabbing a place for himself and aggressively saving some for the Morehouse family.

"I got glares from many a town busybody this morning," he whispered to Clara when she sat down next to him.

"Don't they realize that we're the victims and have to be in the courtroom?"

Her father let out a laugh. "I don't think they care, as long as they get a front-row seat."

Around them, Clara could hear the other spectators gossiping about the events.

"I think that those ruffians who beat up Mr. Butler must have set the fire of their own accord," one woman whispered loudly from the back of the courtroom. "Because the Emmers boy would never hurt anyone."

Another person scoffed. "I saw him kick a dog once."

"Oh, hush up. Think of everything the Emmers family has done for this community. Do they seem like the type that would burn down a store?" another person asked.

On and on the gossip spread through the church, which was serving as the courtroom today. Some painted Michael as a villain; others called Clara a troublemaker for causing such a fuss. John took Clara's hand when one of those comments hit their ears, and she was grateful for the comfort. While the hand-holding might stir more talk, she really needed the comfort right now.

Besides the terrible things a select few were still saying about her, she was also very nervous to see Michael today. She had not laid eyes on him since the day she had hit him with a broomstick—the day he'd started the rumors about her. His eyes had been filled with hate and fire then, and she didn't expect much to be different today.

The judge entered the church, and his eyes widened in surprise at the crowd gathered there. Independence did have its share of crime in recent years—hence the need for a full-time judge—but never had there been such an audience for the types of small offenses typical for the town.

Clara couldn't remember the last time she had attended a trial. Maybe when she was younger and was more curious.

Michael was brought in, his hands in restraints. Clara could see Mrs. Emmers protesting her boy being kept in handcuffs, but her husband told her to hush up. Clara noted that even though they said they weren't buying Michael's way out of this, the family had clearly paid for a fancy lawyer from New York City to come in and represent him.

The man seemed very out of place in Independence. No one else was quite so spic-and-span—and certainly no one had that…whatever was in his hair to make it sleeked back like that.

John wore a suit today, but Clara thought that it made him look dashing rather than snobby like the New York lawyer.

Eliza and Hannah were called to the stand first.

Hannah was nervous and shy about the entire thing, and the audience could barely hear her story, as it was spoken in such a small voice.

"Speak up, girl!" Someone from the back yelled, but the judge just banged his gavel while he called for order and then told Hannah that he could hear her just fine.

"I'm the only one who really needs to hear it," he reassured her.

When it was Eliza's turn, she was completely opposite of her younger sister. She thought this whole thing was a grand adventure and gave her testimony with dramatic flair.

A few of her reenactments of Michael's demeanor outside the shop when he was fighting with Clara had the audience members gasping.

"That will be all, Miss Morehouse. Thank you for your…interesting…testimony," the judge said as he dismissed her.

Next up was Clara, and she shook off the murmurs and whisperers she could hear throughout the audience while she walked forward and swore on the Bible that she would tell the truth. When she sat down, she could see several people from the community give her encouraging smiles. Her family was in the front row, a strong foundation that gave her courage to speak today. When she met John's eyes, she knew that it didn't matter what kind of questions the man from New York asked—she would be all right. She had people who believed in her, who cared for her. And a new life waiting for her in the West.

Her job now was to make sure that Michael Emmers couldn't hurt any other woman in the future. She had to protect them.

Clara answered questions about her interactions with Michael Emmers and how he became more and more aggressive in his advances over time. A few in the audience seemed shocked when they heard how forward the man had been in her own home.

She breathed a sigh of relief when those questions were over but knew that she still had to face Michael's attorney for the cross-examination. Clara said a quick prayer asking for peace and for the right words to say.

"Miss Morehouse, how long had you and Mr. Emmers been in a courting relationship prior to the fire?" The New York attorney came out with a ridiculous question right away.

"As I said earlier, Mr. Emmers and I were never in a courting relationship."

The man huffed, crossing the courtroom to stand in front of her. "Then, why did he come to your home in the evenings, other than to call on you?"

The man puffed himself up, clearly trying to intimidate Clara, but she was made of sterner stuff. "He came over unannounced and uninvited."

The man slammed his hand down on the desk, making everyone in the courtroom startle.

"And what were you doing that made him think that his affections might be returned? Did you give any indication that you were interested in him?"

Clara gave a firm no to that question.

"That's not what Mr. Emmers will attest to. He says

that you pursued him at every turn, eager to marry into his wealthy family."

Clara shook her head. "At the time of his unwanted advances, my family was not hurting for money. I did not need to marry into Michael's family to live comfortably."

The New York lawyer was clearly miffed that he could not break her. Clara noticed a drip of sweat on his brow. But despite his apparent nervousness, he still attacked her with the worst sort of question next.

"But how are you to be believed, Miss Morehouse? There are rumors around this town that you have a less than savory reputation."

From the corner of her eye, she could see her father and John stiffening, ready to jump up to defend her honor. But she didn't need them to do that. In fact, she hoped to avoid it. Anger was exactly what this big city lawyer wanted—something that would make her and her family seem emotional and irrational so he could cast doubt on their credibility. She wasn't going to give it to him.

Father, give me strength, she prayed before leveling a steady stare at the man.

"Those rumors were started by Michael himself," Clara said in an even tone, not letting herself get riled.

"According to you."

She nodded. "According to me, and any number of people you could bring up here who have known me my entire life and recognized those rumors for the lies that they are."

The lawyer narrowed his eyes at her. "You claim they were *all* lies? What about your relationship with Mr. Butler?"

Clara sighed. She should have known it would come

to this. "Mr. Butler and I are engaged to be married. See? I'm wearing his ring."

While most people in town knew this information, there were a few gasps from the crowd. Michael glared at her. She wondered if this was the first he had heard of their engagement.

Clara snuck a peek at John. How did he feel about her bringing up the fake engagement on the stand?

Michael signaled his lawyer, who walked over and exchanged a few words with his client. The lawyer approached Clara again.

"Why did you conveniently become engaged so quickly after you rebuffed the proposal of Mr. Emmers? What kind of woman are you?"

John sat up straighter in his seat and nodded at her, and Clara knew what he wanted her to say. This very moment was why they had established their betrothal, despite the risk to his reputation. No one had ever done such a kindness for her before. And now she had to talk about it on the witness stand—where she had promised to tell the truth. "I'm the kind of woman who waited for a man who I could love to propose."

Clara looked over at John, who had a big smile on his face. That face that had become so dear to her in these past few months. Was he smiling because of what she said? She hadn't lied, exactly. She had indeed waited to accept the proposal of a man who she could love. John Butler was such a man.

Clara blinked. Did she love him? After all her efforts to keep things friendly and professional, had she fallen in love anyway?

She didn't have time to even consider the possibility because the New York lawyer demanded her attention again.

"And what about the late nights Mr. Butler was seen working in your store? Did you just accept his proposal to stop the scandalous gossip about you?"

Clara wanted to grind her teeth at the nerve of this man, but she still kept a calm demeanor.

"I would remind you that I'm not the one on trial here—Mr. Emmers is. But to answer your question, before our engagement, Mr. Butler thought my family would not be moving west with him and he wanted to learn about supplying a general store. My father was not feeling well, so he asked me to help."

The lawyer tried a few more times to get Clara to crack, and to imply that she had behaved improperly, but she answered everything in an even and soft voice. Most people in the audience nodded their heads at her answers. Michael and his lawyer's tactics had not worked, and people knew the truth.

Finally, she was able to step down from the witness seat and return to her family and John. The latter was called to testify next, but before he rose to his feet, he squeezed her hand to let her know that she was fine now. Clara gave him a small, encouraging smile. She knew that facing the big city attorney was not an experience she would wish on anyone.

John's pulse raced as he approached the witness stand. He had started this morning feeling calm and confident about how the day would turn out. But when the lawyer came at Clara so aggressively during her testimony, tension started to fill him. How dare this man accuse Clara of all the foul rumors that Emmers had spread? How dare he even suggest that the man's actions were at all justified?

John was proud of the way Clara had stayed strong

and confident throughout her testimony. When she declared under oath that she had been waiting for a man she could love to propose—what did that mean? That she could love him? Or that she *did* love him? Did she still see them as just business associates and friends? If so, his courtship attempts over this past week had fallen quite short of the mark.

He reminded himself that he still had time. Months of time on the wagon trail awaited them.

John sat down in the witness seat and swore to tell the truth. His testimony went more smoothly than Clara's because there was no dispute about what had happened to him. His attackers had already confessed. They would be taking the stand next, as they had the most incriminating evidence.

John saw Clara wipe a tear from her eye when he talked about the beating he had taken. She mouthed "I'm so sorry" at him and he wanted to stop talking, rush over to her and pull her into his arms. This was not her fault. She had to know that.

When he left the witness stand, he sat next to her and held her hand again. He had been doing that a lot this morning, and she had not pulled away. It gave him hope that they could eventually be more than friends.

A short recess was called after John's attackers testified. The judge announced that he needed time to weigh his decision. From across the room, John watched the Emmers family approach the judge.

"Looks like they may not be keeping to their promise to stay out of it," Arthur said under his breath.

It made John's blood boil that people thought they could twist the law in their favor. He was about to go over and intervene, but he saw the man shoo the couple away with an angry expression. "Looks like their money will do them no good here."

The Morehouse family and John gathered outside, waiting for the verdict. A few well-wishers approached Clara and thanked her for her testimony. A few said they were sorry for ever doubting her. When she was finally through talking to everyone, she approached John with sad eyes.

"I'm so sorry for what happened to you. I knew that you had been injured, but I didn't know how bad it was."

John shook his head at her. "You have nothing to apologize for. Michael Emmers is the one responsible for what happened to me, along with the men who beat me up."

"But if I had never suggested to Michael that you and I were courting…"

John reached for Clara's hand and interrupted her. "I would have done something else to annoy the man. He saw me as competition before you even said anything. And the fact that both you and I stood up to him—it sent him over the edge."

Clara frowned. "Still, if it hadn't been for his infatuation with me, you wouldn't have been so hurt."

John gave her a mischievous grin. "I don't know. I usually find a way to get on the bad side of a fool like that. So, we probably would have come to blows regardless."

She still looked skeptical, and John wanted to hug her. But he didn't know if such a gesture would be welcomed. He settled for holding her hand again and was thrilled when she let him.

"Seriously, Clara, please don't think this is your fault. Emmers is a vile man, and he did vile things. End of story."

Clara was about to open her mouth to protest when her father stepped up to them. John's heart sank a little when she quickly dropped their joined hands.

"He's right, you know," Arthur said to his daughter. "None of this is your fault. Personally, after the show in our drawing room and just now in the courtroom, I blame his parents. I don't think they taught that young man an ounce of responsibility."

John couldn't help but agree. He had met many well-to-do families in his travels and they usually fell into two types. Some had so much wealth and privilege that they thought themselves better than everyone else. Others taught their children that their place in life was earned, and that it carried with it certain responsibilities to lead by example and behave with honor and dignity. The Emmers family was the former, while the Morehouses were the latter.

Clara bit her bottom lip, something he had noticed she did only when she was exceedingly stressed. He prayed that all of this would be over soon so that they could move on with their lives and head west. During the journey, he could only hope that he'd find a way to win Clara's heart at last.

Somehow, he had fallen in love with his own fiancée. When she was on the stand today, bravely answering all the rude and accusatory questions posed to her, his feelings had become absolutely certain. John longed to pull Clara aside right now and tell her how he felt about her, but he didn't get the chance.

The sheriff stepped outside and announced that a decision had been made. Everyone rushed to get back into the church and find their seats.

"I'm surprised they didn't stampede one another to

steal a closer spot," Clara whispered to him as they saw the townspeople cram into the room to hear the verdict.

John took his seat near the front, which thankfully Eliza had saved for them. "I wasn't foolish enough to leave," she said with a knowing look. "We have a prime location."

He thanked her with a wink and waited for the judge to reveal his decision. A hush spread through the courtroom as the man banged his gavel.

"The Emmers family has been a pillar of our community for many years, which is why this case is so difficult," the man started.

John clenched his fist. The case should not be difficult at all—Michael had perpetrated several crimes and should serve time for them.

"But the overwhelming evidence shows that Michael Emmers did commit these crimes, so we find him guilty."

A wave of murmurs went through the crowd. Some must have thought he would really get away with it.

"Because this is the first time this young man has committed such serious crimes, and because his family can vouch for him, we sentence him to one year in jail."

Another round of murmurs went through the crowd. "One year? He destroyed our livelihood and he nearly killed you!" Arthur Morehouse was beet red with rage. His daughters did their best to calm him.

"It's okay, Papa, at least he got some jail time, which will be miserable for him," Hannah said. "Besides, we got that money from his family, so we will be able to start our new store."

John turned to look at Clara, who looked pale.

"What if he comes after me again when he gets out

of prison? What if he tries to destroy our family or—worse—your new town?"

John put his finger under her chin and lifted it so their eyes could meet. "We will be long gone by then. He's not going to bother traveling that far west for some revenge."

Clara relaxed a little. "You really think so?"

John nodded. "Besides, if he does, there will be a whole town of people ready to support you. That's the thing about new towns—everyone is there for each other. And someone like Michael Emmers will not be welcome."

Clara smiled up at him, and his heart skipped a beat at the fact that he was able to make her feel even a little bit better.

As the sheriff was taking Michael away, he turned toward Clara and spat on the ground. The crowd gasped. "This is all your fault," he accused.

Both John and Clara's father stepped forward to defend her, but she placed a hand on each of their arms and moved toward Michael herself. It took all that was within John to not pull her back to a safe distance away, but he knew by now that she could take care of herself and would resent his interference.

Clara looked at Michael Emmers with a calm and serene expression on her face. Gone was the regret and fear from a few minutes ago.

"I forgive you."

She said the words with confidence, and Emmers reared back from them. "What?"

Clara nodded. "I forgive you for everything. While you're in jail, and for your whole life afterward, I want you to know that I'm not going to hold on to this. Any of it. I'm leaving this town to start a new life, and I'm not taking anything of you with me. I hope you find peace."

And with that, she turned and walked out of the church, oblivious to the way everyone in the building was staring after her. John fell a little bit more in love with her at that moment, if such things were possible. She was so brave and strong, and he only wished he could be the same.

John thought back to his conversation with the young minister about forgiving his mother for all the pain she had caused by leaving them. The minister had said that forgiving her would be healing for them both, even though she had passed away.

Clara had made it look so easy. And for a moment, John wondered if it could be.

Chapter Twenty-Two

The following month was so busy, the entire group of people heading west hardly had time to think. There were homes to clean out, wagons to pack, goodbyes to say. Clara felt like she didn't have a moment to sit down. She had gone over the inventory for their new store not once but about thirty times. And then she had her father check it, just to be safe.

The men who they had hired to drive their additional wagons came for lunch one day, and they found they got along with them just fine.

One was a tall man named Clay, who was raised on a ranch after he was orphaned as a boy. He was working as many jobs as he could to save up enough money to buy some cattle for the land he would stake his claim on one day.

Clara couldn't help but notice how Eliza's eyes lit up with excitement over Clay's stories of the West. Nope, that was not happening. Her sister was too adventurous for her own good. Clara knew she would have to keep a close eye on Eliza during the journey west, lest she run off with the first man who promised her excitement. While adventure wasn't something to look down upon,

Clara knew from her experience with Michael that men could promise one thing and mean just the opposite.

Another driver was Raymond. He was an older fellow, but he was still strong and knowledgeable of life on the trail. A happy sort of man, and Clara knew that they would enjoy having him as part of their group.

"I can start a fire in the rain and just about fix a wheel while it's moving," Ray said with a jovial chuckle. Clara didn't know if it was true, but she was sure those would be skills that would come in handy on their journey.

Rounding out the wagon drivers was Micah, a boy barely over eighteen whose baby face made Clara feel like an old woman. He was the oldest of ten children, and his parents had sent him out into the world so young because they couldn't afford all the mouths they had to feed. Clara's heart went out to him, but he seemed thrilled about seeing more of the world beyond Independence.

One thing that was constant while they were preparing for their journey—John came by every night for supper. He was keeping up the pretense of their betrothal, as they'd agreed. They would be engaged until they made it out West and had settled for a time, then they would break up. The thought of that weighed heavily on her.

Ever since the trial, she hadn't been able to stop thinking about her declaration that she'd been waiting for a man she could love. But with all she had to do to get ready to travel west and then open a new store, Clara didn't think she needed to be considering a romance right now.

But John was making it hard for her to ignore her growing feelings for him. He brought her a gift every day—baked goods, chocolates. No trinkets though, because he knew she couldn't fit those in her wagon.

"He doesn't need to keep bringing me stuff and visiting me every day. He has a wagon train to plan," she complained to her sisters late one evening while they were brushing each other's hair.

Eliza and Hannah giggled. "Oh yes, Clara, it's an absolute mystery as to why John Butler is here every day."

Eliza was in a full fit of laughter on the bed now, and Hannah was not far behind her.

Clara knew her sisters wanted something romantic and lasting to develop between her and John, but they couldn't be right about his feelings—could they? "Maybe he's just lonely. We are getting closer to our trip, and he probably is looking forward to seeing his brother. He's homesick. That must be it."

Hannah shook her head. "He's not just lonely. I know you've put romance so far out of your mind that it's hard for you to see it, but think about what you would assume if this was happening to anyone else—if you heard about a man who visited the home of a woman every evening."

Clara thought about when all her friends had suddenly had daily gentlemen callers.

"Do you think…he's courting me?" The question sounded absurd coming out of her mouth. Clara's arms were suddenly peppered with gooseflesh. "Do you think that maybe he's trying to do something about our relationship…romantically?"

Eliza and Hannah nodded, exchanging relieved expressions.

"I'm so thankful it finally dawned on you. I thought we were going to have to act it all out for you."

Hannah giggled. "And I would make a terrible John."

Eliza dramatically stood up to her full height.

"Oh, don't be silly. I, of course, would be John and you would be Clara."

She grabbed Hannah and clung to her tight.

"Oh my darling Clara, I love you so. I'm a fool who doesn't know my feelings. You're a fool who doesn't know yours. Let's be fools together."

Hannah was in a fit of giggles, but Clara could only glare at her sisters.

"Are you quite through?" She didn't know for sure if John really was trying to court her, and she didn't know if she wanted him to or not. This seemed to her to be far from a joking matter. "As of right now, John and I are still just friends. End of discussion."

Her sisters were going to object, but they were interrupted by a knock on the door. "Mr. Butler is here again," Betty said.

Eliza and Hannah just burst into laughter as Clara stormed out of the room to greet their guest. When she arrived in the drawing room, John was pacing it. His shoulders were tight and he had a lost expression on his face. It was obvious that something was bothering him.

"John, what is it?"

He turned to her and stopped his pacing. "Clara. I need to talk to you about something important."

Her heartbeat sped up. Was he here to say he wanted to court her in truth? Clara had no idea if she wanted him to or not. John was exactly the kind of man she had dreamed of marrying someday, but once she'd decided that she wanted to run a store, she had not considered romantic love or marriage to be a possibility anymore. Then, there was the problem of John's five-year plan. There was no way he would seriously consider a true engagement between them when he had to settle for such a long time first.

Still, she was willing to hear him out. "Of course. Please sit down."

John sat on the chair across from her. He was bouncing one of his knees up and down, unable to sit still.

"Clara…when you forgave Michael in the courthouse the other day—how were you able to? He didn't even say he was sorry!"

Of all the things she had expected him to talk about, this most certainly wasn't one of them.

"Someone doesn't have to be sorry for you to forgive them," Clara said. "Forgiveness just means that you aren't going to let your anger at them control your life anymore."

John leaned back and sighed, rubbing his face with his hands. "I've been angry at my mother for so long. It's driven so many of my decisions."

Clara got up and crossed to him. She pulled his hands down so she could look into his eyes. "I know your mother isn't here anymore, but your anger toward her still weighs on you. I've seen it. I think your heart will be much lighter if you can just let it go. It's already impacted you by making you afraid to settle down."

"Your dad told me a few things that helped me get over that part," he said with a smile.

She blinked in surprise. Her father hadn't said anything about a conversation with John. "Well, in that case, I'm so glad you did. But you know that until you find a way to deal with the pain, it's going to keep bothering you. When you finally decide you are ready to settle down, start a family…"

Clara blushed at the mention of children. She was the one currently engaged to him, but once they broke their engagement and he finally found someone to marry, perhaps he would have a family someday.

John nodded at her words. "You're right. I don't know if I can forgive her, but I'll try."

Clara asked him softly, "Would it help if you talked about her a little bit?"

He didn't even know where to start. "She would have loved all the excitement of the trial. She loved when something big was happening and all the neighbors got involved. My father was often a loner and liked us to keep to ourselves, but she liked to be in a community."

Clara nodded, soaking in his words. "It must have been hard for her, then, starting over in new places all of the time."

John gave a little laugh, but his smile didn't reach his eyes. "I don't like to think about how hard it was for my mother. It's easier to always focus on how hard it was for me. That helped me to stay angry with her."

Clara wondered if that mindset helped soften the small boy's pain at her loss. "I think it might make things a little better for you if you try."

He was quiet for a few moments before answering. "I'll think about it. Thank you for listening, it helped me sort out my feelings a bit."

Clara smiled at him, glad she could be of help. "Will you be staying for supper?"

John stood up and shook his head. "I would love to, but I promised some of our fellow travelers I would check in on them tonight."

He said his good-nights and left—with Clara no closer to understanding how he felt about her.

John's next stop was to the camp where some of the families and their covered wagons had started to gather in anticipation of their journey. He found the one that would serve as the home during the trip for the young minister Ed Daniels. He had moved from the home of Independence's minister to the wagon camp early to get to know his future congregation.

"I was wondering if I might have a moment of your time, Reverend Daniels."

The young man turned to greet him and smiled. "Nice to see you, Mr. Butler. Don't forget, I asked you to call me Ed. Reverend Daniels makes me sound like I'm much older than I am."

John nodded and also insisted on being called by his first name. "If everyone called me Mr. Butler, it would get very confusing when we get to the town and my brother is there too."

The two men laughed at this, and John accepted Ed's offer of a cup of coffee and a seat by his campfire.

"What brings you to my wagon, Mr. Butler?"

"It's about my mother," he admitted. "We talked a bit about her when we rode together to Independence, if you remember."

John explained why he was so resentful of his mother, and how he didn't know how to forgive her. Ed listened patiently and thought for a moment before speaking.

"It seems to me that the trial got you thinking about the mother you knew before she left, and not just the one you knew afterward," the young minister said.

John gave him a confused look. "What do you mean? I didn't even know her after—I never saw her again."

Ed took a swig of his coffee before he answered. "All these years, you've only thought of your mother as the woman who abandoned your family. You've focused on that instead of on the woman who used to tuck you in at night. The woman who made you clothes and food. Who sang you songs. That mother."

John reeled at the man's words. What he was saying was true. Once his mother left the family, he'd focused only on the fact that she didn't do any of those things anymore.

"I'm not even sure I remember what she looked like," John confessed.

Ed gave him an understanding look. "I've heard that's pretty common when you lose someone at such a young age. But I bet if you think about it, you can remember more about her."

John closed his eyes and tried to imagine what his mother had looked like. All he could remember was curly hair. It would tickle his face when she hugged him after he brought her flowers. She gave wonderful hugs.

"Vanilla. She smelled like vanilla because she loved to use it in her baking," John exclaimed in wonder. He couldn't believe that he remembered that. A rush of love poured through him toward his mother.

"But how can I reconcile how I felt about her with what she did?" Remembering how much he loved his mother made the pain even greater.

Ed just smiled at him. "You need to grieve her as two different women. Grieve for the mama you knew and the woman who died in the city, all alone, without her sons and husband by her side."

John could clearly imagine the two different women in his mind, and he was surprised to find himself feeling a little sad for the woman who died without her loved ones around her. For the first time, he hoped that she had found some sort of happiness in her life after she left them.

Still, the pain of being that little boy without a mother weighed on him.

"But how do I reach what comes next? How do I actually forgive her?"

Ed smiled and clapped him on the back. "Wanting to is the first step. But you can't do this alone. Thankfully, you don't have to. You have the person Who is the best at forgiving on your side."

Humbled by the minister's words, John knew that he was right. *Father, please help me to forgive her. Help me to be a good husband and father someday to my own children. Help me to love them better than I was loved. Lord, help me to remember the good things about my mother and share them with my new family.*

As soon as John said the prayer, he felt a weight lift off his shoulders. He hadn't realized just how much his anger and pain had been weighing him down until he finally released them. John was ready to start his new life in Butler Valley with his wife and family.

"Thank you, I feel so much better."

"I'm glad I could be of some use already," Ed joked. "Now, I have to tell you, this might be something you have to do more than once. Pain has a way of sneaking up on you sometimes, even after you think you've let it go. The important thing is to recognize it and ask the Lord for help. You may feel sometimes that you have to make the decision to forgive her every day. Keep doing it, until it comes more naturally."

John and Ed sat by the campfire, swapping stories for the next hour or so. His heart felt much lighter. He couldn't wait to share his joy with his Clara.

Chapter Twenty-Three

Today was an exciting day for the Morehouse family—they were going to visit their wagons and do some final checks.

John said they would pull out in three days—rain or shine. Clara had overseen the packing of the wagons, but this would be the first time she would see them side by side and ready to go.

And they would get a chance to meet all the other people heading out. A few were familiar faces from Independence who John had recruited, but other families had come from all over the country to join their adventure to the West.

Clara thought it was all rather exciting to be part of their new start in life.

She didn't take time to count them all, but Clara guessed there were more than fifty wagons waiting to travel with them. The camp was filled with bustling noise—people packing or performing last-minute maintenance on their wagons, children running around trying not to get in their parents' way, strangers introducing themselves, livestock complaining loudly about their change in circumstances.

She certainly would enjoy her last few nights of the quiet in her home.

Clara saw John wandering between wagons, greeting each family. They all were pleased to see him, and she couldn't help but admire the way he was able to bond with people. It was clear he was loved and respected by these future citizens of his town.

He was a good man, probably one of the best she'd ever met. Seeing him like this, as a leader of this little community, was a reminder that he was just as dedicated and passionate about his work as she was about hers. And John had been only supportive of her desire to run her business. She had never imagined she could have a husband and a business…but what if she could?

Clara stopped walking, her mind reeling. A moment later, she snapped herself out of her daze and rushed to catch up to her sisters.

When John turned and saw the Morehouse family, his eyes lit up and a grin slowly spread on his face. Clara's stomach fluttered at the sight as a realization rolled over her like a warm blanket. *I do love him. I've fallen in love with my own fiancé.*

Clara didn't have time to consider the implications of her feelings, because the man in question was just a few feet from them. John said a polite goodbye to the people he was talking to and made his way over to them, his eyes locked on hers as if he never wanted to look away. Could he possibly feel the same way?

"What do you think? Does everything seem all right for our journey?" John asked her father but kept his gaze on her.

Clara nodded, and her father launched into a speech about the readiness of their wagons. She could tell that John was listening with only half an ear.

"Good, I'm glad you all are ready to go. We've been waiting for this for a long time," John said.

One by one, her family members made an excuse to walk away. Within a minute, Clara found herself alone with John. She had never felt nervous around him before, but the weight of her feelings made things heavier between them than they had ever been in the past.

"This is wonderful—everything you've done here, John. It truly is."

His eyes widened, and a sparkle came back in them that she had not seen in a while. "Thank you, Clara. It's been many months of work. I can't believe we are finally here."

John held out his arm for her and Clara linked hers with his, letting him guide her through the camp. He pointed out each wagon and told her about who owned it.

She loved listening to him talk and could do so all day, but unfortunately, they came to the end of the caravan. John seemed hesitant to part from her, as well.

"Clara…would you mind if we spoke for a moment, about something important?"

Her heart started pounding wildly in her chest, so fiercely that she was surprised that he couldn't hear it. She nodded and he led her to a log that had been laid down as a makeshift bench in the camp. Suddenly, nervous for reasons she didn't understand, Clara decided to talk first.

"Did you hear that they transferred Michael to a jail in another town? I heard it was because his mother kept barging in and bringing him comforts from home."

John laughed. "Yeah, the judge told me the cell was starting to look like a fancy hotel room rather than a place for a criminal."

Clara knew that Mrs. Emmers would do everything in her power to pamper her son, but hopefully when he was in custody farther away, the man could finally face the consequences for his actions and come out a changed man.

"I'm just glad we will be a good distance off by the time he gets out of jail." While she had forgiven him, she was more than ready to move on from having him as part of her life. She never wanted to see Michael Emmers's face again.

"He won't ever have another opportunity to bother you, I promise. If he sets foot in our town, I will drag him out myself."

Clara laughed at the thought of John pulling an angry Michael out of town and tossing him into the wilderness.

"That might be worth it to see."

The two grinned at each other, but soon John's face turned serious. She knew he was about to reveal why he had pulled her aside. Clara's pulse increased as he reached out and grabbed her hand.

"I love you," she blurted out before he could get a word in.

John's eyes widened and he froze completely. This was not how Clara had expected this moment to go.

It took John several moments to recover from Clara's outburst. She loved him. *She loved him.* To hear the words out loud, after everything, was earth-shattering. It was life changing.

She must have panicked at his silence, because she started to babble.

"I mean… I understand if you don't feel the same

way or it makes you uncomfortable. We can remain friends and travel together and it will be fine—"

John reached up and put a finger to her lips. "I really want to kiss you now, but I don't think that's wise, given all we've done to repair damage to your reputation. I'm going to sit down here on this end of the bench so I can actually talk to you without being tempted to do something I shouldn't." John reluctantly let go of her and moved to the other end of the log.

She arched an eyebrow at him. "Are you sure that distance will be enough?"

He laughed. "Probably not, but it will have to do for now. I have a few things to say to you."

Where should he begin? Should he tell her the reasons for his five-year plan? Should he admit that it all seemed ridiculous to him now? There was so much to say and he didn't know where to start.

"I love you too" was the first thing that came out, and it was the right thing to say, because her entire countenance glowed with happiness.

"You do?"

He nodded. Was she actually surprised? How could she not have known? "Of course I do. I've loved you probably from the second or third day I was working with you in the store. I just didn't realize it."

She gasped and stared at him in surprise. Clara really hadn't known. "You mean…when you proposed? You think you loved me then?"

John thought back to her rejection, and his frustration that he couldn't convince her to let him help her.

"Yes, I loved you then, and the Emmers situation just gave me an excuse to offer for marriage. I would have proposed to you without that reason, eventually."

She scoffed at that. "Yes, after you settled in your

town for five years. Who knows where we would have been by then?"

He sighed. What a fool he had been. Suddenly, Clara sat up straight.

"Wait. I cannot believe that in my moment of weakness, I forgot all about that we cannot even be together for five years! Why even tell me that you love me now, knowing how long I'll have to wait for marriage?"

John couldn't believe she thought that he would torture her with a love confession followed by a caveat. *Well, you're the one that came up with the plan in the first place, you fool.* John could kick himself for how stupid he had been.

"No, it's not like that anymore. I promise."

She looked at him skeptically. "No more waiting?"

Clara remained silent while John explained the reasoning behind his foolish life blueprint—and his conversation with her father that had convinced him otherwise.

"I don't need to wait to be sure that I will have a home. You are my home."

And it was true. He didn't want to be anywhere but by her side for the rest of his life. There was so much he was anticipating sharing with her. John couldn't wait to show her what life was like beyond Independence as they traveled to new parts of the country.

He looked forward to showing her the beautiful plot of land where he and his brother had chosen to build their town. To sharing his dreams with her. To helping Clara with her own dreams of opening her own store. To building new dreams together with her.

Tears filled her eyes at his words, but she didn't seem convinced.

"But how do I know that you won't change your

mind tomorrow? We don't want to start out this journey with so much new and uncertain between us. Perhaps we should make an agreement to not discuss this, to discuss our feelings, until after we arrive out West?"

The thought of going several months of seeing Clara every day and not being able to kiss her or tell her that he loved her weighed heavily on John. Now that they had confessed their mutual feelings, he wanted to proclaim his love to her every moment of every day. Could he concentrate on what he needed to do to get the group safely to their destination with that big of a distraction?

"If you think you can keep from kissing me that long," Clara teased.

"I don't think I can."

He had said it plainly, but it was the truth. He hoped it was true for her, as well.

"But what are we going to do? I don't want to ruin my reputation with my new community by kissing the man in charge every day."

She had a smile on her face, but her voice sounded tight. John wanted to go down to the jail and punch Emmers for the pain he had caused Clara. But he reminded himself the man was behind them now and the two of them had a whole future to look forward to.

"I have a solution to that—and I want you to know I'm saying this not out of a desire to rescue you or to fix your reputation."

She eyed him warily but nodded for him to continue. Clara gasped when he grabbed her hand and got down on one knee.

"I'm going to ask this again, and with the intention of it being entirely real this time. Clara Morehouse, would you do the honor of becoming my bride? Will you marry me?"

Tears were streaming down her face as she nodded, and he stood up to pull her into his arms.

"It's a good thing we have a preacher coming along with us on this trip. We can have a small wedding one evening on the trail." Clara's grin was contagious, but John shook his head at her plans. She tried again. "Well, I suppose we could wait until we got there, but I think we already talked about how hard that would be."

Waiting until their arrival did have the benefit of Adam being there, but John didn't feel that that was reason enough. His brother would hopefully understand.

Again, John just said no. Clara's eyes widened. "You want to get married *before* we leave? I suppose I can call on the minister and his wife and make the arrangements for us to wed on the morning we leave."

John laughed and disagreed again. "No, we are doing none of those things. But I love how you have a plan for everything." It's why she was such a good businesswoman. He looked forward to her organizing and planning a lot of things in their lives from now on. Her plans were much better than the ridiculous ones that came from him.

Except for maybe this latest one.

Clara was utterly confused by him and he leaned forward and gave her a quick kiss on the cheek. "What are you thinking, John?"

He grinned, holding her close as he calculated all he'd have to do to accomplish his mission by this evening. It could be done, even though it meant he'd have to work extra hard tomorrow on actual business that he'd intended to complete this afternoon.

He pulled away from Clara, kissed her nose and looked her straight in the eye.

"We're going to get married today."

Chapter Twenty-Four

"What?" Clara could not even begin to understand what was happening right now.

John wanted to get married today? It didn't seem possible. This morning their engagement was strictly business—or at least she was trying to keep it that way for her sanity. And now, they were in love, talking about their future—and they might be husband and wife by the end of the day.

"I know it's sudden, but I don't want to go the entire trip without you as my wife," John said smiling. "And you deserve a nice place for your wedding and to start off your marriage. You can wear a pretty dress that's not covered in dust."

Clara had packed only a few practical dresses and her walking boots in her bag for the journey, although she had a few nice things tucked away in a crate for special occasions once they arrived in their new town.

"I would marry you in my dusty dress and boots, just so you know." She was not a snobbish sort of girl, although she did like the idea of looking pretty on her wedding day.

He smiled at her, and she thought her heart would

burst. She loved this man. He understood her and supported her in a way that no one ever had.

"I know that you would, but I want our wedding to be nice for you. And tomorrow we will be so busy with travel preparations."

She hesitated, wondering if they could get everything organized to have a wedding tonight. Clara was sure they could go to the minister and be married in his parlor within fifteen minutes, but she wanted her father and sisters to attend.

John took her slow reaction as hesitance.

"Is it because you want to spend your last few nights in your family home? We can always stay with your family if that's what's bothering you."

Clara laughed. "I don't care where we stay, and of course I want to marry you. I'm just worried about being able to pull it off tonight."

John whooped and picked her up, spinning her around. "Let me worry about that. You just go home and get ready. Tell your family, and I will send news."

She huffed. "Are you saying I need to go and look pretty while you handle all the work? I think you're marrying the wrong woman, then."

He laughed and hugged her close. "You're right. I just wanted to get everything taken care of so you wouldn't have to worry. Do you want to stop by the minister's house together on our way back to your house so you can be in on the details?"

She nodded, relieved.

The minister was surprised but pleased that they would call on him in the middle of the afternoon.

"Thank you for giving me an excuse to take a break from working on my sermon for Sunday," he teased, welcoming them into his drawing room.

Mrs. Bolton brought in a tea tray. She was beaming with joy to have so much company in one afternoon. "We are seldom this busy, but we had to perform three emergency weddings this week. A few young women of Independence are marrying and getting out of town on that wagon train. It happens every time."

Clara blushed at her words, wondering if the woman had guessed why they were here.

"Oh hush now, love. I think it's sweet. They are young couples in love and the thought of being parted for months is too much for them to bear." Reverend Bolton added way too much sugar to his tea, almost as if to prove just how much he liked things to be sweet.

"Well, they could be sensible like that Gordon girl. She got married, but then stayed here with her parents while her man went on ahead to settle their land. Then she went out there when he had an actual home built. I can't imagine what all these young women are thinking, heading there to nothing."

Reverend Bolton took a sip of his tea. "I think it's very brave of them. Besides, they have their love to get them through."

Clara felt a wave of thankfulness toward the man.

"So, what brings you here this afternoon?" the minister asked.

John shifted nervously in his seat, not wanting to announce their intent after Mrs. Bolton's little tirade. Clara, however, had no such qualms. She stared down the woman, wanting to see her expression when she announced their news.

"We would like you to marry us, tonight. Hopefully at the church if you are able."

She was rewarded by Mrs. Bolton turning beet red

and apologizing profusely for the things she had said. "I didn't mean anything by it, I promise."

Clara just smiled at the woman and said she understood, then suggested that perhaps she should be kinder to the couples who were coming in here. "You are privileged to witness the joining of two hearts so many times—that is such a blessing."

The woman was suitably humbled and began helping them make plans for that evening. They didn't need any fancy decorations or a big meal; they just wanted her family beside them.

"Are you sure you don't want to wait until we get there—so your brother could be by your side?" Clara worried John would feel left out with only her people who would be in attendance. But they had all sort of adopted John, so she supposed her family was his already, as well.

"No, he will understand. I promise. He will just be thankful I came back at all," John explained.

Clara smiled at that. He would go back to Butler Valley all right, but with a wife.

A few hours later, Clara brushed at the skirt of her dress nervously as their carriage approached the church. She had expected to walk there, but their neighbor had offered his carriage when he heard of their intentions. In fact, many of their friends in Independence had contributed to the festivities. Apparently, Henry had overheard them making plans. (That boy had eyes and ears everywhere in town.) And he'd spread the news. Only a few weeks ago, Clara thought they didn't have many friends, but now it was being proven otherwise.

All her gowns were packed away, so Clara had intended to wear what she had on hand. But then her friend Esther Warren, who was almost exactly the same size, dropped by with an evening dress for her to wear. It was the color of lilacs, and it hung off her shoulders to show off her lovely pale skin.

Her sisters had pinned her hair up, making her neck appear even longer.

"You look absolutely beautiful," her father told her through teary eyes as he helped her down from the carriage. Another family friend handed her a bouquet of flowers picked from her garden, and Clara knew this day couldn't be any more perfect.

But then they entered the church, and she gasped in surprise. The pews were filled with friends and customers who had supported the family for years.

The people who had canceled their orders during the Emmers scandal obviously were not in attendance, but those who had remained loyal to the Morehouse family had showed up to support Clara's wedding. And to say goodbye and thank them for their years of dedication to the town.

Clara tried wiping tears from her eyes, but it was no use, because they were running down her face. Her father handed her a handkerchief, but he was also considerably misty-eyed himself.

"I'm a mess," she said with a blubber, and her father chuckled.

"You are a lovely mess, and besides, I don't think your future husband minds at all."

Clara turned toward the front of the church, where John was standing in anticipation. Though he was far away, and her eyes were blurry from crying, she could see the expression of love on his face.

He wore his best suit. He must have dug it out of his

wagon this afternoon after they parted. "He looks so handsome."

Clara realized that every eye in the church was on her, and she was delaying the entire wedding by standing there crying.

"You ready to do this, Clarabelle?"

She smiled up at her father, so thankful that he had been able to overcome his grief to be here for her today as she married the man who'd helped make that happen.

"I wish Mama were here." She hadn't meant to say it. Clara didn't want to make him sad again, but he just smiled and patted her hand.

"She is here. She's always with us. And she would be so proud of you today."

He held out his arm for her and she linked hers through his. Clara passed many friends smiling at her on the way down the aisle, but she could see only those beautiful chestnut eyes of her groom staring at her.

When they reached the front, her father handed her off to John, and the two men nodded at each other. When she felt John's rough hand reach for hers, their fingers sliding together naturally, all the nervous excitement she had been holding in her body melted away.

"You look… There aren't even words. *Beautiful* is the closest, but it doesn't do you justice." John had whispered to her, but a few ladies in the front row made happy sighing noises when they overheard.

Ever the charmer, my soon-to-be husband, Clara thought, even as she blushed at his praise. The minister started the ceremony, but Clara barely paid attention. She could only focus on the warmth of her hands connected with John's and the fact that, in just a few minutes, they would be linked together forever.

She paid more attention when she heard John's voice as he started his vows.

"Clara, I always thought my plans in life were set, but you came along and changed all of them for the better. It doesn't matter where life takes me, as long as you're by my side. You're my home, and I'm going to do my best to make all your dreams come true. I promise to never stand in the way of you doing all the amazing things you are capable of. I love you, and I'm honored that you have chosen me to love."

Clara's breath caught at his words. She never expected to find someone to love and support her so completely, just as she was.

The minister cleared his throat, indicating it was her turn to speak. She braced herself and turned to meet John's eyes, which were sparkling with tears.

"John, I had no plans at all when it came to love or marriage. Thank you for sharing your dreams with me and wanting me to be part of them. I can't wait to go on this new adventure with you. I promise to love you forever. And I will never leave you. Never."

She repeated it because she knew just how deep the wounds caused by his mother ran. He smiled at her as the minister continued the ceremony.

Before she even realized what was happening, John slipped a plain wedding band on her finger and the minister was declaring them husband and wife. John swept her into his arms for a kiss.

Everyone cheered—her sisters the loudest of all. The couple walked hand in hand out of the church and to the hotel for their celebration supper.

Clara could hardly believe that she was no longer a Morehouse but a Butler. But watching her husband interact with her father and sisters, she knew that he had truly become part of their family, as well. She couldn't wait to meet his brother and hoped that he liked her.

But what if he didn't? The thought was the only thing that marred her wedding day.

John wondered what had happened in the first five minutes of marriage to upset his new wife. "Why are you frowning? Brides are supposed to be happy. Are you having any regrets?" His voice was teasing, so she would know that he had no concern about her joy at being wed.

"I was just thinking about your brother. My sisters and father have accepted you as one of their own. What if he doesn't feel the same?"

John lifted her hand to his lips and kissed her knuckles one by one. He reveled in the affection that he could now show her freely. They had gone from a fake betrothal to husband and wife in a matter of hours. But John had no regrets.

"I love you. My brother loves me. So, by proxy, of course he will love you, as well. Besides, you have one thing that will make him prefer you to me."

She gave him a questioning look.

"A head for business. He is the brains of our operation. I'm the charm. I expect the two of you will be able to talk all day about numbers and figures until my eyes cross with boredom."

In truth, John looked forward to putting his two favorite people in a room together. He would not be bored, because he would be busy trying to distract his wife from work. He grinned just thinking about it.

Tomorrow, they would begin their long journey west, to their new home.

It would be slow and hard travel, but as he felt Clara's

arm move through his, he was grateful that he didn't have to do it alone this time. For many, it was a new adventure. For John, it was a whole new life.

Epilogue

About five months and many miles later

Clara leaned forward as their wagon reached the top of the hill. This was it. Their new home, their town was waiting for them on the other side. Butler Valley. She held her breath as they came to the top. The valley below them was beautiful. There was green grass as far as the eye could see that seemed brighter in the sunshine. A small river—or creek, she couldn't tell— ran through the valley, and near one of its banks there was a small cluster of buildings.

John's brother and his team had been very busy while waiting for them to arrive. Clara hoped her new store would be in one of those buildings. She couldn't wait to get started. Her husband leaned over and gave her a kiss on the cheek.

"I can't believe how much there is. When I left, it was nothing. And Adam came out here with no more than a wagon filled with supplies."

Clara couldn't help but grin at the excitement that was reflected with her husband's voice. She had not thought it could be possible to love John more than on her wedding day, but the many months they had spent together on the trail had brought them closer together. They'd laughed as he taught her the art of cooking over a campfire, and she'd burned the coffee every morning until he took over.

They'd grieved together at some of the losses the wagon train had endured, and some of the setbacks they had experienced on the trail.

They'd spent hours every evening talking and became very familiar with each other's company because they had to remain in their wagon for several days at a time when the trip came to a halt due to a rainstorm.

She turned to him for comfort when they all worried about Eliza's health because she became ill on the journey. Thankfully, she recovered, though she was still not back to her full health.

There had been good moments on the trail as well—weekly church meetings, where they all gathered around a campfire and the men each took turns sharing God's word. They sang the songs they could remember without their hymnals.

Hannah had started story time for the children on the journey, reading them a chapter out of a book each evening after they stopped for the day (providing their mamas time to prepare supper without children running underfoot).

Their journey had brought them all closer together, not just the two of them in their marriage but the whole community of wonderful folks who would be building this new town with them. They were all family now.

And that family's growing, she thought as she patted her stomach to acknowledge the new life in there. John had been thrilled when he learned of their coming baby and had promised to build her a home right away.

"I don't mind. I love our wagon." It was true. She had started to see the little covered wagon as their home now and would always remember it with affection.

John just shook his head at that. "Our child is going to be born with a solid roof over its head, and not one made of canvas."

She just laughed at that and told him to do his best. But she didn't mind either way. He liked to tease her that the baby was part of his new five-year plan—the one where they would have a bunch of children who would come with her to the store or to his office.

Clara smiled at the thought, knowing their journey west was actually the first step in that plan.

John turned to her, and pulled her over so that she was right next to him. "Do you like it?"

She grinned. "I love it."

John let out a cheer, and others around them joined in. Everyone was relieved that their long journey was over and they could begin the next part of their lives.

"Let's go home," John whispered into her hair.

She lingered in his arms for a few more moments, whispering back that she already was home.

* * * * *

Dear Reader,

Thank you for choosing John and Clara's love story! It's so much fun to explore what life was like in the community that sent pioneers off on their journey west on the Oregon Trail. I have loved historical Westerns since I was young. Never could I have imagined, when curling up with books from the church library to keep myself entertained while my dad wrote his weekly sermon, that someday I would be writing my own.

The West was built by not only brave entrepreneurs like John but by bold and strong women like Clara. I love how supportive John is of Clara's ambition. It never occurs to him to expect her to be anything other than who she already is. Writing about John's journey to forgive his mother and find his home was very special to me. The choice to forgive and not let bitterness cling to your heart is tough, but it is worth it in the end when it leads to happiness.

I hope you enjoyed reading about John, Clara and the whole Morehouse family as much as I enjoyed writing about them.

Thanks for reading!
Julie Brookman

LOVE INSPIRED

Stories to uplift and inspire

Fall in love with Love Inspired—
inspirational and uplifting stories of faith
and hope. Find strength and comfort in
the bonds of friendship and community.
Revel in the warmth of possibility and the
promise of new beginnings.

Sign up for the Love Inspired newsletter
at **LoveInspired.com** to be the first
to find out about upcoming titles,
special promotions and exclusive content.

CONNECT WITH US AT:

f Facebook.com/LoveInspiredBooks

🐦 Twitter.com/LoveInspiredBks

LISOCIAL2021

Get 4 FREE REWARDS!

We'll send you 2 FREE Books plus 2 FREE Mystery Gifts.

FREE Value Over **$20**

Both the **Love Inspired®** and **Love Inspired® Suspense** series feature compelling novels filled with inspirational romance, faith, forgiveness, and hope.

YES! Please send me 2 FREE novels from the Love Inspired or Love Inspired Suspense series and my 2 FREE gifts (gifts are worth about $10 retail). After receiving them, if I don't wish to receive any more books, I can return the shipping statement marked "cancel." If I don't cancel, I will receive 6 brand-new Love Inspired Larger-Print books or Love Inspired Suspense Larger-Print books every month and be billed just $5.99 each in the U.S. or $6.24 each in Canada. That is a savings of at least 17% off the cover price. It's quite a bargain! Shipping and handling is just 50¢ per book in the U.S. and $1.25 per book in Canada.* I understand that accepting the 2 free books and gifts places me under no obligation to buy anything. I can always return a shipment and cancel at any time. The free books and gifts are mine to keep no matter what I decide.

Choose one: ☐ **Love Inspired**
Larger-Print
(122/322 IDN GNWC)

☐ **Love Inspired Suspense**
Larger-Print
(107/307 IDN GNWN)

Name (please print)

Address   Apt. #

City   State/Province   Zip/Postal Code

Email: Please check this box ☐ if you would like to receive newsletters and promotional emails from Harlequin Enterprises ULC and its affiliates. You can unsubscribe anytime.

Mail to the **Harlequin Reader Service:**
IN U.S.A.: P.O. Box 1341, Buffalo, NY 14240-8531
IN CANADA: P.O. Box 603, Fort Erie, Ontario L2A 5X3

Want to try 2 free books from another series! Call 1-800-873-8635 or visit www.ReaderService.com.

*Terms and prices subject to change without notice. Prices do not include sales taxes, which will be charged (if applicable) based on your state or country of residence. Canadian residents will be charged applicable taxes. Offer not valid in Quebec. This offer is limited to one order per household. Books received may not be as shown. Not valid for current subscribers to the Love Inspired or Love Inspired Suspense series. All orders subject to approval. Credit or debit balances in a customer's account(s) may be offset by any other outstanding balance owed by or to the customer. Please allow 4 to 6 weeks for delivery. Offer available while quantities last.

Your Privacy—Your information is being collected by Harlequin Enterprises ULC, operating as Harlequin Reader Service. For a complete summary of the information we collect, how we use this information and to whom it is disclosed, please visit our privacy notice located at corporate.harlequin.com/privacy-notice. From time to time we may also exchange your personal information with reputable third parties. If you wish to opt out of this sharing of your personal information, please visit readerservice.com/consumerschoice or call 1-800-873-8635. **Notice to California Residents**—Under California law, you have specific rights to control and access your data. For more information on these rights and how to exercise them, visit corporate.harlequin.com/california-privacy.

LIRLIS22

IF YOU ENJOYED THIS BOOK
WE THINK YOU WILL ALSO LOVE

LOVE INSPIRED SUSPENSE
INSPIRATIONAL ROMANCE

Courage. Danger. Faith.

Find strength and determination in stories
of faith and love in the face of danger.

6 NEW BOOKS AVAILABLE EVERY MONTH!

LISXSERIES2021

IF YOU ENJOYED THIS BOOK, DON'T MISS NEW EXTENDED-LENGTH NOVELS FROM LOVE INSPIRED!

In addition to the Love Inspired books you know and love, we're excited to introduce even more uplifting stories in a longer format, with more inspiring fresh starts and page-turning thrills!

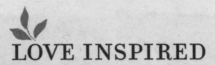

LOVE INSPIRED

Stories to uplift and inspire.

Fall in love with Love Inspired—inspirational and uplifting stories of faith and hope. Find strength and comfort in the bonds of friendship and community. Revel in the warmth of possibility, and the promise of new beginnings.

LOOK FOR THESE LOVE INSPIRED TITLES ONLINE AND IN THE BOOK DEPARTMENT OF YOUR FAVORITE RETAILER!

LITRADE0222